I0600191

HIGH WATER HEAVY

CORBIN MUCK

For requests and permissions, or to order additional copies of this book, write to:
CorbinGMwriter@gmail.com

ISBN: 979-8-9938353-0-8

Cover design by Jonathan Sainsbury
Book design by Caerus Kourt

For my bub, Mariska

HIGH
WATER
HEAVY

1

"Huh," Buck said, "So that's the scheme?"

Karl blinked back slow and flat and empty, "What is?"

"This. Here. Now. Lunch."

"What about it?"

"Come on, Karl, don't play dumb—we both know you're no damn good at it."

"You've lost me, pal."

Buck reached for the paper and read back the listing, "'*Downtown offices for rent. 501 Columbia Street, entrepreneurial and modern, viewings available by appointment.*' 501 Columbia. That's—what—a block from here?" he asked, looking around the restaurant. He hated places like this, the kind where the fat cats came to shuck oysters and watch their fish-eyed, second wives bully the waiters, but at least now he knew why Karl'd been so damned insistent.

Buck chucked the paper back across the table. "So, what times our appointment?" he asked.

"What appointment?"

"Uh-huh."

Karl shot Buck a vinegar-dipped look of mock confusion, "Really, pal, it's nothing fishy. I just wanted to grab a bite someplace where my shoes don't stick to the floor, that's all." Then, after much too short a pause, he added, "And anyway, that's today's *Oregonian* you got in your mitt there—fresh off the newsstand. You were with me when I bought it outside. How am I supposed to have arranged anything since then? You seen me use a phone, have you? Or do you figure I've been sitting here tapping a message out in morse under the table?"

Now that was just insulting. There was no way Karl hadn't seen that ad already. He was a fiend for all things typeset. It had served him well during the war, when a couple breakfast keystrokes in England had meant bombs over Germany by lunch, but you'd think the hip-deep slurry of inky parochialisms falling out the presses back home here in Portland would have eased him off a bit. Nope. He read all three of the city's broadsheets front to back every morning and had the habit of sharing the choicest bits as if he were Moses fresh from Sinai.

Buck looked at his watch, "We got time to eat or is it just drinks?"

"It must be exhausting to see such conspiracies around

you all the time, eh, pal? To be so paranoid? Should I be worried you've cracked? Is it the job? Have your nerves given out? Well, if that's the case, might be that you should call it quits and go work a truck route for a while. A little break might do you good. I hear those guys do alright long as they don't mind a load going missing every now and again."

"Thanks for the tip."

"Anytime." Karl flagged down a waiter and ordered them a pair of steaks and some coffees to go along. "They pan fry the ribeye here," he said, crossing his arms and leaning back, immensely pleased with himself, "You're going to love it."

"Uh-huh," Buck said again.

"Alright, pal. *Alright.* You got me. Bit of a friendly ruse, that's all. But keep an open mind, would you? It's just an office; just a place to hang your hat. You don't like joints like this? Fine. Don't eat here. Go back across the river every goddamned day for lunch if you want, but we need an office."

"We have a—"

"—A *real* office, Buck. One that's close in on the happenings—not some eastside rat hole; one that's done-up nice; one that says *these guys can be trusted; these guys can be discreet.* You think any of these Goose Hollow housewives are coming across the river to see us when they smell the wrong perfume on their guy's collar? Or

3

when somebody's young precious over at Multnomah Athletic disappears, you think they're looking as far as Albina for a bloodhound? Not a chance. Rome ends at the Willamette for these people, pal."

Buck considered that as the coffees arrived, "OK."

"What?"

"OK, I said."

Karl's brow shot up. "Really?"

"Yah."

"And you'll consider it? I mean, *really* consider it?"

"Sure. Why not?"

"Well... well, good. Alright then. Good. That's all I ask. This could be really good for us, Buck. Better class of client, better rates, better everything. I know you're used to the old office, but this is a great opportunity for us to move up the ladder."

"It's the '*old*' office already, huh?"

"You know what I meant."

Sure, he did. That was the problem. But Buck let it go. If Karl cared enough to go full cloak-and-dagger on this, it was only a matter of time before he won out anyway. Much as Buck hated to admit it, Karl had a point about the office. Not a lot of deep pockets on Alberta Street, and most folks up that way had no need for the kind of professional certainty that he and Karl could offer. What could a private detective tell them that they hadn't heard through the walls already? Or that the whole block hadn't known since Tuesday? Problems are the human condition, but its money that makes for mysteries, provides for the extra apartments, fills the secret accounts, and grows the great green hedge where the rich go chasing.

They changed the subject. Dodgers. Red Sox. The rain, the heat, the river. A gal Karl was seeing up Terwilliger. But with the pretense exposed, lunch lay like a spent match between them, and when the steaks finally arrived, Karl was more than ready to start in on hardier fare, "Did you call the message service this morning, by the way?" he asked.

"Not yet."

"There was a promising one for you. I took the liberty of calling them back and doing a little reconnaissance."

"Nice of you."

"Don't worry, I'm not poaching; this one's yours all over. Apparently, the cops found some guy by the name of Thomayer face down in Skid Row with a needle sticking out of his arm. But the guy's sister—who goes by the name Whitmore now—says it doesn't add up," Karl said, sawing at his steak. He didn't work Skid Row. It wasn't his bag—place was closer to Hong Kong or Harlem than it was to the rest of the westside. Brothels. Gambling. Dealers. The city's rotten old heart beating strong as ever from inside its puffed-up chest, but with so much caked-on grime that the cops didn't even try anymore. They just took their kicks and made sure none of the blood made it past Burnside.

"Which part of a dead junkie on Skid Row doesn't add up?"

Karl chewed on that for a while, taking first his time and then a sip of coffee before answering, "Don't know."

"Thought you talked to the sister."

"I did."

"She didn't say?"

"Nope."

"But you asked?"

"I told her you'd call; told her that you were the man for the job. Tell you the truth, she was pretty frantic over the phone. She wasn't making a lot of sense, and she didn't seem to like me much. Who knows—might be bullshit—but for what it's worth, I called my guy at the coroner's office, and he said it looked like Thomayer was a first timer. Apparently, he'd had trouble finding the veins. I guess they'll know more in a couple days, but—and here's the kicker—guess where they found the guy? Specifically, I mean?"

"Where?"

"Outside *Bon Vivant*'s."

"Huh." Now it was Buck's turn to chew. "They mention *Bon*'s in the paper?"

"Sure did."

"Maddy must've been pissed."

"You'd know better than me."

"Less so these days. Did *Bon*'s mean anything to the sister?"

"She didn't say anything specific about it, but, like I say, she was pretty defensive on the phone, so… yah, probably. How's the steak?"

"Bit rich."

Karl snorted, skewering a last, bloody bite, "Anyway, there yah go, pal, that's the case; that's what I got. The rest I leave in your capable hands. I told the sister you'd call her today. Now hurry up and finish, our appointment is at one."

Ten minutes later they were a block up Columbia Street, shaking hands with Mr. C.C. Dunleavy of Dunleavy Commercial Properties, a stocky man with ten fleshy, home-grown fingers and an extra he'd had imported from Havana. He was bald, flat-faced, bespectacled, and every time he looked at Buck he seemed to be swallowing a laugh.

"Of course, money can't *buy* respectability, gentlemen," he intoned, puffing emphatically at his cigar, filling the empty office with his voice, "But it *can* buy *proximity*, and I can tell by the look of you two, that a little bit of proximity is all you need. Same story for all you boys, isn't it? You've served your country, you've faced the trials of combat, and now you've come back to take your rightful place at the head of the community. You got married, you bought the house, and if you don't have kids yet, well, I'm sure that's something you're *feverishly* working on, eh? Eh? Eh?" He allowed himself a long, knowing exhale. "Now's the perfect time, then, to get yourself situated. Lay a foundation. Get a sense of the commercial landscape.

Because what use is peace without prosperity, gentlemen? And that means business—business and fine, upstanding *businessmen* such as yourselves. And no matter what line you're in, there's profound advantages to having an office down here." He swept a cloud of blue-purple smoke towards the rain-dappled glass, "Through that window, gentlemen, you'll have a full view of city hall. While just around the corner is the courthouse, the sheriff, and all the finest enterprises of the city. Three blocks over, you have museums and parks for the kids, while, for a night out, you and the wife have the Paramount just up the road, along with all the finest dining in the city. A sea of white tablecloths and four-page wine selections. When you're down here, gentlemen, you're standing on the surface of the sun, watching the everything that's anything in this fine state orbit around *you*. That's gravity. That's science. That's prosperity. That's what we're talking about when we're talking about proximity. Right people, right place. The rest follows." He snapped his fingers. "Pretty straight-forward, isn't it, gentlemen?"

Karl nodded, admirably pretending like he hadn't already heard the speech. "See, Buck? It's got a real office for each of us. And this could be a lobby where we can have folks wait with a bit of dignity, not just have them stand in the hallway under that burnt-out old bulb. I bet the heat even works. Few months, maybe we get a secretary? We can keep the message service for any after-hours calls, sure, but to have the personal touch? That's the ticket."

"Sure, Karl." Buck said, taking stock. The place was divided into three rooms—two ready-set private offices connected by a long reception space, with a chest-high window running the full length—each of the three sections bigger than the entirety of what even Buck was now starting to think of as the *old* office. But Karl wasn't one to leave a thing up to chance. He went at ambiguity with a club. It's what made him a good partner, a good detective, and, most days, what made Buck like him. A marrow-drinker. Easily agitated, hard to shake. Still, sometimes listening to the big man go on and on like he was, it was hard not to feel like a post being driven into the ground.

No feature could escape his praise. There were windows with good morning light. Saved on electricity. Looked clean. Looked open. Nice big floors where they could lay a couple rugs or one of those big plants with the palms? One of those they grow down south? Why not in the corner there? Frosted glass for the offices; clean and thick and well-insulated. Nice doors. Nice locks. The whole place nice and quiet at the back end of the hall. This and that and this again. More and more.

"And what line of work did you say you gentlemen were in again?" Dunleavy asked once Karl seemed close to the end.

"We're detectives."

"Aha."

"PIs," Buck corrected.

Dunleavy nodded along with genial disinterest, pulling

9

a rental contract from his inside pocket and handing it to Karl, "Good, good. And, tell me, what did you do in the war?"

"I was in England with the bombers," Karl answered, "Army Air Corps. They call it the Air Force now."

"Yes, very good. You know, my son Liam was a pilot too, though he was in the Pacific. He won the Navy Cross, which made his mother very proud. A few others too—medals, I mean. As I say, his mother was very proud."

"What'd he fly?"

"I'm not sure exactly. Liam is very modest. Very modest indeed, much like you gentlemen. But I believe he flew off a ship he and the other boys called, 'The Fighting Hannah'. Isn't that a fine name for a ship? You know, his office is down the hall, maybe we can drop in on him when you're on your way out? I'm sure he'd jump at the chance to meet another *flyboy* and swap war stories!"

"I wouldn't want to interrupt his work."

"Not at all, it'd make his day," Dunleavy turned to Buck, "And you, Mr. Bordell? Where did you serve?"

"Southeast Stark mostly."

The property manager cocked his head ever-so-slightly in confusion until Karl broke in, "Buck's got flat arches. He wasn't *able* to fight overseas."

"Oh, well, that's not your fault, son," the man said with a father's condescension, "Everybody did their part, didn't they? Tell me, Mr. Stevenson, did you come home with any medals?" Dunleavey asked, confidently mispronouncing Karl's last name.

"Just the big one, I'm afraid."

"Well, that's the only one that *really* matters, I suppose. Liam would be the first to agree, despite the Navy Cross and all."

"Here, here. Say, mind if we take the paperwork home with us? Give things a good look and get back to you?"

"Of course, gentlemen! Things are going fast, but I can keep this office on hold for you into next week while you make up your minds. I can tell that you two are just the sort we'd want around here."

"That's very generous of you, sir."

"Not at all. Now, unless you have any other questions, should we go see if Liam has a moment to meet a fellow aviator?"

"I'd love to, sir, but Buck's got some appointments this afternoon to keep, so we better hustle back over to the eastside. Gotta make our hay while the suns shines, isn't that right, partner?"

Buck shrugged, biting his lip, "I got time."

"You do, do you?"

"Yep. Plenty."

Karl's face slid into the wide, toothy smile he always trotted out for clients. The fake one. "Oh, good."

"Excellent! Follow me, gentlemen!" They tramped down the hall together, but Dunleavy junior wasn't in his office after all, so they continued on and said their goodbyes in the lobby. Shakes. Hats. Coats. And promises for next time. "Oh, and Mr. Stevenson, if you were thinking of financing through the Servicemen's Readjustment Act, rest assured that we are exceptionally experienced in navigating that particular program. You're in good company here. I'd say almost half of our offices are leased out to veterans currently."

"I'm sure we'll feel right at home."

"That's our hope exactly."

They shook again. Nodded. Smiled. Tipped hats. And then Buck and Karl were back out on the gray, spittle-slick streets of Portland's business district, where the buildings all had Christian names, and the proud patricians of so second-rate a berg play-acted Rockefeller. Karl fit in down here—not with the clannish little owls themselves, but with the statues their money had sponsored. He was big, broad, and blonde, solid and Swedish, a slab of marble gone walking. He wore good suits, had nice shoes, and spoke as if he were a star pupil confessing minor sins. Buck wasn't like that. He was shorter, thicker, and too liberal with a stare. Old clothes. Bit grimy. Tie loose. No jacket. A blue, twice-patched, herringbone vest. His nose had been broken three times, and each time it had set back worse than before. He kept his hands in his pockets a lot, his Stetson cocked back, and his stubble mangy. His eyes were gray during the day, but at night they had the habit of taking whatever shade of neon was on offer.

The two walked quiet, reached the car, dodged trams northward, and had just started crossing the Burnside Bridge when Karl asked, as if to no one in particular, "So? What'd you think of the office?"

"Quite a bit of dough, isn't it?" Buck offered from the passenger side. He'd glanced at the contract. Gotten the gist.

"It's an investment."

"So you've said."

"But what about the office itself? The space? What'd you think?"

"It was nice. Good to know you'll get along with the neighbors. You and Dunleavy—thick as thieves already, huh?"

"He's alright."

"If you like presumptive sons of bitches."

"What'd you mean?"

"He really painted quite the picture back there, didn't he—waxing poetic over all the wives and kids and homey little bungalows that we have lined up. What'd you tell him, exactly?"

"I didn't tell him anything. He's just used to working with a certain type of fella, that's all. Fellas like us—ambitious; on the rise."

"Well, you didn't have to lie."

"What's the lie? I don't know about you, pal, but all that domestic stuff's coming for me soon enough. I didn't lie."

"Not that. I mean the stuff you said about the war."

"What, that? I was in the air corps, he just *assumed* I

13

flew. I would've told him right off I was a typist—I'm not ashamed of that. Alright, guess I see your point though; guess he is a bit presumptive. But who cares? It doesn't make him a bad landlord."

"No, I don't mean that either—I mean that thing you said about me having flat arches. Lie about yourself all you want—"

"—I didn't lie, I just didn't correct him, that's all."

"Well, I can correct folks just fine on my own."

"Come on. You heard how he was going on about that kid of his and all the fucking medals he'd won. He didn't seem like the broad-minded type to me. I thought it would just be easier that way."

"Easier?"

Karl looked over, "Yah, Buck, *easier*. People don't want to hear you talking about all that conchie shit. It offends people. Not everybody's as tolerant as I am. And you like to goad."

"Fuck 'em. It's my business."

"That's where you're wrong, pal; long as we're partners, it's *our* business. Together. Shared." The hum of the engine. The bell of a passing tram. The wipers battling hard against the rain. Karl cleared his throat and tossed the contract over. Buck flipped through it again, the words hitting his eyes like so much splatter on the windshield, bursting and blurring and falling away.

"I'll lose clients," he said.

Karl shrugged. Face dead. Coy to the last. "And gain others. It'll even out."

"*Bullshit*. Outside of Skid Row, I'm only ever on the eastside. Nobody knows me up Terwilliger. This doesn't help me a lick, and you know it. So—*partner*—if we're doing this, we're doing it sixty-forty. No matter how the cases shake out each month; no matter if the rent goes up, down, or sideways. You're sixty, I'm forty. That's the deal."

"What about fifty-five, forty-five?"

"No."

"Fine. Deal. Should we have it drawn up?"

"Have what drawn up?"

"The pay split."

"Do we need to?"

"Well, no, of course not. I trust you, and you trust me, but it's just that it might be good to have something we can both refer back to in case there's—you know—any confusion later on."

"Oh," Buck grunted, "well we wouldn't want any confusion, would we?" And so—in the spirit of prudent record keeping—he drafted a little memorandum for future review at the bottom of the contract, reading:

> *I, Buck Bordell, at 2:03 on the afternoon of Tuesday, May the 25th, 1948, got royally screwed.*

2

'Course, for all the ink spilt towards change, the next day kicked off pretty typically—with Buck sweating, hungover, and walking towards the same kind of spruced up, cedar-sided doll house where a healthy portion of his cases came from. The eastside had some alright spots these days; some deep-pocketed pockets where the houses were real trim. This one was yellow. Newly painted by the looks of it, with blooming rhododendrons out front, and a clean swept porch. Bright and fresh and hermetically middle-class.

He knocked.

Nothing.

Knocked again.

Waited.

Christ, it was hot out today. Been that way all month,

despite the rain. He'd done his best—sleeves rolled, vest open—but it was no good. The sweat was thick on him already, and the sunlight seemed pinned to his collar.

Getting nothing at the door, he edged into the rhododendron to try and look through the front window. Place was empty inside. No lights. No movement. Not a fucking thing.

"Hello? Mrs. Whitmore?" he hollered, words steaming onto the glass.

He and Whitmore had spoken just that morning. She'd asked him to come by and hear about this case of hers in person. Annoying, then, for her to leave him standing there like some door-to-door dickhead who can't take a hint. Real annoying. He trampled over a few pink blossoms on his way out of the bush and onto the grass. Stood. Hands in his pockets, eyes on the gable, listening to the 'cross street *tak-tak* of the sprinklers. He threw his hat onto the dash, door lolling, and smoked one. Burned his forearm on the chassis. Tried the house again. "Fuck it," he grunted, mounting up and starting off. But as the car rounded the corner—and he'd started trying to remember where he could find a payphone 'round here—a woman darted into the street, wearing a white and red, rose-petaled summer dress, house slippers, and a frantic expression. Had a dog with her too. Little guy. Squirmy. A terrier maybe. And she was waving him around as if he were a checkered flag over at the Downs.

Huh.

Buck didn't stop exactly, but he slowed enough for the lady to take it as an invitation, sticking her curly, blonde, green-banded mop in through the passenger side window, keeping pace and demanding, "Are you detective Bordell?"

"Buck's fine," he answered.

That was all she needed to hear. She and Fido hopped in, "*Drive!*"

"Sure."

And he did. One block. Another. Turn after turn. But the gal didn't say anything. She just sat with her chin pressed hard into her shoulder, looking back, scrutinizing every car parked or passing, while the dog panted on her lap. He thought about the pistol he kept locked in the glovebox over on her side. Best not to mention.

Buck glanced over, "What's your dog's name?"

She gawped at him for a long moment. "I don't have a dog."

"Sure," he said agreeably.

"Oh, you mean… well, this… this is… *Bertram*," she said, reading the collar, "Did you see anyone back there? Back at the house, did you see anybody waiting around or anything? Did you see a truck with wiring all over it? A white one with a dent in the door?"

"Don't think so."

"Are you sure?"

"Not really."

She turned, "You *are* Mr. Bordell, aren't you? Of Bordell-Svensson Investigations? The one I spoke to on the phone this morning?"

"I am."

"Well, how do you do, Mr. Bordell? I'm Doreen Whitmore. Was I wrong in thinking that you were *supposed* to be some kind of detective?"

"Private eye."

She chucked the dog into the back seat, "And a blind one, at that. Just drive."

"Where to?"

"Around."

"OK."

On they went. Around and around and around with the little dog yipping away until Whitmore deigned to dangle back a hand for him to wriggle against—a gesture she seemed practiced in.

"Not your dog, huh?"

"He's borrowed. I'll bring him back after we've talked." They nosed onto Belmont Street and the lady's attention returned to scrutinizing its every moving inch. Bird's nests. Grocery bags. The insides of people's pockets. Straining and peering and staring at the inscrutable tangle as it crawled along around them.

"And when, exactly do you figure we'll start the talking part?" Buck asked.

She didn't answer. Shook her head. Waved him off.

Directed him to turn again, quick as they'd come, towards Lone Fir Cemetery, where the sight of its stunted little mausoleum tower seemed to calm her significantly, "Pull over," she said.

He obliged, shuttering the engine and opening his door. "What the hell are you doing?" she asked.

"Getting out."

"We shouldn't."

"We'll roast in here."

"They'll spot me."

"Who?"

She stared at him as if he were the dumbest man who'd ever lived or breathed or spoke, and certainly the dumbest to have done all three, right there, at the same time. "I told you—*I don't know*. But fine—if you *insist*." She flung open the door. Stood. Started for the cemetery pathway. Turned, "*Well*, Mr. Bordell? Are you *coming*?" And then she was off again before Buck could respond, hot-footing it so fiercely that she was liable to ignite the grass. Buck watched her go. She was a looker for sure; one of those soft featured, round-hipped, All-American gals they used to have on the newsreels doling out rationing tips. Not his type, really. But the mutt was mad for her. Moment she'd gone, he started yipping and carrying on. Buck scooped him up by the belly and went to follow.

At first, she was like she'd been in the car. Skittish. Suspicious. Hurrying between the moss-laden names of moldering pioneers and the firs they fed. The ground smelled warm, dry grass crackling underfoot. The air buzzed. They did a lap 'round the headstones, and then another. Molasses thick in the air. Bertram and Buck panting together, waiting on Whitmore. Finally, under the sharp shadow of the mausoleum eaves, she stopped. "I suppose you read the papers?"

"Not if I can help it."

She didn't seem to hear him, "I suppose you heard how they... *found* him? *Where* they found him?"

He nodded.

"We started seeing each other regularly again two months ago... it'd been... well, we hadn't seen each other for too long before that, but things were getting better. We were talking again. He came over and had dinner with John and I just a week ago. He seemed so good. So like himself. I would have been able to tell if he'd been..." she drew her shoulders up and sighed deeply, "It just doesn't make sense. I know Eli frequented that *Spindelman's Music Hall* downtown on occasion, and I know they get up to all kinds of things down there, but he loved his music, my brother. That's it. That's all it was. He was too smart; too... *together* to mess around so *publicly* like that."

"Mess around how? Don't suppose you mind being a bit more specific?"

"I trust you know full well to what I'm referring."

"Guess you'll have to."

21

"We needn't get snippy, Mr. Bordell."

"'Course not, miss."

"Missus."

"Right. Sorry. It's only—and I don't mean to be insensitive—but I didn't come to hear a eulogy."

"I know full well why you came."

"Well, then you'll know it's a good idea for me and you to be explicit about things—no matter how uncouth. Otherwise, I spend half my time chasing euphemisms."

A throat clearing rattle of irritation from the lady, her voice tight, "What I mean to say is that Eli was a good man. Not without flaw, of course, but upright, if you take my meaning."

"I don't."

"Well, among other things, he was wary of illicit substances."

"He tell ya that himself, did he?"

"He didn't have to. It was obvious."

"Look, no disrespect meant, but most the *upright* seeming fellas I know got something or other proppin' 'em up that way—obvious or not."

"We're not talking about too many Tom Collins' on the weekend; we're talking about *heroin*. You know, I don't doubt that your cynical little flourishes are very impressive to *some* people, Mr. Bordell, but you shouldn't count me among them. My brother mixed socially in a way that was ill-advised, perhaps, but he was not a junkie. He had his faults, his vices if you like, but any listing of the great and the good of this city would not easily omit his name."

"OK."

"He isolated *himself*, you know. He was proud. He was stubborn."

"OK," Buck said again.

"John routinely invited him to the Portlandia mixers, to the socials and to the fundraisers for Mrs. McCollough Lee. You know of her, don't you? Mrs. McCollough Lee?"

"Nope."

"You should. She's to be the next mayor. She's going to finally make this city respectable—clean it up."

"Good for her."

"Such ambivalence is understandable coming from a man like you, but Eli's reticence was inexplicable. When John and I married, things between my brother and I grew... strained. It was natural. As we got older it became more and more obvious that our lives were taking us in different directions and, for a while anyway, neither of us quite knew how to, I don't know, *articulate* that to one another. But whatever our past squabbles, we were coming together again. And then he learned that I was pregnant, and he was to be an uncle, and he was over the moon about it. Things were good. Not perfect, but good. We'd moved past the unpleasantness. When he came over last week, he brought me a record for Pete's sake, as a peace offering or a joke, I don't know which. He knew I don't care much for jazz, but I appreciated it all the same."

"And did you happen to see his arms that day?"

Whitmore's stare damn near broke skin. Unblinking. Unimpressed. Another familiar gesture, Buck assumed.

"It might've been a mistake, my calling you," she said.

He spit. Shrugged. "That mean you want your dog back?"

"Are you always so antagonistic towards the people who intend to hire you?"

"Time to time."

"It's bad business."

"Look, I reckon you know more mayors-to-be than I do, but I've seen lots of fellas take the slide, and you'd be surprised how far down a guy can go before anybody notices; how quiet it all is until it gets loud. And if that's the case here, I figure it saves me time and you money. But maybe you just wanna be indulged? If that's the case, I suggest you go somewhere else. I'm not one of those Grand Ave stumble-fucks who'll give you the run around long as the checks keep clearing. So—*respectfully*—it's not bad business. Bad conversation, maybe. But *good* business in *my* business means clarity. You to me; me to you. If you don't *want* that, hell, there's a dozen outfits who'll take you on, no questions asked. But with me, your money buys plain-speaking."

"And the speechifying?"

"Free with the consultation."

"Well, you're wrong on one count—I *can't* go to any *Grand Ave stumble-fuck*, as you so eloquently put it—my husband happens to be an important man with his firm, and the prominence of his position compels him—and I, for that matter—to avoid being drawn into anything too sordid. He doesn't even know I'm talking to you. Nor will he, *understand*?"

"'Course."

"If I'm wrong, you get your fee, and the scandal of my brother's death fades in time. But if I'm right, the whispers will be dispelled outright."

"A murdered brother is more socially convenient than a junkie, that it?"

"It's a crude way to put it."

"Uh-huh."

"My reasons are many. I want the truth. I want discretion. And it happens that you come recommended in both departments. You worked for a friend of mine last year. She said you were... *prickly*, Mr. Bordell, and I see that she was right, but I suppose your being prickly has its advantages for the customer."

"I aim to please."

"You aim badly."

"You don't know the half of it. What makes you so sure something happened to your brother, anyway—something other than the obvious, that is?"

"The papers said Eli was found in an alley outside of a

place called *Bon Vivants* in Old Town. They implied that he had been a… customer there. Do you happen to know what kind of establishment *Bon Vivants* is, Mr. Bordell?"

"Dimly."

Doreen made a sour face, "I'm sure. Well, what you'll understand then—however vaguely—is that my brother had *no business* being anywhere near that kind of establishment. It wasn't to his taste. You take my meaning?"

"I'm with ya."

"Good." Her shoulders inched downward; hands together. They walked on, Buck shuffling the mutt from arm to arm, listening, "Eli and I were close as children. And once both our parents were gone, all we had was one another and no room for secrets. He was older, but not by much. I think I was the first person who ever really knew."

"You tell that to the cops?"

"More or less."

"And what'd they say?"

"Much the same as you."

"Well, that's embarrassing."

"In fact, the only one who *hasn't* lectured me so far is Mr. Takahashi."

"Who's that?"

"The other detective I've hired."

Buck stopped. "What?"

"After speaking to Mr. Stevenson, your associate, I—"

"—Svensson—"

"—The man's rude, whatever his name, and I didn't much care for the way he spoke to me, so I made a few additional inquiries and was given Mr. Takahashi's number."

"And you hired him?"

"Yes."

"So, why are you talking to me?"

"I want *you* looking into this as well. My friend at the Portlandia Club spoke quite highly of you."

"Portlandia? That would've been Karl, not me."

She took him in for a long, quizzical moment, "You know, it's funny, you remind me of Eli, in a way. He could be so willful."

"Flattering. But this Takahashi guy? How's he supposed to factor in?"

"You'll work together."

"Will we?"

"You'll have to. After Eli's death, I transcribed an address book of his and put together a list of places he frequented—like that dreadful music hall for instance. It isn't much to go off of, but I gave it to Frank yesterday and paid him a week's advance. I did try contacting you first."

"Frank, huh?"

"Yes. Mr. Takahashi."

"Well, call *Frank*, and get the list back."

"You'll share it."

"No."

"Why not?"

"Because that's not how this works. With one guy askin', a question's just a question. It's casual. Just talking. But when you have two guys running around making a bunch of noise, it starts to look like some J-Edgar-boy bullshit, like an investigation, and when that happens people clam up. They disappear. Trust me, it works best solo."

"No."

"No?"

"I want to ensure results. Mr. Takahashi stays on."

"Why?"

She shrugged, "I like him."

"But not me?"

A pause. "You come recommended."

"You've mentioned. What if I save myself the headache?"

"Well, that'd be disappointing. But I'll tell you the same thing I told Mr. Takahashi; that if you find proof that something happened to my brother, there's a one-thousand-dollar bonus in it for you. On top of your normal fee, of course."

"That's a lot of scratch."

"I believe in incentivization."

"Good business, huh?"

"Exactly."

"And if I get you your answers all on my own? What happens to the bonus then?"

"Why don't you want to work with Mr. Takahashi?"

"I told you already."

"Is it because he's Japanese?"

"The guy could be from Timbuktu for all I care."

"Because that would be an ugly, ugly thing, Mr. Bordell. The war's over. You have to leave it behind you if we're to move forward as a nation, do we not?"

"I was a conscientious objector."

"Really?"

He shrugged, spit, and shifted Bertram to wipe the exasperation from his brow.

Whitmore went sour again, "I'd have preferred your being a bigot."

"Sorry to disappoint."

"But Eli would have approved. He was a lofty sort of man. Yes. Yes, alright. I want you on the case, Mr. Bordell. Will you take it?"

Buck sucked a tooth, thinking. The thing was so obviously a goat-rope he could already smell the manure. But he reckoned he could shake this Takahashi guy early, get some dealer to squeal, work over Whitmore a bit, and take both shares of the two g's, easy. Yah. Doable. "OK, but before I go agreeing to anything, I got another question for you."

"What's that?"

He held out Bertram, "Who's fucking dog is this?"

3

"Well, I told you, didn't I?"

"No, you didn't."

"Sure, I did. I told you she sounded off when I talked with her on the phone. That she seemed a couple cents short of a dollar."

"That's not what you said."

Karl shrugged. He didn't care. In fact, he was barely listening. For the past hour, he'd been carefully transferring his archive of case files into moving boxes. "You taking Franklin?" he asked without looking up.

Years ago, a client had given Buck a framed photo of the then president in lieu of final payment, and Buck had kept it on his desk ever since. He liked FDR well enough—even if he'd never voted for him or anybody—but he'd kept the portrait mostly so clients would have a sympathetic expression to turn to while spilling their guts. It was the best he could do—not having a wife or a girlfriend to be pictured instead—and, without it, his side of the office looked like a wasteland. He kept no notes, read no novels, didn't go in for knick-knacks, and liked to keep his gun in the car. He had won no prizes, been bestowed no awards, and garnered no diplomas. He did have a small collection of bibles his father had sent him over the years *in* the desk—with their disintegrating corners and marginalia scarred pages—but a fella in his line wasn't helping business any by showing off the gospels. He'd tried updating the portrait to Truman for a while there, but he got tired of talking about the bomb, so he went back to good ole' Delano.

Karl continued, "Maybe use the governor in the next spot? The governor would be better. If we're going to have more bigwigs in and out of the office, it might get us some points. Maybe after the election you switch over to whoever wins? What'd ya think?"

Now it was Buck's turn not to care. He leaned back in his chair, mulling, "Anyway, it turned out to be the neighbor's dog."

"You don't say."

"After Whitmore hopped the fence, the mutt wouldn't stop barking, and she thought the noise might give her away, so she decided to take him along."

"*Give her away*? To who? What'd you mean?"

"She said she'd seen a couple of guys pull up in an old pickup and try jimmying the door just before I got there. She legged it out the backdoor when she saw 'em—hence the fence jumping. Says she'd seen the truck drive past the house two or three times already that morning before her husband left for work, like they were waiting for it to be empty; says she remembered seeing it specifically because, apparently, it had chicken wire all over it, like from a farm or something, and it had a big dent in the driver's side door. She figures it had something to do with what happened to her brother."

"Chicken wire? She's pulling your leg, pal. I bet she made the whole thing up just for attention. I bet she's not even related to the dead guy."

"Gave me his yearbook photo," Buck said, flashing the picture from his pocket.

"Alright, so maybe she really is his sister, that doesn't mean her story adds up. Sounds like she's bored to me— probably figures she can string along some sap for a while and keep herself entertained."

Buck shrugged. Karl cocked an eyebrow.

"Don't tell me you believe her?"

"Why not? Far as it goes, it *is* odd that they found the guy outside *Bons* like that."

"I'd have thought plenty of guys wash up down there."

"Sure, they do, but Charlemagne's always quick to scoop

32

'em up off the sidewalk and chuck 'em someplace else. They keep a tight ship over there, far as it goes."

The big man kept on packing, flipping through an immaculate folder labeled '46, A-G. "Alright. Fine. But it's still kind of thin, don't you think, Buck?"

"She seemed sincere."

"Did she now?"

"Yah."

"Yah?"

"*Yah.*"

"And which part of her struck you as most... *sincere*, exactly?"

"It's not like that."

"Sure, pal."

"It's not. She's married. Baby on the way, apparently. Not that you could tell."

"See?" Karl snorted, "You meet the husband?"

"Doreen said to keep him out of it," Buck said, rubbing his face. "God, it's hot today."

"Hey pal, whatever, it's your case. Long as the money holds out, what business is it of mine? She pay in cash?"

"Check. In the husband's name. Said he signs a couple dozen at the start of the month for her to fill out as needed. She promised a bonus too, if I can scare up some proof of foul play."

"How much?"

"Two grand."

That got Karl's attention. "Well, alright, sure, in that case, I can see the angle. Still, if it were me, I'd circle back around to the husband—whatever she says. Last thing we need is some guy kicking down our door at the new office, screaming about how we've been taking advantage of his wife's condition or something. You don't want to get sued, do you? For *real* this time, I mean?"

"It'll be fine." Buck stood, "I do need a favor, though. Think you can get me a copy of the autopsy report from your guy down at the coroner's office? Just so we can rule some things out?"

"Sure, pal. No problem."

"Thanks. OK. Figure I've put off talking to Maddy long as I can. Better get."

"Well, pack your stuff first, would ya? I'm driving a load over this afternoon after I finish my side. I want us out by tomorrow."

"Sure. One sec." Buck pulled a carton of cigs from the top drawer, Dad's postmarked bibles from the bottom, and set it all down in a box beside Mr. Roosevelt so he might have some things to keep him occupied on the trip. "There. OK, see ya."

Couple minutes later, Buck was driving west over the Willamette. Water was high today. And quick. Radio'd been buzzing about it since yesterday. Figures. All month it'd been rain and heat and heat and rain, May like a dog's mouth, so 'course the river was going to be bucking. He knew the feeling.

Oh well. Best to barrel through; to make your back so sleek with sweat that sin might find no purchase. That's what Dad would've said. Thundered, more like. Frothed.

He really should throw out those fucking bibles.

Le Bon Vivant was right in the center of Skid Row. A well-kept, brick two-story rising up off the street. Maddy had started the place with nothing but two other girls and a case of cheap champagne back when internment had cleared out the neighborhood and things were going cheap. Six years on, the place was an institution. A fixture of the community. Like the Shriners, or the post office. 'Round the clock, guys came by to get a little time with the cuckoos working upstairs, while other fellas popped corks in the beaded, red-draped whirlpool of the bar below. Maddy was always in the thick of things. Leading from the front. Table to table. Wink to smile. A font of gossip and jokes and double entendre. Back when Buck had first known her, she'd been Madison Irving of Troutdale. But her pretensions had since emigrated. Now, far as anyone knew, she was Madeline Le Blanc of Toulouse—a canny entrepreneur who'd smuggled her continental charms out of Vichy and over to the City of Roses. And it had to be said that the Madame had acclimated quite well. Her English was phenomenal, if strangely accented, while—out of red-blooded, Yankee-doodle fervor for her newfound home—she kept her French to the occasional *bon mots*, and to the curation of the atmosphere. There were French wines on offer, French cheeses, French music, French chairs and paintings and light fixtures. All of which spoke fluently enough on her behalf to fool the wanna-be sophisticates with neither the dough nor the sense to take their Francophilia someplace private. As it was, *Bon's* was among Buck's first stops whenever somebody'd lost a husband or a brother, son, father, uncle, cousin, friend, mechanic, lawyer, pharmacist, partner, or priest. Maddy didn't mind the occasional walkthrough, though, long as she got a piece. He liked her. She liked him. They had history. Long history. They respected each other—professional to professional.

"The fuck you doing here, Bordell?" she asked, taking him by the arm with a gracefully coercive motion the moment he stepped through the door, "You should have called. I got a councilman upstairs."

"Which one?"

"Never you mind *which one*. You really should have called."

"Was in the neighborhood. Since I'm here, can I snag you for a minute?"

She snorted contemptuously. "I *wish* it ever were that long with you. You *do* take advantage of one's *noblesse oblige*."

"Nice one. Been taking classes?"

"Shut up, Buck."

"OK."

"Come on." She dragged him into the bar and through to her office. She was wearing a red Foyle dress with white cuffs, and had her black hair done up in the most triumphant victory rolls he'd seen since VJ Day. Crimson lipstick. Considerable wedges. She crossed carpet the way scissors cross paper, and if the hangdog looks nipping at her heels were anything to go off, a couple of the barflies were hopelessly in love with her.

Most stayed quiet. But a few were bold, drunk, and bolder still.

"Maddy! Maddy, where'd you go just now? Come have a drink with me!" one of the slack-jaws sputtered as she passed.

"Buy something worth drinking, Hughey, and *peut-etre*," she answered lightly.

Another, "I got the brandy, Maddy! You like the brandy, don't ya?"

"*Bien sur*, gentlemen, *bien sur*, I will be back soon, but I've got some business at the moment," she patted Buck's arm.

Howls. Lamentations. The shaking of the walls and tearing of collars.

"You're one lucky son of a bitch, mister!"

"Ditch the stiff, Maddy, come on!"

"It's the good brandy! Come on! Maddy! Come on!"

The door shut behind them. Maddy's office was small

37

and orderly. There was an impressively ornate desk with laid out, ready envelopes, and little bouquets of cash set besides—freshly plucked. Mean streaks of sunlight came in from an east-facing window. Against the opposite wall, finishing a plate of biscuits, was Charlemagne, the biggest bear of a body man Buck had ever seen, presently licking the honey off his paws.

"Charlie," Buck said with a tilt of his hat.

Charlemagne sucked at a finger. Then another. Then took a long breath, set the plate aside, and nodded, "Buck."

Maddy threw herself behind the desk, "Charlie, dear, can you go and see that Hughey finds his way out the door in about five minutes? There's hot air enough already today."

"Yes, ma'am."

"And Emma said one of those starched boys in the back booth tried to short her last time, talk to him, would ya?"

"Yes, ma'am."

She lit a cigarette, "And when you're done with all that, if Buck here is still kicking around, skip the nice stuff and just throw him out."

"Yes, ma'am," the big man said for a third time but with fresh relish.

Maddy smiled, "Thanks, Charlie. That's all of it." The big man stood and once he'd lumbered out the room, she continued, "Now, Buck, to what do I owe the pleasure?"

"Hoping to talk to one of your girls."

"Usually, a guy pays for something like that."

"I'm a friend to the worker, Maddy, I don't mind paying long as it's by the minute, not the hour."

"Standard rate?"

"Fair enough."

She flicked some ash into a clam-shaped tray, "Let me guess, it's about this guy Thompson, isn't it?"

Huh.

"Thomayer," he corrected.

"Whatever."

"Been reading the paper then?"

She scoffed, "'Course I read the papers. But you're sucking hind on this one, Buck; some *Japanese* beat you to it. He came by an hour ago and caused a scene, so Charlemagne saw him out. He was upsetting the girls, the customers. It happens. Every once in a while, we still get a couple of them coming around here and acting like we owe them something—like it wasn't them who shot first. The nerve of it. Some of my girls were sweet on boys who sailed off and never came back too. I got a business to run, Buck. Girls to look after. It's a touchy subject."

He nodded unenthusiastically, "Seems like it. What was his name?"

"Who? The Jap?"

"Yah."

"Don't know."

"Was it Takahashi?"

"You deaf or something? I said I don't know. Go ask him yourself, he was still out there last time I checked, leaning on a light post. What is it with these people and surprise attacks, you think?"

Buck went to the window. The street was bustling. "Where?"

"You're the detective. Figure it out."

"OK. Hold on."

"Damnit, Buck, I was jok—" but Buck lost the rest as he hurried out to the street. Now was his chance to catch Takahashi and get the list off him. Then he could cut the bastard out altogether. He could handle Whitmore; could talk his way into the full bonus. It wasn't personal, he just couldn't have some asshole getting underfoot. Getting in the way. Cocking things up. Wasn't how he did things.

Takahashi wasn't hard to find. All Buck had to do was follow the stares far as the street corner, where the kid stood lock-legged, with a paper-cutter mustache, the smile of a grocer's boy, and the eyes of a truant officer. He was twenty-four at the oldest, done up in duds typical for the neighborhood—the same ole' jacket, suspenders, and flat cap hanging off every other Joe Nobody—but since internment a Japanese fella stuck out down here whatever he wore. Buck went straight over, hands in his pockets, sidling up, grinning big and broad and stupid, "Name's Frank, ain't it? Frank Takahashi?" he asked.

The kid paused. Looked around. Smiled back politely.

"Do I know you?"

"No, but we got a friend in common. A Mrs. Doreen Whitmore." He stuck out his hand, "Name's Buck—Buck Bordell—how are ya?"

"Oh, right. Nice to meet you." Cautiously, he shook, "Mrs. Whitmore told me you'd be in touch."

"She did, huh?"

"Yah, she called this morning."

"Well, good. Good-good."

Another pause.

"How'd you know I was here?"

"Great minds, kid. Natural place to start, ain't it? Speaking of, I hear you got thrown out of *Bon's* already. Hell of a thing when a guy can't even find welcome in a cathouse, ya know? Hell of a thing; hell of a world. What'd ya make a scene or something?"

"It was them causing the scene."

"Maddy says otherwise."

"Is she the madam?"

"The owner."

Kid shrugged, cheery little kick to his voice, "Well, she's lying. I just asked a question, and she started in on me."

"Don't take it personally. Maddy can be a bit territorial, that's all."

"*Territorial*," Frank repeated philosophically, "That's rich."

"Is it?" Buck asked, reaching for his cigs and sewing

41

up the smile tearing 'cross his face with a fresh-lit little needle, "You can't be too surprised she took that kinda talk poorly."

"I didn't say that to *her*, of course."

"*Smart.*" He took a drag, "But you went in guns blazing, huh? Asking about Thomayer, and all that? What'd she say?"

"Other than calling me a '*Jap*?'"

"Yah, other than that."

"Nothing really. She just sicced the big guy on me. What'd ya make him? Six-four? Six-five?"

"Don't know."

"Six-five, I bet."

"Well, don't take all that too personal either—getting thrown out by Charlemagne's a rite of passage."

Cheery, "If you say so."

"And I do. Smoke?" Buck offered. The kid passed, but Buck lent him some anyway via a long and level exhale. He was generous like that, "So... me and you, huh? Paired up. You do much of this sorta thing before?"

"Lots in the army."

"They got PIs in the army?"

"No, I mean the being part of a unit; a squad—that part."

"Well how 'bout the PI part?"

"Nope."

"Yah, me neither."

"But if it's what the lady wants, I suppose we best figure it out. That's the job."

"Took the words right outa my mouth, kid," Buck said, plugging up another smirk. And then, after a spongy, blue-thin minute, ventured, "Still… the specifics might be tricky."

"You think?"

"Well, there's two schools of thought, isn't there? There's the divide and conquer approach—which maybe you'll be partial to, given your army experience—and then there's the option that we treat this case like some kinda three-legged footrace and spend the whole time tripping up on one another, which doesn't seem ideal."

"I think Mrs. Whitmore envisioned us sticking together."

"Sure. OK. But joined at the hip? If you try getting back into *Bons,* you're just gonna get chucked out on your ass again."

"You and the madam are friends; you can vouch for me."

"Fat fucking chance. I don't got *that* kinda pull. Nobody does."

The kid was practical enough to agree, but Buck could tell the implication irked him. Ego's a tricky thing when it comes to bird-dogging—a fella needs some piss to go with his vinegar; some animating enmity—but this ain't the business for preening, self-satisfied little pricks who

43

think the world gives a hot damn about a shaking finger. No, a fella's gotta take it as it comes and give it back into the ribs; gotta know when to bite and when to chew.

"What'd ya say, kid? Daylight's burning."

"Yah, sure, why not? Go ahead. I'll wait."

"There we go."

"Do you need a pen?"

"What?"

"A pen. Do you need one?"

"What the hell for?"

"For the notes you're going to take."

"I ain't taking notes."

"What if you forget something?"

"Then I forget."

"What if it's important?"

"Then I won't."

Kid cocked his head, scratching at the side of his mouth, "Gotta say, friend, that doesn't make as much sense to me as it might to you."

"Don't worry, I'll pan your nuggets for ya and leave the rest. Trust me, most the time, more's just more."

"Not sure I agree on that count either."

"Well take it 'round the corner. Maddy can see ya standing here and it's winding her up."

"Fella can stand where he likes, can't he?"

There was that pride of his, cracking out and sizzling on the sidewalk. Buck smiled and flicked a salute into his hat brim, "Suit yourself."

Back at *Bons*, Maddy had obviously been watching the scene through the window, stewing. "What'd he say?" she asked, lighting a fresh one.

Buck waved her off, "Oh, you know."

"No, Buck—no, I don't know. You told him to beat it, didn't you?"

"Sure."

"*And*?"

"And, I don't know, kid got a little huffy, I guess. Said something about somebody being a thief and him not going anywhere—I don't know," Buck said, sucking a tooth thoughtfully and sitting on the desk edge, "Something like that anyway. You know how some guys get—only excuse they need to kiss the train is for the conductor to blow the whistle."

Maddy spun back to the desk and took up the phone, "We'll see about that."

"'Bout what? Who ya calling?"

She glared at him, brow arched and jaw set.

"What the *cops*? Ah, come on, Mads," Buck grunted, too quick to hide his distaste, "Really?"

"What'd you make yourself a friend out there, or something?"

"No."

"Then what'd you care?"

"I don't. It's just… kid's prideful, that's all."

"Prideful about *what*, Buck? I own this place fair and square."

"Nobody said you didn't. Just no need to call the flat-foots is all I'm saying. Give him a minute, he'll wander off."

"And what's that—the Buck Bordell guarantee? Thanks, but no thanks. I've known you too long." And then, into the phone, leaning so hard into the accent she almost cracked the plastic, "*Bonjour monsieur*, zis is Madeline Le Blanc for officer McClean. *Oui*, I will 'old." She pressed the receiver into her chest, looking over, "You sticking around or what?"

"What about me talking to some of the girls from the other night?"

"I can save you time, they won't know anything. The papers got it wrong, this guy Thomas didn't come in that night."

"Thomayer."

"Sure."

"But maybe some other night? Maybe he was on his way and just didn't make it. Maybe one of the girls would know?"

"You're set on asking?"

"Long as you don't mind."

"Of course, I mind, but if it'll get rid of you faster and keep Charlie focused on the patrons, then *d'accord*. Polly and Sue were working late that night, but Sue's booked, so Polly will have to be enough."

"That's fine. Which room's hers, again?"

Maddy laughed sharply, "Come on, Buck, don't act like you need directions."

He stood. "How long?"

"Ten minutes enough?"

"No."

"Too bad. Now go… Ah, 'allo Monsieur McClean, I 'ate to trouble you, *mais…*"

Buck lost no time. He hot-footed it out the office and through the bar, stalked by Charlie's jaundiced, big-cat eyes while the rest of him purred disquietingly into some slump spilling off his stool. He went up the stairs, past some faceless schlub on the landing, and on back to Polly's room at the end of the hall. Light off. No murmurs. Clear as clear got 'round here. Inside, he found a baby-faced blonde with a scrunched nose reading some worn dime store paperback with a smiling cowboy on the cover. Her preference for the cowpoke was obvious. She rolled her eyes as Buck came in, languidly flipping to the next page, and shaking her head, "*Oh,*" she said, "Hi, *Buck.*"

"Hiya, Polly."

"Thought you was banned 'till June."

"You're thinking of Bert."

"Who's Bert?"

"No time for small talk I'm afraid, Pols—think I can bend your ear for a minute?"

"*Pssht.* You know, a fella of mine got in a heap of trouble 'cause of you. Good customer too. Haven't seen him for weeks."

"Sorry about that."

"No, you ain't."

"It's different this time. I'm looking into that stiff from a couple days back. The one they found outside."

"Lookin' how?"

"Just looking, you know, don't know too much yet. I was hoping you could help me out."

"Me?"

"Yah."

"Why?"

"Weren't you working that night?"

Polly glanced at the nightstand. Each room was rigged with a switch that connected to an emergency light downstairs. All it took was a quick flip and Charlie would come charging. "Maddy know you're here?"

"Uh-huh."

"Really?"

"Would I lie to you?"

"Sure you would. Everybody lies to me. That, or they don't talk to me at all."

"Come on, Pols, don't pout. It's all been worked out downstairs." He came over and sat beside her on the bed, one leg splayed lengthwise and the other planted, "Cig?" he offered.

"Yah."

He handed one over, letting her sink into a few drags

before breaking out Eli's picture. "This guy look familiar?"

"Nope."

"That was quick."

"He don't. Sorry."

"Look again."

She did. Shook her head. Another drag.

"Think any of the other girls might know him?"

"How should I know?"

"The name Elias Thomayer mean anything to you?"

This time she waited a beat. Tapped her chin. Pushed her hair off her ear. Same result. "*Nope*," she said like she was smacking gum in her mouth.

"What about the other girls?"

"You think I'm some kinda mind reader, do you, Buck?"

"You all talk, don't you?"

"Yah, but not about him. And not about you either, just so's you know."

"Shame." He slipped the picture back into his pocket. "What about that night? Last Sunday it was; you remember anything odd that night? Hear anything? See anything?"

Her eyes fluttered, bouncing off the wall and up to the ceiling over the course of a long, long drag, "I told you, I don't know the guy."

"Anything odd that night? See anybody hanging out, keeping to themselves? What about the windows, you have 'em open, right? It's been hot as hell, 'course you had 'em open."

"Yah, the windows were open. So what? Come on, Mac,

I didn't see nothing, I didn't hear nothing, and I don't know nothing neither."

He thought for a minute.

"What about a white pickup? One that was all dented up, maybe? With, uh, *chicken wire* on it? Something like that?"

Her disinterest hiccupped for a second. "Nope," she said, recovering. "Or, I mean, there's lots of pickups out here, aren't there? What am I supposed to remember every one of 'em?"

"So, you saw something?"

"No. I mean, how should I know? This is a busy block, pal, and the view's not so good from the bed, is it? I don't keep tabs."

"You're sure?"

"Yah, I'm sure. You're being a real pest, you know that?"

"It's the job, Polly."

"That ain't no excuse to be wasting a girl's time, hitting her with questions she don't know nothing about. There's no dignity in that. That's fly work, fella, *buzz buzz.*"

She had him there. "What about when all this came out? You hear any of the girls say anything?"

"Jeez you're a broken record. I only heard what Maddy said about it. She wasn't happy on account of how the papers threw us into the story, not with the money she spends to keep us outa there. Imagine that, huh? Some newspaperman taking our dough only to turn around and come after us? It ain't right. There should be a law."

"Tell the chief next time he's through."

"*Ha. Ha. Ha.*"

"Speaking of, I assume Maddy hasn't had any problems with the vice boys since the article?"

"What'd you think?"

"So, it's just the principle that's upsetting her?"

"Yah, that's it—the principle."

He lit one of his own, "You seem a little nervous, Polly."

"'Cause you're *making* me nervous. I told you I don't like being pestered."

"Yah, you did. Just seems like you're being cagey is all."

"Well, I ain't."

"OK."

"And you don't get to just come in here and call me a liar. I don't have to stand for that."

"I didn't say you were lying."

"No, but that's what you meant."

"Come on, Pols, throw me a bone here. What'd you know?"

"Nothing. The guy wasn't here; I got nothing for you."

"What about that truck?"

She reached for the nightstand. "Why don't you ask Charlemagne, buddy boy."

Buck shot up. "No, no, no, I'm leaving." He fished a dollar out of his pocket and handed it over, "Thanks, Polly. You've been swell. Call me when you get your memory back."

"Go to hell, Buck."

He tipped his hat and hurried out. Polly followed him

out to the landing, arms crossed, foot tapping. That was enough for Charlemagne. The big guy moved to block Buck's path, but Buck went wide, squeezing past a pair of lip-biting silver hairs and the wall. But when he tried to shut Maddy's office door behind himself, a big, meaty palm held it firm as steel.

"Time to go, Mac."

"Yah, sure thing, just gotta talk to the boss for a sec."

Charlemagne looked past to Maddy. She sighed heavily, "This time it's *exactly* a minute. Start counting, Charlie."

"I talked to Polly," Buck said quickly, "It's just like you said, she didn't know the guy."

"See," the madam said convincingly enough.

"But she *did* say something about some truck or something that came by that night. Might've been white? One that was all dented up or something? With wiring all over it? I don't know. She said it was suspicious somehow. Anything on that?"

Maddy tightened. "I don't know what she's talking about. We get lots of traffic on this block. How are we supposed to keep track of it all?"

"Uh-huh."

"What's that count at, Charlie?"

"Twenty-six, ma'am."

"Count faster, would you? Buck here is really starting to bore me."

"OK, OK, Maddy, no need for that. I'm going."

"Good."

"Can I use the back stair without Charlie clobbering me?"

"The back stair? Why?" She glanced outside, "Ah. Still dodging the precinct boys, are we? Is that what it was about earlier? Don't worry, *mon cheri*, I wouldn't call the fuzz on you. I wouldn't need to. We're *friends*." Buck risked a step further into the office to get a better look out the window. There were two cops standing either side of Frank down the block. Close. Crowding. Buck recognized one of them.

He frowned, "Ah, Maddy—why'd you have to go and fink on a guy like that?"

"Thought you didn't care."

"I don't. 'Course I don't. But the cops, Maddy? McClean? Thought you were bluffing earlier."

She ground out her cigarette with her immaculate, blood-red nails. "I don't bluff, Buck. You know that. Count, Charlie?"

"We're at forty-four now, ma'am. Forty-five. Forty-six. Forty—"

"—Best get to going, Buck."

So, he did, bolting past Charlemagne and back through the bar, "Wrong way, Mac!" the body man hollered after, but Buck ignored him. There'd been a change of plans. Cutting the kid out of the case was one thing, but if the cops went and roughed up Takahashi moments after Buck'd left him on the street corner, the kid might get the idea that Buck'd had something to do with it and go squawking to Whitmore. He couldn't have that. Plus, the idea of word going 'round that he and the beat boys had their hands in one another's pockets was more than he could bear.

Outside, Buck beelined it for Frank and the cops, hollering as he came on, "Hey! Hey, McClean, I thought that was you! How was the policeman's ball this year? You go stag again?"

The crewcuts menacing the kid turned; the nearest—McClean, the one Buck recognized—was thick-necked and fat-headed as a buffalo. "Fuck off, Bordell," he said wearing one of those terrible, gone-wrong grins that came standard with the badge.

"Sure thing—once you're done hassling my associate here. He's got a train to catch."

McClean jabbed his nose in Frank's direction, "You know this guy?"

"Oh, sure. We go way back. Bosom buddies."

"That make you some kinda Seamus, too?" the other copper barked, feeling ignored.

Buck eyed him, "Jesus, Pat, what's with the rookie? What happened to Behan?"

"Made detective," McClean answered.

"Yah? Makes sense. I always figured him for it eventually. Has the look, you know?"

"True."

"Some guys just can't handle the beat."

The rookie again, "Watch what you say, Seamus. You...
you goddamned Seamus."

"Hey, pal, that's real good! Learn a couple more words
and you'll be ready for the circus." The crack was a
bit of a risk. You never knew how a rookie was gonna
react these days. Most of the ones coming up now had
missed the war—even the few who hadn't, had spent it
sorting mail or something—and *all* of them had missed
the wood-smoke, dog-ass days of the old town, so they
tended to be pretty loose with the vinegar. Had things to
prove. Worse, they really did seem to respect that shiny
badge of theirs. The fraternal this; the benevolent that.
Say what you want about a guy like McClean—and there
was *plenty* to say—but he knew better than to go in on
that delusion. It's corrosive. That's why so many of these
new guys flamed out so fast; why they spent a couple
years bungling, bashing, and hassling before they traded
up or traded out. The lifers? The full pension boys? They
were thugs alright, but they knew it. Thick as pig shit to
a man, but clear-eyed.

So, when the rookie took a step, Buck was pretty sure
he'd be getting a fourth nose break out of the deal, but
McClean stopped it dead with a wheezy gurgle that was
as close to a laugh as he could muster. Buck wasn't sure
why, exactly. Maybe they were too close to *Bon*'s to make a
scene, or maybe it was too damn hot out, or maybe it was
just that McClean didn't like the guy any more than Buck

did, the sneery little pissant. Lucky, whatever the case.

McClean turned back to Frank. "Look here, pal, you're disturbing the neighborhood, and we can't have that. You gotta clear out. Right now."

"I'm just standing here, officer" Frank said, voice level, eyes straight.

"That's loitering."

"Loitering isn't a crime."

"Says who?"

"The Portland city code."

"It is when you're menacing folks."

"Menacing? I'm just—"

"—You got something wrong with your hearing? You know full well what you're doing out here, and you're going to clear out or things are going to get nasty."

"Come on, Franky, let's ditch the flatfoots, huh?" Buck said, angling a shoulder in between Frank and the cops, taking the kid by the elbow, "We got that train, remember? I am still driving you, aren't I? Cars just 'round the block, Frank. Come on, let's go." The kid brushed him off. Twitched. Smile puckering. Choking on something; choking bad. But he kept his cool and drank the middle distance. Face like plaster—dignified, cheery, and fixing for a crack soon as the batons started swinging. Buck pressed, "Come on, Frank; come on, let's go."

McClean leaned in, voice dead, "You gonna go on and listen, son? Are you?"

Horns down the street. Couple of shouts. The heat. The glare. The sunlight thick on the air, like juice squeezed from a vice.

Quiet, "You hear me, you *Jap bastard*?"

"The kid hear's ya, Pat."

McClean let the rancid look slide down his face, and stepped back, "Good. You fellas have a nice day now."

"Officers," Frank said, pinching his brim and stepping off on his own. Buck hustled after. The walk was tense as hell. The kid had done good. He hadn't bubbled over or doubled back; didn't go stomping, screaming, threatening, or otherwise making an ass of himself. He didn't lash out. Didn't lose it. No. He kept his hands unclenched and his eyes ahead. He kept alert. He swallowed the poison. He was livid, that much was obvious, but even if he didn't know what to *do* with all the bile, he at least knew what *not* to do; he at least knew that a man's pride grew back quicker than his teeth. That was good. A start, really.

"So," Buck asked at the end of the block, "You hungry?"

4

Delancey's was quiet most days; a used-up matchbook kind of place where the serious boozers came to take the high dive into oblivion. Red letters on the window and green, glass-shingle lights over the booths. Bridles on the wall. Crosscutters. Cig smoke so thick you could scoop it out the air and onto your toast. On weekends, brakemen from the railyard down the hill would blaze through like the express to Seattle and be there sounding the whistle 'till dawn.

But today was Wednesday, and Wednesdays were quiet.

"What do ya think of the place?" Buck asked, lighting one up.

Frank nodded.

"You'll come 'round. The grub's better than you'd think. Can I get ya a beer?"

"It's three o'clock."

"Thanks for the update. Beer?"

"Sure."

Buck hollered over to Raul the bartender to load them up a couple snub noses. "So, how long you been in the racket, Frank?"

"Got my license last year."

"Getting many cases?"

"I stay busy."

"It's hard starting out. You can't let guys like McClean get to you."

"He doesn't, and I don't."

"Oh, no? 'Cause it seemed he had his finger *right* in your eye."

"I've seen worse."

"I bet. You spent much time in Skid Row?"

"I grew up in *Japantown* if that's what you mean—3rd and Couch. Made milk money folding sheets at the Royal Palm Hotel and unloading crates for Mr. Ito at the grocery. Bussed over to Benson for high school. Played cornerback."

"I meant since the clear out."

"Not so much, no."

"But you know who Maddy is? You know about *Bon*'s?"

"I know that it used to be old man Tanaka's hardware store."

"Well, least a fella can still get a screw thereabouts, huh?" Buck joked reflexively. Frank's smile didn't budge an inch. Didn't laugh. Didn't move. He just let the crack roll off him and onto the liquor-stuck floor as Raul brought over two fresh bottles of lacquer, "*Comida*?" he barked.

"What kind of pie you got?" Frank asked.

"None kind."

"Hush puppies?"

"No."

They haggled like that for a while, with Frank eventually landing on the chicken. After Raul had gone, Buck asked, "So which camp? Heart Mountain or Minidoka?"

Kid's brow slid up a tick, surprised, "Heart Mountain. But I didn't care for Wyoming, so I went to Italy. Then France. Then Germany."

"War hero, huh?"

"Did my part."

"And now you're back."

"And now I'm back."

Buck nodded. Frank nodded. And the beers nodded a couple times too. Frank tried wiping some crud off the table. It didn't budge, "How about we talk about what you heard at *Bon Vivant's*. Lady's not paying us to drink and gab."

"You reckon she's crazy or what?"

"Who?"

"Whitmore. Seems a couple cents short of a dollar to me—seems to have a lot of fantastical ideas and not a lot of facts. When a guy turns up dead the way her brother did, there usually isn't much more to it than what you find cold on the street."

Philosophical again, "She seemed lucid to me."

"*Lucid*, huh?" Buck cleared his throat, "They all seem like that when you're starting out. Look, kid, you seem like a nice enough guy but I'm here to tell you that folks lie in this business. They lie about what happened, they lie about who it happened to, when and where and how, and they lie about the why most of all. Sometimes they don't do it on purpose, but that doesn't mean *we* don't end up holding the bag. It's a small town, really, and a fella's reputation can go dog-shit quick if he starts carrying water for cranks. And a fella like you's got it hard enough as is."

"It's nice of you to be so concerned."

"I'm just trying to get things straight, kid. We're supposed to be the professionals here. If word gets 'round that we're the types to take some Laurelhurst housewife for a ride, well, that has an impact on both our reputations."

All that dropped into Frank without even a ripple. "I believe her."

"You do, huh?"

"Just a feeling."

Buck snorted into his longneck, "Cute, kid."

"And since we're a couple fellas straight-shooting over here, I'm gonna have to ask you to stop calling me that."

"What? *Kid*?"

"Yah."

"Don't mean nothing by it."

"Then I suppose it'll be pretty easy to stop."

"Now-now, don't get tough on me—it's McClean you're mad at. You're welcome for that, by the way."

"I had it."

"Really? Seemed to me like you were about two seconds from getting your jaw busted."

"That shames them, not me—reveals them for the thugs they are—which helps in the long run. It's good to figure out who you can work with and who you can't."

"Been finding many cops you *can* work with, have ya?"

"Here and there."

"Yah?"

Kid shrugged affably, "Well, it's important to stay open to the possibility, anyway."

"If you say so."

The kid plucked out a notebook, "Let's talk about the case. What'd you hear at *Bon Vivant's*?"

"Nothing," Buck answered, and it was even kinda true. It was what Mads *hadn't* said that was interesting. It was that she'd pretended to forget Thomayer's name. Twice. Maddy'd never forgotten a name in her life, much less the one that'd got her dragged into yesterday's edition of the *Oregonian*. She'd been nervous too. Brittle. That wasn't like her either. She was hiding something when she gave him that line about the truck and the traffic—the one she'd coached Polly on.

"You didn't hear *anything*?"

"Nothing important anyway."

Frank pushed his patience down onto the creased, blank, waiting pages, "Indulge me."

So, Buck did, recounting his every step and every word. Only parts he left out were all the parts that mattered. Frank took it down rote, ignoring the food Raul brought, his digestion otherwise engaged. He sat there listening and nodding and enshrining each and every meaningless detail. Page after page. Talking to him was like standing beside one of those pale water, pin-prick lakes up on Mt. Hood. Whatever you chucked in just sank and sank and sank down all clear and cold and considered, and when it finally came to touch bottom it looked as natural and true as if it'd been there since the beginning of time. It was boring, really.

"You should eat. Raul gets moody if ya let things get cold."

"Do you think anybody might be lying? This Polly, maybe? Or Maddy?"

"God, she'd hate it if she heard you calling her that."

"Well?"

Buck shrugged, "It's possible."

"But you don't think so?"

"No."

"Why not?"

"Well, it's like I told ya, Maddy's territorial, so she wouldn't cover for somebody treating her place like a dumping ground, and she's in like a tick with the down-

63

town crowd; the rackets, the pinball, hell, even Big Jim tips his hat her way—nobody wins by fucking her over."

"Maybe."

"Definitely."

"But if that's the case then how'd it end up in the papers?"

"Fluke."

"Or—if she's as untouchable as you say, as connected—maybe that's the point and somebody's using her to send a message. Maybe they were using Thomayer too."

Huh.

It wasn't the craziest thing Buck had ever heard. Not that the kid needed to know. "That's a lot of maybes so far, Franky boy," he said, flagging down Raul for another round, "An *awful* lot of maybes."

"It's just a thought."

"Yah-yah, I get ya."

"Well, what about you? Do you have any theories, or is this just a paycheck job?"

"I didn't realize you were working *pro bono*. That's noble of you."

"I didn't mean it that way."

"Suppose that means you won't be wanting the bonus then. Maybe you should call Whitmore and tell her. There's a phone at the end of the bar there. I'll even lend you the dime."

Frank sighed and tucked away his ledger, "You know, I knew a guy like you in the army. He was touchy too."

"Touchy?"

"No offense meant, you understand—we all got our hang-ups. I just meant to ask why you took the case. We only get the bonus *if* we find something the cops haven't, and if you don't *believe* we will, then you're here *just* for the paycheck, not the bonus. See what I mean?"

"I get ya."

"Good."

A pause.

"Well?"

"I like staying busy."

Frank took a long, incredulous look 'round the bar, "So you say."

"How's a fella like you get into the PI business, anyway?"

"It seemed like a good fit," Frank answered.

"How's that?"

"Well, it seemed like the kind of job where I could help people."

"And is it?"

"Sometimes."

"What about when some bastard pays you to find somebody who don't wanna be found; or when some miserable son of a bitch has you out digging his dirt for him?"

"I don't take those cases."

"Don't get 'em you mean."

"No, I get offers, I just don't take a case unless it seems like it's for someone who doesn't have any other options, or who the police aren't listening to—that kind of thing."

"Yah?"

"Yessir."

Frank turned then to his grub, eating slow and cheery and methodical. Eyes alive. Shoulders loose. Ready in the way that only some dumb fucking kid could be. So, Buck sat smiling and nodding and sipping away easy, like there wasn't but one word perched on the tip of his tongue.

5

They ended up splitting the list that Doreen had put together of Eli's old haunts. Frank took the clubs and the music hall, and Buck the neighbors; Frank the charitable groups and Buck the office; Frank a couple family friends and Buck some diner called *Hattie's Bonnet*. Once done, the kid left his number and took off. But Buck hung 'round for a bit, bickering with Raul and making calls. He tried Mrs. Whitmore first, but a man answered so he hung up. Next, the message service, but they had nothing new. And last, the Albina office, hoping to catch Karl before he shut off the line. No luck. So, he decided to get out of there; decided to walk over to the new spot; decided to take Frank's half-drunk beer along as consolation until he could do the same with the bonus. He'd of preferred to be rid of the kid already, of course, but the situation required a bit of finesse and it was a fat-fingered kinda day, everything sticking to everything else. The town knew it, crawling along like it was, the Willamette too. The river was high today—higher than yesterday for sure. As he crossed over, Buck spat some stale beer off the side of the Steel Bridge, adding his little bit to the proceedings.

God, it was hot.

He stopped in for a few glasses of water and a fortifying half-pint at one of the scuzzy joints off Burnside. Then, onward. By the time he met Karl at the new office, his buzz had started to go a little sour, and he was so damn sick of sunlight that when the big man suggested they slink down into some basement someplace, Buck didn't argue. Not that it would have mattered. Karl was all schemes today. Momentum. Pushing and rising. Must've gotten the idea off the river. He wanted to get the office in order tomorrow. Hang some pictures. Buy a plant. Make things comfortable. Hire a girl for the phone.

"That's fine, Karl," Buck said lighting one up as they hit the sidewalk.

But the big slab wasn't satisfied with that. Agreement wasn't enough. He wanted conversion. So, all along their short, shimmering road to Damascus he proselytized on behalf of the Holy Sisterhood of Typists. "I had my reservations at first too, pal, but the rates are good, real good. Hell, we'll *make* money with someone taking the calls we'd miss while we're out. That message service is a racket. It's the personal touch we need. If we had someone who knows us, knows our business and the kind of people we work with, folks are going to trust her to relay their messages—lot of folks aren't comfortable doing that with some mercenary service like we got. And the girl wouldn't just be waiting around collecting a check until someone calls. She could be proactive; could follow up on client bills; call around. It just makes business sense, doesn't it? People like a pretty face there greeting them; someone to give them coffee, and tell them which chair to sit in. It's a good idea, pal. Don't you think? I mean, why else would the big operations go that way? I looked into it, and it looks doable."

"Yep," Buck agreed. It was too hot to talk theology, and Karl let off as they passed beneath an iron sign carved in the shape of a cannon, and stairs leading down from the sidewalk where, at their bottom, some cloudy-eyed guy with brass buttons up and down his vest stood barring their path. "Evening, gentlemen," he said in a tone taut as a tripwire, caught somewhere between hostility and obsequiousness, "Are you members here at *Armstrong's*?"

"I am, and Mr. Bordell here's my guest," Karl said as he flashed a card. The doorman glanced at it, his rictus expression holding strong, "Ah, yes, good to see you, Mr. Stevenson. Go on in."

"Thanks, Mitch." Hitting the air inside was like catching

a cold. Stuffy. Chilled. Swimmy. There was cool air blasting out the vents overhead—enough to prickle a guy's mop sweat if he was standing—but it wasn't near enough to keep up with the rolling brays of hot, hoarse laughter echoing off the walls and the body heat besides. The tables were small, and the chairs were big, old, and uncomfortable. Amber light. Low ceilings. All the clientele with pallors pale and boozes bronze. A golden-haired portrait of Custer supervised the bar, while an even more grandiose scene of his death beside the Little Big Horn ran the wall opposite. The whole place smelt like wet straw and spilt rye.

A cop bar. Just the goddamned worst.

The waitress led them to a table in the back, and through her Karl made his dispensations to the PPD boys. Whiskey for a captain over at the bar, gin for a hook-faced lieutenant glowering in the corner, and a beer each for two absolutely blotto sergeants slow-sinking to the carpet. He seemed to know most everyone, and while his mouth continued espousing the virtues of the secretarial class, his eyes bounced between the front door, the hitch-post, the tables, and back again. He was unshakeable. Bullish. Buck tried changing the subject—baseball, the weather, or whatever world news he could half remember, for Christ's sake—but Karl kept on. It was enough to force a guy's hand.

"All I'm saying, pal, is that when people walk in—right— doesn't it make sense if there's someone there to meet them? It makes things feel like an institution. People like that. People trust institutions. They want—"

"—How's that gal of yours up Terwilliger? Things still rosy with her?" Buck asked abruptly.

A pause. A shrug. A drink. A slight deflation at the corners of the mouth. "Yah, pal, it's going swell."

Uh-huh. Buck had half-figured that was the reason they'd suddenly needed a secretary so badly. Karl never had been one to much distinguish between the personal and the professional.

But he was quick to make a pivot of his own, "And how's that goose chase of *yours*?"

"Don't know yet."

"*Ha.* Yes, you do. Did you ask Southpaw about it?"

Buck shook his head lazily and looked up at the roof-beams. Somebody'd nailed a bunch of horseshoes on them. Dollars too. For luck, he imagined. Both types.

"What? What'd I say?" Karl asked, knowing perfectly well. "Are you and him still on the outs? I honestly can't keep track."

"We're fine. Hopefully it doesn't come to that. Look, speaking of your buddies over at the precinct, I need a couple more things from your guy."

"Sure, pal. Whatever you need."

"Police report, witnesses, tips—the works. Anything the lugs bothered to write down."

"Sure, sure. I could probably have all that for you by Friday, same as the autopsy."

"Thanks, Karl."

"Fat lotta good it'll do ya."

"That's the idea."

Karl snorted derisively and swirled a finger inside the lip of his glass. He watched over Buck's shoulder as the rounds he'd fired off started to make impact. He nodded. Waved. Ripped open too tight a smile. All teeth, no eyes. Then, when the gratitude died down, he came home. "Just be sure to watch yourself on this one, 'K, pal? We got a reputation to protect," he said.

Buck laughed, "Right. *We*."

"What do you want from me here. You know how it is. It's a small town—"

"—Yah, yah, save it. I've already given that speech today. Let's talk about something else, for Christ's sake. Please."

A long pause.

"To who?"

"What?"

"Who'd you give the speech to? That Spanish guy over at *Delancey's*?"

"Raul's Puerto Rican. And no. No. There's this kid—I, well, Whitmore—the sister, the one you charmed—she hired another guy to work the case. We're on it together now. Doctor's orders."

Karl gaped. "You're kidding."

"Nope."

"And you agreed to that?"

"Sorta."

"Why?"

He considered. "She asked me to."

"That's hysterical." Karl leaned back in his seat, swaying like a pine catching breeze, "*Jee-zus*, Buck, what kind of a stick this gal been hitting you with? She must be some kind of something to have you domesticated so quickly. *Jee-zus*. You know, if you needed help you could have just *asked* me."

Buck let that pass, and the next few like it. He took a long look over his shoulder. More PPD brass were trouping in by the minute, and the place was really starting to get loud. A couple string players on a makeshift stage were trying to muscle in on the merriment, but their elbows weren't near sharp enough.

He turned back, "How 'bout you, Karl? Anything good?"

"It's *all* good on my side of the street, pal, all of it. I make sure to keep it that way."

"Yah, yah. What about that thing you've been working up in Montgomery Park? How's that going?" Buck asked, knowing the gist already—an office feud gone wrong. There'd been insults. Deferred promotions. Letters slipped under doors. Even a bit of shouting, if you could believe it. But now, some guy wanted some other guy tailed; wanted dirt. Real white-collar kind of mess. On its own, all that wasn't much worth talking about, but case talk had always been the most reliable bridge between Buck and Karl. They'd been working together fourteen years now—minus the two Karl'd spent in England—and it wasn't that they'd grown apart since the early days of losing runaways, botching stakeouts, and snarling at the world—it was that they'd never been too much alike to begin with, and they'd only recently begun to notice. It happens. Fellas change. Not in big ways usually, but they tense a little or fatten or soften or break like shale, and it's not 'till the grays start coming in that they realize what'd seemed like kinship in the reediness of youth, had long since stiffened into something else.

Still, things'd been hairy back when. Shared and hungry. A thing to stand on. So, after they'd warmed themselves up talking over the Montgomery Park thing, they started in on the old times—the dodgy shit from before the war when nobody knew about them and their bungling. They picked up on the whiskey. They laughed. And as the bristles ground down, Buck even started to remember that Karl could be a lot of fun when he wasn't acting the scold and looking past you.

But the spell broke when the waitress came over with a double-pour of something clear for the big man and said, "Excuse me, Mr. Stevenson, but Lieutenant Behan sent this over. He would like you to join him at his table if you're so inclined."

"Tell him I'll be right over," Karl answered.

She nodded and went.

"Behan, huh?" Buck asked, shaking his head.

The big man waved to the far end of the bar, "Mareman too."

"Oof. Mareman. What an asshole."

"And two others I don't recognize. Desk guys maybe. You could come on over with me, you know."

"No, thanks."

Karl shrugged. It hadn't been a real offer anyway. Behan and co. had sent over *one* drink, and *one* invitation. Beat cops might've struggled with that kind of math, but Behan was brass now, and the brass boys could count *that* high at least. Buck didn't take it personal. Karl'd been setting bait all evening, and he wasn't the kind of guy to hold a fella's catch against him. Still, the big man hung back for a while. He pulled a cigarette for each of them, eyed the scuzz left at the bottom of his glass, and they took the drags and dregs together. Just like old times. Then, "You know, Buck, it wouldn't kill ya to make a few new friends."

"Already hit my quota for the day."

"Yah, well, there's friends, and then there's *friends*, isn't there?"

"Well, hell, Karl, I got *you*, don't I?"

The big man stubbed out and stood. "Yah. Yah, you do. See ya tomorrow, pal."

Buck didn't hang around. He went out and past and up. Night like a breaking fever. It was later than he realized. He could smell rain on the sidewalk. Warm. Seeping. Mixed with the gas and the crud and the grind of black polished shoes. He took off his hat and waited for something clean to wash down from the sky, but nothing came, and the stinking sweat stayed put where it lay, turning cold until the walking brought on a warmer coat. Quick. Breathing steady. A rhythm. He went north. Like water he followed the night downhill. He stopped once. Drank. Smeared the ink. Kept on. Stopped again. Eyes flattening. Smelling, each time, that same hint of rain but feeling only the brackish, bubbling storm of brow and back. Walking. The bridge. He could hear the water below; could almost taste its dragged-up murk; could feel its blind rush for the black lined horizon. That line. A comfort. Long. Swallowing. Numb. He reached home, poured a last, and hurried after.

6

Next afternoon, the rain was thumping, and Buck was driving northeast up Sandy Boulevard; past its small lots of somber, gray-sided houses, and clattering screen doors to what used to be the home of Eli Thomayer. He'd been to *Hattie's Bonnet* for lunch, but the only thing on offer'd been a heaping helping of hagiography—which was the same dish he'd had all over town, working his way down his half of Whitmore's list.

Thomayer had been a real solid kind of guy. Swell. Genial.

Salt of the earth.

Cream of the crop.

Top of the heap.

All that and then some.

Buck tried getting more. Really did. Bite of something burnt; bit of something bloody, but no, all anybody had for him was the same 'ole sweet butter biscuit, so he listened, nursed a coffee, wrote his condolences on a napkin, and went to see what the neighbors might say.

Thomayer's place was a two-storied house on Siskiyou; green tissue-wrapped in the overhang of an adolescent willow with a pair of straight-pruned laurels running on either side. The cracked sidewalk sloped up into red painted stone steps which led to a wide, hidden porch whose shade-wrapped seclusion was spoiled by the big, bold, yellow *memento mori* PPD had taped across the door. No sound but the rain. Curtains drawn. Neither of the next-door neighbors were home. The street was quiet and cool and empty. It was nice, especially after yesterday. Revitalizing. Gray-green smelling. Buck looked around, sipped his third coffee of the morning, and looked again.

From Thomayer's stoop, he could see right down the barrel of 71st, and there, one lot down off the eastern corner, he noticed a well-worn porch with its chairs angled this way and a guy pretending not to stare.

Perfect.

"Morning!" Buck called out, crossing the street. The guy acted like he didn't hear until Buck was standing square in front of his house—moss on the shingles, a cracked step, uncut grass. He tried again. "*Morning!*"

Slow-eyed acknowledgement. The porch-sitter was

older, somewhere in his sixties, slop-jawed, with a dramatic widow's peak and a widower's wardrobe of suspenders over stained plaid. Couple Folgers spittoons set either side of him and big, unused boots with spiderwebs thick 'cross the laces by the door.

"What'cha want?" he growled.

"I was hoping to ask you a couple questions about your neighbor over there." Buck pointed back down the street.

"You mean the fairy? He's dead."

"I know."

"'Bout damn time, that."

"Ya think?"

Gravy-guts eyed him up and down, "What'cha with vice squad or somethin'? I been calling y'all for months about that goddamned sodomite."

"I'm not a cop. I'm a private investigator."

"What'cha doing around here? Paper's said he was a dope fiend. Died downtown, they said."

"Mind if I come up outa the rain? Was hoping we could talk for a minute."

"You're fine where you're at, mister."

Buck came up anyway. He shook his hat out under the landing. The old man scowled, hocked a bit of crud into the nearest can, and stared hard. "Thanks. Did you know Eli well?"

"No, sir. No, I did not."

"Just spied on him, then?"

"Spied? No, mister, I didn't do no spying. It's just that I got eyes, don't I, and it don't take no hot shot investigator to see what that deviant was up to. Them kinds always think they're so clever as to hide it; they sneak around and lie and play-pretend like they ain't out here fixing to turn the neighborhood into some new kin'a Sodom. No, mister, I got eyes, and the Lord's got eyes too, and we mean to use 'um." He sputtered—choking on all that righteousness until it dislodged in a yellow glob the size of a silver dollar and was hawked into a can. "He got his judgement. And if you're lookin' at me for tears, mister, you're lookin' in the wrong place."

Buck took out a cigarette.

"Don't smoke that here, damnit" the old man snarled, "I got the asthma. 'Bacco smoke gives me fits."

"So, I'm gathering that you and Thomayer didn't socialize much?"

"*Socialize*? You accusin' me of something?"

"Just neighborliness."

"Ain't no being neighborly with queers, mister."

Buck stuck the cig in his mouth and looked back towards Eli's house.

"Don't you go lightin' that up here! I told you, you ba—"

"—You got yourself a good view here. Can see that top window pretty well, can't ya? What's that up there? The bedroom?" Buck asked, "Could see a lot more if it weren't for those shrubs and everything. Bet that's why they're there, though, huh? Or might those be the vines of Sodom with their 'clusters of bitterness?'"

"Leviticus."

"Deuteronomy, actually," Buck grunted back, flipping open his lighter.

"I told you—"

"—White truck with chicken wire on it and a dent in the door, seen one of those recently? Last week or so?"

"No."

"And you'd know, wouldn't ya? I hear you and the Lord both got yourselves a good set of peepers."

"I'll not have you mock—"

Buck lit the cig, took a long, smooth drag and blew the smoke straight on into the other guy's face. "Alright, well, thanks for the chat, pal. It's been swell," he said, but the guy was too busy going berserk to have heard. Sputtering and stomping and gnashing with chew-stained teeth. Shouting some misquote—Revelation this time. Oh well. Let the bastard choke on that too. As for Buck, the gospel always made him hungry, especially garbled. It reminded him of Dad and of bark-topped benches; of sweet-sour Sunday-breathed homilies, and of fasts unbroken till dark; reminded him of piety boiling in the cedar boughs, and how it stuck there—stuck and glimmered like dew.

'Round the corner was a Greek place. He ate quick and went for the phone.

"Hello? Whitmore residence."

"Mrs. Whitmore, it's Buck Bordell. Got a minute?"

A pause.

"I'd prefer if you didn't get into the habit of calling me at home, Mr. Bordell."

"I've been careful."

"I'm sure. I can come by your office Saturday morning. If you've found something, we can talk then."

"OK."

Another pause.

"So, did you?"

"Did I what?"

"Find something."

"Not sure yet. That's why I'm calling."

"Where are you? It's very loud."

"Matzu's. Place's got good lamb. You ever been?"

"Yes, I've been to Matzu's," she said, realization heavy in her voice, "Are you going to Eli's?"

"Just been."

"Is Mr. Takahashi with you?"

"No."

"But you *have* spoken to him? Per my request?"

"I have. We've met and everything. Nice guy."

"Well, then you shouldn't have any trouble describing him to me."

"Not at all." So, he did. Painstakingly. Eyes. Mustache. Hat. Suit. Tie. Gait. Notebook. Handwriting. But Doreen broke him off before he could get to the shoes.

"Alright, Buck, alright, you've made your point," she said.

"Glad to hear it. Listen, was thinking I'd get inside your brother's house and take a look around. Did he keep a key under the mat or anything like that? Leave any windows unlocked?"

"No. Eli was very protective of his home."

"I bet. I just met the neighbors. What about you, do you have a key?"

"Not at the moment, no. Eli didn't have a will, so the house is in probate until they determine an inheritor."

"Which'll be you."

"Yes."

"Perfect. Then it won't hardly even be trespassing, since I've got your permission."

"My permission for what?"

"To go in."

"Do you really think that's necessary?"

"In my professional opinion—yes."

"I suppose that's what I'm paying you for."

"Suppose it is."

"Do what you have to if you think it'll help, but be discreet. Is there anything else, Buck?"

"Seen any more farm trucks since the other day? White, dented, both, or otherwise?"

"I'm hanging up."

"Oh. Wait. You should know, I moved offices recently.

We're on the westside now." He gave her the address, and the phone number, but he could tell she wasn't writing any of it down. "When should I expect ya on Saturday?"

"I'll come by at ten o'clock."

"OK. See ya then."

"And I'll expect Mr. Takahashi to be there as well."

"You will, huh?"

"Will that be a problem?"

"Doesn't seem too efficient to me, but hey, it's your dime."

"Yes, it is. And Buck?"

"Yah?"

"Don't call here again."

When the line went dead, he sat in the car for a while, smoked a couple, listened to the rain, and digested. Today was moving right along, wasn't it? Speeding up, even, and it'd be shame to get sloppy or sluggish or stupid and wind up pinched on account of a disgruntled neighbor and the lamb special. Whitmore didn't *technically* own the house, and he didn't trust the beat boys responding to a B and E to be particularly open to a nuanced interpretation of probate ownership. He'd go in, take a look, and get out. Quick as quick.

Just to be safe though, he parked a few blocks up and around the corner so nobody casual could trace him car to house, and from the side which gave him the best chance not to be spotted by his new friend on 71st. He walked fast;

hat down and collar up, pick hook stowed in his sleeve. The side-yard was fenced, but he hopped it easy, and, once over, he pulled on a pair of rawhides.

He tried the windows.

Locked.

Wide steps, twisting his foot in the soggy ground, mangling the shoeprint.

He made his way 'round back.

Clear. Quiet. Nothing but droplets watching from the leaves. But when he went to try the door, it just swung open, no tickling required. He stepped through and tried to lock it behind him. He couldn't. Busted. Somebody'd broken in already and made a real mess of things, and now the pins couldn't reset. Clumsy fucks whoever they were. Careless.

He moved on through the house, taking stock. Clean. Ordered. Nothing obvious missing. A watch on an end table, silverware in the drawers, bowl of spare change on the counter, record player and a *Cab Calloway Orchestra* vinyl waiting on top. The downstairs was neat, untouched, unpilfered. Strange. Same with the bedroom. Pristine. Pictures on the wall with Thomayer shaking hands, standing in groups, smiling, clean-cut. But the upstairs office was a different story. There was a filing cabinet up there, with the locks busted, and nothing inside. Same with the desk. Locks forced; drawers spotless. But they'd left the typewriter. Nice one too. Same as Karl's. What kind of a guy has an office, has a desk, has a filing cabinet, and a top-of-the-line typewriter but no paper? No files? Not a shred of nothing?

Buck went deeper. Closets. Cupboards. Drawers. He checked the water tank in the toilet, ran his hand under the counters and the tables, picked the grout, and dug around in the cushions. In the trash, he found a twice-folded playbill, reading: *Spindelman's Music Hall proudly presents: The Tillis Brothers, May 23rd.*

Huh.

He pocketed the playbill, backtracked, slipped out the gate, and let the dead echo of Thomayer's place wash out with the rain. He had a couple stops he'd thought of making today, but they could wait. Back in Matzu's, Buck called the number Frank had left, but a woman answered. Looks like Karl was on to something with all that secretary business.

"Hello?" the gal repeated.

"Yes, hi, this is Buck Bordell, I'm looking for Frank."

"Sorry, honey, you must've gotten a bad connection, 'cause there's no one here by that name. Take care now," she said, and hung up.

Huh.

He tried again.

Same voice, "Hello?"

He hung up and scrutinized the number. It was written in such a clear, deliberate hand that there could be no confusion about it, and Frank didn't seem the type to screw that kinda thing up. Man for details if there'd ever been one. Buck chocked it up to the kid getting slippery and drove over to the new office. Thought he'd sit for a minute on his own. Acclimate. Mull. He poured himself half a hand of amber and set the playbills on his desk so's Franklin could assess.

So Thomayer had been to *Spindelman's* the night he died. Made sense. The music hall was a well-known sore spot for the westside well-to-dos; the lewdness of the place was legendary, and its bar was a known haunt for all manner of drifter and degenerate. There'd been efforts to shut it down entirely, speeches, protests, boycotts, and—so Buck'd heard—ceaseless hysterics in the press. Harshest of all, in a town where any ole' lean-to could get a liquor license, *Spindelman's* had had its petition denied in perpetuity by the fine fathers of the city; and thereby was indecency banished forever from the streets of Portland. Job done. The end. Amen.

Just then, Karl flew into the office, followed by a whirling-whip-bang sound of drawers open-closing, coat strap canvas snapping, and the sloppy, deflated whomp of a wet hat hitting the floor. "Miserable fucking weather, ain't it?" the big man hollered from behind the rapidly clouding glass.

"I prefer it."

"*Ha*! You would!"

"How's the head?"

"Fine, pal! Sweet of you to ask."

"Pretty tame with the boys in blue then?"

"Oh no! No, no, no! They got after it, alright! I just paced myself is all! You ought to try it!"

"Uh-huh."

A few pounding footsteps brought Karl from his office over to Buck's, "Take a look," he demanded wearing his *real* smile—the shaggy one with the canines popped out—and chucking over a thick bundle of business cards that read:

Carl Stevenson and Buck Bordell, Private Investigators

———

Discreet. Professional. Licensed.

———

501 COLUMBIA STREET, OFFICE #206, PORTLAND, OR

"Swell, aren't they? Got them on a rush order up the street—what do you think?"

"Nice paper."

"Yah, pal, of course it's nice paper. Folks like the feel of something substantial. Why do you think banks always have so much marble? So much stone? There's a comfort in heft, you know? Reliability. Person looks at a card like this, and that's what they feel, right? Heft! What about the wording? Sounds pretty good, doesn't it?"

"*Discreet. Professional. Licensed*," Buck intoned, flipping the stack over to where the new phone number was listed on the back. "Very official. Yah. I like it."

"Yah?"

"Yah. Sure. That part looks real good, Karl, but they spelled your name wrong, and they put 'Stevenson' instead of 'Svensson.'"

"No. They're right. I got it changed," he said, still admiring the cards, "Nobody outside of Coos Bay ever pronounced '*Svensson*' right anyway. Don't know why my folks didn't change it when they came over in the first place."

"It's your name."

Slightly irked, "So?"

"The cards are nice, Karl. Real nice."

"They are, aren't they? That stack's for you, and if you need more, I got a whole box back over in the desk. Help yourself."

"How much do I owe ya for 'em?"

The big man leaned hard in the doorway, waving him off, "Ah, don't worry about that. Say, I called my guy about all that stuff you wanted, and he says it's not going to be a problem."

"Well, thanks for that too. I owe ya double."

Karl nodded, scratched his chin distractedly, and flipped one of the cards back and forth to admire it, "Sure, pal, sure, don't mention it. Talked to Liam on the way in."

"Liam?"

"Dunleavy the younger. Mr. Flying Ace?"

"Oh. Right. I remember."

"Turns out, the flyboy's a bit of an odd bird."

"That so?"

He nodded sagely, "Yep. I tried swapping war stories, but he didn't seem interested."

"Maybe the war wasn't as much fun out in the Pacific."

"Oh yah, must have been terrible—warm ocean, sunshine, and native beauties waiting at every port. I had to spend the whole damn time in England, and England's a lot like Oregon, pal—gray and gloomy, and I think fonder of the Luftwaffe than I do the dames." He straightened, "Anyway, I just wanted to bring the cards by and see what was up. I got to drive out to Lake Oswego tonight and follow up on some stuff. Are you staying a while?"

"Naw," Buck said, "Think I'll catch a show."

7

When Buck got there, *Spindelman's* was in full swing. Marquee blazing. Ticket booth besieged. Its every inch— theater, lobby, bar—boiling with humanity. There was no chance for a seat, so Buck wedged himself along the back wall with the other late arrivals. It was drag tonight. A broad-shouldered Mae West trotting out the hits. Raucous. These shows always brought in the everybody else kinda crowd; the all-kinds caucus scorned by the city fathers— from the West Hills gadfly angling for a bit of pearl clutch- ing back home; to the streetcar hop-ons and switchboard girls; to black folks over from Vanport, and jump-pass *braceros*, all mixed into row after row of pan-Scandie, new world *paisano*, and bog Irish who'd paused, for sake of the show, their clamoring for place within the obliviating ranks of lily-white brotherhood. Everybody together. Everybody crackling as one. A bonfire of *bon homie* in which the city's enmity burned away and was replaced by something else—something new and fresh and free and bone deep.

Which was pretty and all, but, you know, bullshit.

'Cause as the houselights rose for intermission—as the smoke cleared, and the brass went cold—the city was still there, bright and bare, same as ever. It with its covenants and clans; it with its aggrievements wrought in iron; it with its orphan blocks, its clear-outs, its move-downs, and its Victorian gables crowned in laurel. Way it was. Ticket or no.

Buck followed the crowd to the so-called 'saloon' that *Spindelman's* had out front—a big room off the lobby with two swinging doors and a bar where the strongest pour your dollar got you was a bit of day-old coffee. Buck bobbed around for a while. Took stock. Then, when the show kicked off again and things cleared a little, he started asking 'round after Thomayer. But *Spindelman's* was a place for revelry not recognition, and something about being flashed a dead guy's yearbook photo seemed to make folks uneasy. So, it was tough going, but Buck kept at it until, sitting on a stool with his back against the bar, he saw a woman in high-waisted, tweed trousers stride in; a fabric carnation pinned to her blouse, and her men's wingtips clacking 'cross the tile. She was tall. Long gait. Pencil-hipped. Pixie mopped. Calligraphy in place of eyebrows. By way of an introduction, she threw out an order for a ginger so-and-so, before sitting down beside him. "So," she said, drumming her fingers on the bar top, "we've been getting complaints."

"Oh, yah?" Buck said.

"Apparently, there's been some guy in here holding down the bar and asking questions. Hear tell he's spoiling the fun."

"Sounds like a pest."

"Sure does," she said as her drink arrived. She took it without looking, jabbing the straw like a pick into its icy, coppery, gingery guts—churning the viscera and taking a sip. "Apparently, he's asking after a certain *illicit* substance too."

"Naughty."

"Very. Unless of course, he's vice squad."

"Is that what they're saying?"

She shrugged, "Might be. But they're wrong—the guy's not vice. Know how I know?"

"How?"

"Vice don't have that kind of attention span. Five minutes footsie—ten tops—before they get bored and start making people turn out their pockets. Know what else?"

"What?"

She kicked Buck's stool, "He's in the wrong seat."

"Maybe he didn't realize they were assigned."

"No, no, no, it's just that if he *were* vice, he'd sit like all the other vice boys do—so's he can keep a weathered eye on the men's room and scoop a couple fellas up on the degeneracy charge."

Buck turned. Inspected. The bathrooms were near the door, just back and off. "Huh," he said.

"Yep."

"Sound like a real pack of charmers."

"It's them that got the badges, sailor, not us."

"OK. So, if our guy's not vice, what is he, then—besides a spoilsport? Figure he's a junkie? Guy could do a lot worse than coming to a music hall looking to score."

"You're right in general but wrong in this case, sailor. We're a clean venue."

"Uh-huh."

"*And besides*," she said, taking Buck in, "He doesn't seem the type."

"There's a type?"

"'Course there's a type. And he ain't it."

"Ya sure about that?"

"Sure as sure goes. He's tight up in the shoulders, you know? But loose around the mouth."

"So, what is he then?"

"Well, if he's not vice and he's not looking to score, then odds are he's some kind of private detective—we get almost as many of them types down here as we do vice squad, and, of the three, most times, it's the gumshoes who're the biggest headaches. Know why?"

"Not yet."

She laughed airily, smiling and stirring and *stab-stab-stabbing*, "See, it's like this—vice guys come in two flavors. Two and only two. You got your payolas, and you got your puritans. But thing is, that's all surface, you know? Once you get past the schtick of it, they're *basically* the same guy. Simple men with simple needs. They're *honest*, you know? Reliable in a backwards kind of way. Unimaginative, anyway. They do the same things in the same ways over and over again. They're pricks of course—and bastards to a man—but manageable. And the junkies? Well, they're even simpler, aren't they?"

"But your average PIs a bit more complicated? That it?"

"Exactly."

"Not sure I buy that."

"No, no, no. It's true. With them, it's tricky. Wanna know why?"

"Desperately."

"It's because your average PI don't know what he is. He's conflicted. He *thinks* he's smart, but he's really, usually, a bit of a dope. Sometimes your garden varietal, and other times, sailor, *oof*, it's brutal. These klutzes, I tell you, they're blunt and they're obvious. It's weird how often. You'd think it's a requirement or something. But don't get me wrong, all that by itself wouldn't be too bad except for—and this is the kicker—they usually have all these questions, right? But no idea where the answers are supposed to get 'em, and if *he* doesn't know where he's going, how am *I* supposed to know? How is anybody? What do you do with a guy like that?"

"You could let him buy you a drink."

She *tap-tap-tapped* his arm, ginger as the hint on her breath, "I'm flattered, really, but wrong tree, sailor. Wrong one altogether. But you see the pickle I'm in?"

"I do, yah."

"Mmhmm."

"'Course, why not just leave the guy be? Once he realizes all you got here is fizzy water, he's liable to get bored and wander off all on his own."

"Ah, if only. I'm afraid it's a question of appearances—presentation, sailor, you get it. Something just *has* to be done, so's the regulars can *see* something being done, get me?"

"Well then, it sounds like you don't got a lot of options; sounds like you'll just have to throw the bum out."

She pursed her lips in a mock pout, "You think?"

"Yep."

"Darn."

"But do you have the muscle to get him out the door?" Buck asked, glancing around. It was all stink-eyes staring back at him, but nothing serious. No jump-ups. No menace. Hard, but brittle. "That's the question."

"Muscle? Sure—Rachel Spindelman, nice to meet you."

"Spindelman, huh? You always take such a hands-on approach to business?"

"It is my name on the sign, sailor—mine and Dad's."

"Nice you see it that way."

"How else is there to see it?"

"Well, speaking as a former junior partner in the ole' family enterprise myself, it never seemed to me like it was quite *my* name on the sign. But maybe it's different when it's a marquee instead of a chalkboard."

"Ooh, let me guess," Rachel said flicking at her chin, "I bet it was some kind of family store; I'm thinking out off towards Molalla? Estacada, maybe? Dad ran the counter and Mom the back? Vittles and vitals for the dirt road crowd? Something pastoral like that; like a Rockwell painting or something. But you got impatient, didn't you, sailor? Didn't have the stomach for sweeping and stocking and waiting around, so you legged it into town. And now, store's gone, isn't it? The old man sold it off rather than let *you* have it? Or maybe he lost it years ago? Fire, I bet. No, no, no, no maybe you *did* get it in the end, but then, one bad bet over at the Downs and it was gone forever. That about right? Come on, it's something like that, right?"

"Nope."

"Damn."

"Happens Dad was in your line, actually."

"Snake charming?"

"Showbiz."

"You don't say?"

"Oh, yah. He had one hell of an act, too. Nobody could make you feel the lick of hellfire so much as Dad. And that was with nothing but a fir stump to stamp on. Small potatoes. If he could've had a stage like yours? With those lights and all those people to breathe into? Shit, he might well have brought on the second coming."

She gave him a crowbar kinda grin, "You see the show tonight?"

"Yah."

"And what'd you think?"

"I liked it. Brimstone was Dad's act, not mine."

"I see." Rachel posted an elbow onto the bar and let her head fall onto her palm, grinning, "From gospel to gumshoe, and a lover of the arts to boot," she tutted, "I suppose it's not the least original thing I've ever heard."

"I try."

She swirled. She jabbed. She waited. Then, "Alright, go ahead."

"With what?"

"With telling me why you became a PI? You speak in full sentences; you look like you dress yourself. You're a real overachiever as far as snoops go. Heck, I bet if you tried you could parlay all this mediocrity of yours into being something halfway useful; like dogcatcher or something."

"*Useful*, huh? You really think so?"

"Sure, sailor, sure."

"Too late for me I'm afraid," Buck said ruefully, plucking one of his and Karl's new business cards from his jacket pocket and sliding it over, "I'm locked in. It's a sin to waste good stationery."

Sympathetic, *tut-tut*, *pat-pat*, "Ah well. Shame."

"Besides, it's not such a bad gig, really. It suits me. Gets me out of the house."

"Plenty other ways for that."

"If you say so. What about you, Ms. Spindelman? When and how and why did you choose to be a… what would you call it? A music hall heiress?"

She snorted, "*Heiress*. Yah, right. You know what year my father started this business, *Mr. Bordell*? Nineteen-hundred-and-thirty-four. You know how hard you have to work to keep a music hall open during a depression? Hard. *Damn* hard. And do you know what my father did before that? He unloaded trucks in Jersey for thirty cents an hour. And before *that*, as a boy, he sold Yiddish newspapers on the streets of Wroclaw to buy him and my *mumes* their ticket over."

"It's a nice story," Buck said.

"You think? Try hearing it every day." Her eyes leveled. *Jab-jab-jab*, "*Heiress*. You got me all wrong, Mac—I *work*. Because what we do here is delicate; because people trust that that name out on the sign—my name—means something." She waved the business card back under Buck's nose, "That what this means? Or are you like all the other knuckle-draggers out here looking to make trouble, only with a bit of schmoozing thrown in?"

"Been told I come recommended."

She stood. "Wanna know what *I* recommend?"

"I can guess."

"Bet you can."

"Look, I'm not here to fuck anybody over on account of a little after-hours liaison, OK? And I don't wanna make any trouble for you either. Happens that the guy I'm checking up on is already dead. Smack. You think he might'a got it 'round here?"

She stared. Nothing, and a whole lot of it. "I told ya once already. *We're clean.*"

"Yah-yah. What about this?" He said, handing her the picture of Eli, "You recognize this guy? Eli Thomayer. You recognize that name?"

"Sorry," she said, but wasn't.

"Would you tell me if you did?"

And again, "Sorry."

"And if I were to tell you the guy was here the night he died? What then?"

Only her eyes this time. *Sorry*. Rest? More nothing. And piles of it.

"OK." He stowed the picture.

"Make you a deal, sailor? How 'bout I comp your

drinks, and you're gone in five. How's that? It'd be a shame to get nasty after we've had such a nice chat."

"Thought you said I was barking up the wrong tree?"

She signaled to the bartender, "You are. Wrong fucking forest entirely." Then, she was gone. Buck listened to her quick-clacking away as all those brittle, peripheral, prickling glares up and down the bar sat counting the seconds for him. They needn't have. He was a man of his word. Reasonable. And even if he couldn't get anything out of this place, God knows now Frank wouldn't either.

But all those glaring faces forgot him in an instant once a new crowd started filtering in, because amongst them were some black folks dressed to the nines and ordering a round of lemonades. Just like that, Buck was onside again. Guy two seats down, nudged him, muttering under his breath, "Fucking Vanport. This used to be a white man's town."

8

Dope wasn't hard to come by downtown, and the simplest explanation was still the likeliest—Thomayer was new to the junk game. He bit off more than he could chew and wound up dead. Even if he hadn't gotten the stuff at *Spindelman's*, there were plenty of other places where even the jumpiest, middle-class newcomer could walk away with an easy bag. So, sure, he'd gone to a show the night he died, and he'd gone home afterwards, but then he must've gotten restless, come back out, and drove over to Skid Row looking to keep the good times rolling. All it would take for Buck to confirm that story would be a little legwork. If he could track down a dealer or one of the usual looky-loos who might recognize Thomayer from the picture, that'd be that. Case closed. Hell, little luck and

Buck'd be throwing down a good chunk of that two grand bonus onto the bar at *Delancey's* by this time tomorrow night. No Franky boy. No Southpaw. Easy.

Still, the details nagged.

Something'd been off with Maddy. It wasn't that she'd lied—she lied all the time, especially to Buck—it was that she'd lied so badly; so unnecessarily. Why go to the trouble of stonewalling like that? And coach Polly to do the same? What'd she care? It wasn't ideal, sure, but a woman in her position had dealt with a lot worse over the years than a dead junkie and a bit of bad press. And come to think of it—why hadn't whatever tidy sum she mailed twice-monthly over to those hacks at the *Oregonian* and the *Journal* been enough to keep *Bons* outa the story altogether? Not to mention why there'd been any story at all, with Charlemagne so practiced in keeping the block clear of any and all limp-limbed drags on Maddy's good name.

Buck took his time getting back up to Skid Row, mulling things over. After *Spindelman's*, he stopped someplace quiet. Had one. Had another. Mulled some more. By the time he'd finished, it was getting late, and the good-timers were due for a shift change. All throughout the neighborhood, the whomping swing of thick, porthole-windowed doors pumped like a string of bellows to blow the staggering packs of them out onto the cobbles, stiff as deadened leaves, while a pair of mounted policemen sat like statues under the flickering streetlamps. Buck gave *Bons* a wide berth. First, he stopped over at a postage-stamp sized pool hall where a couple pairs of pushers stood 'round the back tables holding cues, handing out baggies, and stuffing twenties into the corner pockets. He asked them about Thomayer, but their only answer was to choke up on their sticks and start edging towards him, so he backed off and went to trawl the pinball parlors instead. It was slow going. Crowded. Hard to parse. The parlors were always hopping down here. In Skid, they were mostly run by Big Jim Elkins, and because he and his crew kept the windows clean and the washrooms presentable, a fella felt marginally less cheated by an Elkins machine than he did by some tampered old model stashed in a backroom someplace. Buck found himself a box near the front and slow-played a couple, watching the money changing hands around him. Place was thrumming with commerce. Straight bets took the lion's share—the ones run by the house bookies—but there was plenty of side action going on. He was particularly interested in the two shutterbugs he spotted taking surreptitious shots with their Kodak 35s and jotting names for a bit of blackmail later. He didn't recognize either of them, but he could tell by the routine that they worked for Southpaw. One dropped out before anything could be done about it, but the other—a moon-faced guy in a flaking, ill-fitting bomber's jacket—kept right on pinging down deeper and deeper into the cacophony of rolling silver, so Buck was able to get the drop on him. "They say you're the man to see for a couple candids," Buck said, coming up alongside and taking him by the elbow.

Guy turned, "Who? Who says?"

Buck nodded vaguely towards the front of the parlor, "You know—*they*."

"Well, they're wrong."

"Don't be like that, pal, My money's green as the next guy's."

"Nice try, *officer*,"

Moon-Face went to pull away. He almost managed it, slippery as he was, but Buck held on and they wrestled like that for a while, pushing and pulling and see-sawing back and forth, mute but for the occasional grunt. Buck couldn't have the guy legging it, but, at the same time, causing a scene would be bad for both of them. They'd be thrown out. Barred. Worse, depending. That was the downside of working one of Big Jim's joints—the bookies got *real* touchy when it came to anything that might sour the mood and scare off any of the more delicate punters, so Buck was forced to thread the needle between oh-so-delicate subtlety and a dose of directness.

"Christ, settle down, would ya?" He said, bits of spittle glistening in his stubble after catching a twisting, errant shoulder to the jaw, "I just wanna talk. Just for a minute. Nothing serious."

A pause. Braced. "Who are you? Who are you, really?"

"Southpaw's tied up unexpectedly tonight, he sent me over to snag Sunday night's film."

Suspicious, "You know Southpaw?"

"Uh-huh."

Slow. "And... Sunday? What's so special about last Sunday?"

"All Southpaw said was that he wanted the film. You know what he's like."

Moon-Face went slack for a second, considering Buck in the dim light. Then, like a fish sputtering on the dock, he started thrashing all over again, "Horseshit," he hissed, "If you really knew Southpaw, how come I ain't never seen you down at the track?"

"What day do you go? Saturday, right?"

"Yah, Saturday, just like everybo—"

"—Well, I go Fridays."

"Fridays? Fridays, my ass, there ain't no big races run on Fridays! You stink of booze, shithead, and no way Southpaw's got you working negatives for him soaked like you are." Sneering, "You know what? You *know* what? I think you're full of shit, and you better fuck off before I hurt you," the guy spit back, jerking his arm away hard and sending them both slow-tumbling into one of the machines. Sprawled against it, they froze. Waited. Braced.

But nobody noticed—nobody important anyway.

Back at it. Staggering. Wrestling.

"Calm down, would ya? I told ya, I just wanna ask you a ques—"

"—*Fuck* off, I said."

"And *I* said settle down. If you'd j—"

"—That's it, shithead, I warned you. You're getting a blade whoever you are. I swear—"

Buck snatched Thomayer's picture out from his pocket and practically pasted it onto Moon-Face's big, pink forehead. "Shut up. You ever see this guy before? Last Sunday, maybe? Any other time? Ever take his picture out there on the street?"

"You didn't hear me, did you? I said I got a fucking blade for—"

"—Yah, yah, I heard ya," Buck said, trying to mask the raggedness in his breath. He would gas out soon. Moon-Face was stronger than he looked. Buck'd have to speed things along. He edged his elbow straight into the guy's ribs and started digging and digging, "Spit it out."

Gritted teeth. Bit of snarling. Then, "Fuck you."

Buck leaned harder.

"Gah… Jesus—*no*. I didn't take his picture, OK?"

"You sure? Think hard. 'Cause if I find out different down the road I'll get you burned at every Elkins joint in town."

"I'm fucking sure*!*"

Buck let the guy go and sent him crashing down onto the carpet. He scrambled up, "You're not fooling anybody, boozer," he said, flashing a knife from his pocket before thinking better of it and racing for the door. Buck watched him go, rolling his shoulders. He'd pulled something in the scuffle. Hadn't gotten much to show for it either.

So, for the sake of his joints, he tacked. He went 'round hunting for dope clumsy as he could—the way Thomayer might've—and while he dredged up a few more pushers that way, they all hightailed it even quicker than Moon-Face had once the questions started. He hit the lounges and the clubs and the card rooms where he knew some of the part-timers well enough to get what passed for a straight answer next, but not a one of them had seen hide or hair of Thomayer. And, sure, maybe it was damn stupid of Buck to take any of their denials at face value, but, for one, he didn't have much choice, and for two, it all added up, in a cock-eyed sort of way—in so far as it *didn't* add up.

Or, shit, maybe he was just tired.

But however tired he may've been—or however drunk—he wasn't enough of either to go groveling to Southpaw. Least not yet. The night was starting to fray anyway. Go quiet. Hole up behind drawn curtains and twice-bolted doors. So, he sat down on a fruit crate and watched as the last beacons of commerce blazed on against the creep of morning. Brightest of them all was *Bons*, with Charlemagne working the door, ushering in the late arrivals, and lingering on the stoop once they'd gone to drag a watchful eye up and down the empty sidewalks. He could probably see Buck from up there, but nothing distinct, just the shape of him; just another blurry-faced nobody slouching beneath the far end of the streetlights.

Satisfied, Charlie turned and went back inside.

Not much more to see. Not much more to do. Not for hours. Hours and hours.

Buck leaned against the drained-out cool of the brick-work, lit one, and waited for the sky to come back purple.

9

Some guys are too conscientious for crowds; too considered for the bird-shot barrel-walk of their fellow man. They turn shoulders. They slip by. They'll scuff a shoe on the pivot long as it keeps their sole out the gutter.

That was Frank. Clean. Waylaid. Scuttling like a chickadee.

Buck sat on the car hood, scarfing down a donut and watching him come on. When he got close, the kid tipped his hat with such mechanical politeness that Buck couldn't help but scowl a little.

"Good morning," he said.

Buck spat, "Mornin'. Got ya a donut."

"More of a pie guy, myself."

"Go on, don't be a prick. They're in the front."

Frank's mustache twitched a little, but he didn't budge.

"What about some coffee?"

"No thanks."

"It's right there."

"No. Thank you. We should get going."

"Well, look at you—just raring to go. Why don't ya let me settle for a minute. I spent half the night trawling around looking for any dealers who remembered Thomayer. So, you know, it's pretty early for me."

"It's nine."

"Can always rely on you for the time, can't I?"

Kid leaned on the hood uninvited, "I was out last night too, as it happens."

"Were ya?"

"Yah. I think I got something down at that music hall *Spindelman's*."

Buck chewed on that. Chewed and chewed and chewed. Finally—reluctantly—he swallowed, "Oh yah?"

"Seems promising."

"Huh. You don't say."

"Yah." Frank set his fritter down untouched, brushed a finger 'cross his stache, and squinted up at the gleaming, broken glass windows of the eastside warehouses. He shuffled. He brushed again. Couple workman passed by in coveralls. Shift whistle. Shouts. The acrid, hot weather smell of warming tar.

"Well, come on, Franky, spit it out for Christ's sakes."

"Apparently, Thomayer's been down at *Spindelman's* three, four nights out the week for the past month or so. Apparently, he comes for the show and then, after, hangs around with the house band at a jazz club over on this side of the river—*particularly*, he runs around with one of the trumpeters, a Mr. Louis Nathans—and nobody's seen *either* of them since the night Thomayer winds up dead."

"And who'd ya hear that from?"

"From somebody who knows."

"Who?"

"Promised I wouldn't say."

"*Jesus*," Buck grunted, shoving the last bit of sugary dough down his gullet while Frank nodded like some kind of two-bit sage.

"Not trying to be secretive, you understand?"

"God forbid."

"Just gave my word is all."

"Uh-huh."

"Anyway, they say he's missing—the trumpeter, I mean." he shrugged. "Musicians. I gather someone going AWOL in their circle isn't too uncommon."

"So, you heard this from someone in the band, then?"

"I said I wouldn't say."

"You get an address for the guy?"

"145 NE Sacramento."

Buck lit one up. "Albina?"

"Yep."

"Shit, that's right up by *Delancey's*. What'd ya say we tip one back on the way?" The kid made like he was going to protest, but Buck held up a hand, "Jesus, Frank, it was a joke. Come on. Eat a donut and lighten the fuck up, huh? You got a gun?"

"No."

"No?"

"Not on me."

"What'd you mean *not on you*?"

"It's at home."

"Fat lot of good it's doing ya there."

"That's where it does me the most good. The last thing I need is for some trigger-happy cop overreacting."

"Don't ya got any pockets?"

"It's too big for that."

"What'd you mean *too big*? What's it, a bazooka or something?"

"It's a B-A-R."

Buck laughed, "Jesus. Really? Like the machine gun?" Kid nodded.

"How'd ya get your hands on such serious kit?"

"Probably shouldn't say."

"'Course not."

"What about you?"

He flicked his cig, "Glovebox. Come on, let's go."

They drove to Albina. No place in Portland had changed

so much as Albina. It had been fashionable once, back when the trees were coming down, and the long, lonely iron of the railyard was all that connected Portland to the markets back east, but tastes had changed, and the tycoons of yesteryear had gotten sick of all that thunder chattering their China off the shelves, so they picked up sticks and legged it for the westside, leaving their high gables to be carved into twelve room boardinghouses for the porters and brakemen and mechanics they employed—black fellas, most of them—and when one of them got tired of renting a stained mattress and sharing a shitter, only places that took his tender fell somewhere in the seven blocks between Union Ave and the river. But while Albina was surgically delineated to the real estate boys, to the laymen it had come to mean less a place on a map and more a color on a skin.

Outside 145 NE Sacramento, three guys were playing cards on a table they'd dragged out to the lawn, two in mechanic's jumpsuits, and a third in a loose-fitting argyle, collar crisp, hair conked, and a caterpillar crawling 'cross his lip. They eyed Frank and Buck as they got out—not that the kid noticed, with his nose pecking feed out that damn notebook of his—but Buck made the trumpet player as the odd man out. It was the way he sat; way he dressed; way the kings and queens jitterbugged in his grip, finger to finger.

"You fellas lost?" one of the jumpsuits hollered, "Or

you some a' them Jehovah's People or whatever? We get some of them, time to time."

"*Witnesses*," the other jumpsuit said, nodding to himself, "Jehovah's *Witnesses*."

"Yah. That's right. You fellas some of them? 'Cause I can't be messing around with no Jehovah's Witnesses, or my mama's on the first train up out of Montgomery straight here to whoop my ass."

"That's right."

Frank cleared his throat, "We're private detectives actually, licensed and bonded. We're looking for Louis Nathans. Do you know him?"

"Nobody here by that name," the trumpet player said a hair too quick, throwing down a run of cards. The overalls followed suit. Shook their heads. Shrugged. Muttered. Tried not to look like they were trying not to look.

"Do you live here?" Frank asked the guy.

"I got me a room, if that's what you mean."

"Have you been here long?"

"Be a year in June."

"But you don't know a guy by the name of Nathans?"

"Can't say I do."

Dutifully, Frank took the note. "Anybody around here you think might?"

They couldn't think of a soul, poor bastards. You could tell it really gutted 'em not being able to help. Buck then, rocking on his heels, "Say, you think I could trouble you fellas for a bit of coffee?"

"Fresh out I'm afraid."

"Ah come on, big house like that? Bunch of fellas? Working nights? Working mornings? House like that never runs dry of joe. I'd pay."

"We're in the middle of a game, mister."

"And I hate to interrupt, but Christ almighty, fellas, I tell ya, I'm gonna need the boost," Buck swept his hat off and slapped it against his thigh, "Looking at a long, long, long day of knocking on doors and kicking up a fuss. Silly, really, 'cause you'd think it'd be an easy thing; all's we need is a signature for the insurance company."

Nathans's gaze slid over, curious, "Insurance company?"

"Yah, yah, apparently this guy Nathans saw some accident downtown involving the son of the fella signing our checks, and he's the protective sort. He wants to make sure his baby boy doesn't get screwed over. So, he's hoping Nathans, being a witness and all, can sign a statement that helps things land the right way, if ya get me."

"Sure, mister. I get ya."

"Hell, wish somebody'd pay me for my signature." Buck said, grinning, "*Whoops*. Wasn't 'sposed to say that part."

"What we talking?"

"Just a gesture."

"How much?"

"Ah, well... no offense, fellas, but figure we'll work that

out with Nathans. If—that is—we ever find the guy."

The trumpet player stood, tucking in his shirt and smiling wide, "Where are my manners, mister? You still want that coffee?"

"What about your game?"

Nathans tossed his cards down without looking, "Rummy."

Buck and Frank followed him into the house. It was old, with a high, bare-walled foyer, thin carpet, and a blocky, sagging staircase wrapping up the far wall. Three stories. Doors and doors. Big, yellow-glass windows open to the alley. Quiet but for the groaning of the boards, the bubbling of the percolator, and the empty, swinging sound of Nathans diving into one cupboard after another. He'd found the coffee easy enough, but mugs were another story. "Shared kitchen," he explained, "anything you don't want broke or stole, you sure don't keep down here."

"I know how that goes," Buck said, "I lived up the street for a while."

"No kidding?"

"Yah, one of the big ones up there on Graham. The green one. With the turret and the hole in the roof."

"*No kidding*? Give me a sec, would ya? Let me run up to my room—get you your mug."

They listened to his steps pass like a shudder through the house. Buck leaned over, "Hey. Hey, Frank. What'd ya think? Maybe next time we call ahead? Maybe wear a

117

couple of nametags? Might cut down on the confusion."

The kid scanned the kitchen, "In my experience, truth leads to truth and lies to lies," he said.

"The fuck's that supposed to mean?"

"It means that I'm not so sure how forthcoming Nathans is going to be after he realizes you're lying to him."

"Well, he sure as shit wasn't gonna get chatty in front of those guys out there. And anyway, I always ask for coffee."

"Why?"

"Tricks 'em into thinking I'm a guest."

Frank shook his head, "And if he's up there loading that piece you seemed so worried about?"

"Calm down—guy's a trumpet player, for God's sake. But, you know, maybe just keep your ears open for the slide of a shotgun."

Nathans hustled back then, spinning the ceramic triumphantly, "Found that mug for you."

"Let's trade." Buck said, chucking Thomayer's picture onto the table.

Nathans froze, looked at the picture, at Buck, picture, Buck, and at the picture again, realization sliding down his face like grease off the wall, "Ah, man, *shit*, I knew I—*shit*."

"Mind if I call you 'Lou,' Lou?"

"Man, fuck you."

"OK."

"I should'a... *fuck*."

"Go ahead—get it outa your system."

"*Shit.*" Pacing. Looking. Half-starts. Head out the hallway, checking. More pacing. "*I...*"

"Did you know Mr. Thomayer, Mr. Nathans?" Frank asked.

"I don't know anything."

"Is that a yes?"

"Really. I don't. And I don't want to be involved either—whatever it is."

Buck went for the coffee. It tasted like dirt, "Well now, Lou, it's gotta be one or the other don't ya think?"

"You met at *Spindelman's*," Frank continued, "A couple months ago?"

"I don't know he—yah, yah I knew him, but—"

"—And you were with him the night he died?"

"Lot of people were."

"Guy in the band says you two had been running together for a bit."

"*Running together*? What's that 'sposed to mean?"

"Their words, not mine."

"Whose?"

Buck chuckled, taking another sip, "Good luck with that, kid's a vault."

Frank again, "It doesn't matter who."

"Look, I didn't do nothing."

"Nobody said you did. It's like I said out front, we're private investigators, not cops, and we're not here to get you into any kind of trouble. We're just trying to figure out what happened to Mr. Thomayer. Honest."

"And it's like *I* told *you*—*I don't know anything*—not really."

"What do you mean *not really*?"

Just then a guy in a half-buttoned bellhop's uniform came into the kitchen, looked at everybody and decided the coffee wasn't worth it. Lou cupped his face, muttering into his palms, "You guys can't be here. People talk. You gotta go. I can't... *shit*."

"You want us to leave?" Frank asked.

"Yes goddammit!"

"You sure?"

"Yes."

"OK."

"OK?"

"It's your house, Mr. Nathans. It'd be better if you talked to us, but, end of the day, it's *your* house." And just like that, the kid stowed his notebook, stood, and walked out the door.

Buck took another sip, watching him go, "Huh."

"What about you?"

"Oh, I don't know what the hell that was, but I'm not going anywhere 'till you talk."

"Goddammit."

"Let's get it over with, come on—you knew Thomayer, and you were with him at *Spindelman's* the night he died—what happened? You get loaded together?"

"No."

"You dipped ink and when he started to go sideways you dumped him down in the Skids, right?"

"I didn't dump nobody nowhere, man. I don't touch no dope."

"Come on, pal, I wasn't born yesterday."

"*I don't touch it.*"

"And if I were to take a look at your arms, huh?"

"You'd find a couple of moles," Lou snapped, tugging at his sleeves.

"What about Thomayer?"

"Clean far as I ever saw. He just liked the tunes."

"That why you ran together?"

"Man, we didn't *run together*—whatever that's 'sposed to mean—we just… we just spent some time is all. Just time. I barely knew the guy."

"I hear it was more than that."

"Well, you heard wrong."

"OK. So, what's the problem, then?"

"You come barking up my tree and you're asking *me* what the problem is? Like I don't know how it looks? Like I don't know what happens any time they got themselves a nice, white corpse and a black fella to pin it on?" Lou brushed past Buck on his way to the sink and consoled himself against the rust, running the water, wetting his palms, and dabbing his neck. "Like I don't know," he said again.

"You got me all wrong here, Lou. I ain't looking for lazy answers. I wanna know what happened, and if ya tell me, hell, I'll get right outa your hair; but if I get to the bottom of this coffee and you haven't given me anything I can check up on, well, I tell ya, pal, it'll start to seem like there's a reason."

The tap ran and ran and ran and ran and ran. Lou on his elbows. Head down. Then, "Other night, I was playing that Tillis Brothers thing—their horn man had the flu or something—and Eli, he... he came around to see the show. Now I told you and I meant it, me and Eli weren't nothing serious, this kinda thing happens, you get guys hanging around, getting chummy with the band... and it comes and goes, right? But Eli... I don't know, he wanted *more*, I guess. I told him. But... anyways, he was always wanting me to come over, you know? And you got eyes—I ain't saying no to a night away from this place. That night, I finished the gig, right? And me and a couple of the other house band fellas take the Tillis guys around the corner from here, over to Jumptown, where the real music's at. You gotta make your appearances at these things. One week it's us hosting them and down the road shoe's on the other foot," He cleared his throat, "So, I hang around a while, have a couple, and then take off to meet Eli, and we go to his place. But we aren't there long."

"Why not?"

"He got a call."

"From who?"

"*Sackler. Tom* Sackler. Eli said it a couple of times—like

I was supposed to remember—he said, 'I'm going out to meet a colleague of mine; I'm going to meet *Tom Sackler*.'"

"He say where?"

"Vanport. He said he'd be back in two hours, and if he took any longer than that, I should put on the Hi De Ho Man."

"And let me guess, that's the last you saw of him?"

"Yes."

"You play the record?"

"It was Eli who loved all that Cotton Club stuff—I'm on Dizzy's side of the whole thing. I practiced instead. I never get the chance over here—you can hear guys *breathing* through these walls."

"So, when'd ya play 'till?"

"Two in the morning, give or take. Slept a couple hours and slipped out at five."

"You see anything? Hear anything?"

Lou looked over, "Like what?"

"That a no?"

He nodded.

"What'd you think happened to him?"

Carefully, "Papers say it was an overdose."

"Uh-huh."

Lou sighed, screwing up his mouth, "Look, I grew up in Mississippi. Biloxi. Little shack off Lameuse Street. You ever hear much about Biloxi?"

"No."

"It's on the Gulf; got water all around it—warm water, not like here—and hot air, boy. God never made a place more perfect for washing off the crud. And I started sweeping floors at the cannery when I was eleven, so I had plenty for washing off. But in Biloxi, the beaches are just for *white* parasols, get me? So, me and a pal of mine—Percy was his name, son of a son of a push-broom from the cannery—started swimming Back Bay at night after our shifts. We was odd, him and me, and we had good times together out there in the water. We used to joke about how, no matter what we did, the crawfish smell stayed on and that it was only the good sand beaches on the Gulf side that could get it off and that next time a hurricane came and blew away all them parasols, we would run ourselves straight into that steel-wool kin'a water, bucking and crashing, and only then would we be clean enough for the Lord to recognize. But Percy must'a gotten impatient waiting on the hurricane. Because one day he didn't show up for shift, and the next they found him face down in the bayou."

"He drowned?"

Lou straightened, switching off the tap, "I told Eli that story too; told him that water's water and there's strong currents everywhere for odd boys like us. Best to find high ground where you can, and the highest I've found is up on that stage, playing them tunes."

"So, you didn't tell anybody about Eli's call with Sackler?"

"I don't need any more problems than the ones I got already."

"Fair enough. And if I find out you're lying?"

"You know where to find me."

"Yah. Right. High ground."

Frank was waiting outside, leaned up against the car, scribbling away. Must've wiled away the time gossiping with the jumpsuit twins. "Get anything?" he asked.

"Not really," Buck answered as they piled back into the car, "You?"

"Depends if you think it's anything that Lou clogged the sink last week?"

"Nope."

"Then no." They drove over to Williams Ave. Air wobbling, wet and warm. Buck parked it at the grocers' and bought a pint of whiskey and a couple sodas inside while Frank baked his ass on the chassis and wrote his memoirs. Minute crept by. Wiping sweat. Shuffling. Spitting into the gutter. "Why do you think he was so nervous?" Frank asked without looking up.

"Who?"

"Nathans."

"Dunno," Buck said, swigging from the bottle, "Some fellas are just the nervous type. Got ya a pop if ya want."

Frank shook his head, rolling the pen in his fingers, "That back there wasn't just the nervous type, Buck. He knew something."

"Eh."

"What'd he say?"

"I told you, nothing really."

"Try me."

Buck considered stonewalling the kid wholesale, but if he was going to check Nathans's alibi—the midnight horn playing—he'd need him to talk to the neighbor back on Siskiyou on account of Buck having left that bridge in cinders. Paid to have a second, for the moment anyway, "Nathans said he spent the evening with Eli, went back to his house, practiced for a while, and dodged out in the morning. No dope, no strife, no nothing."

"And you believe him?"

"I figure we'll check up on it."

"How?"

Within the hour, they were 'round the corner from Eli's house getting ready to call on Ole' Mr. Upright Snarls, Soldier of God, about the late-night trumpet. Wind stirring. Gray sky, bright and bleeding.

"You're not coming?" Frank asked after Buck gave him the need-to-knows.

"Better if I don't."

"You don't say."

"Tell him you're with vice. That'll get him blabbing."

"He's not going to buy me as vice."

"Why not?"

"They don't hire Japanese Americans."

"Think he knows that?"

"*Everybody* knows that."

"OK, so tell him you're president of the North Portland Morality League then, for Christ's sake."

"Fine. Mind trying to get Mrs. Whitmore on the horn while I'm over?"

"Will do," Buck said, saluting. But he didn't. Had a stale donut instead. Splash of brown to go with. Only managed the one though. Turned out, Frank wasn't gone long. He piled back into the rig and they drove on.

"Eh?" Buck asked, offering the bottle, "Trouble ya for the time, mister?"

Frank ignored him, turning in his seat to watch 71st street melt into the distance behind them. "God, what a miserable bastard."

"Told ya. Get anything?"

"Yah. He said he'd been watching Eli's house that night. Said he'd seen Thomayer's car leave around midnight and that he'd heard the horn playing for two hours after that, until about two. Rest was… editorial."

"So, Nathans's story checks out."

"Maybe. He still could have left and met back up with Thomayer afterwards for all we know. We shouldn't rule him out entirely, the way he was acting."

"Sure, sure. We'll check the police reports when we get 'em to see if the times match up. Which, speaking of, what the hell was that back there?"

"What?"

"You always just up and leave every time you're asked?"

"It was his house."

"It's a boardinghouse."

"I got what you might call a special interest in respecting a man's wishes when it comes to matters of the home."

Buck stared at Frank. Said nothing. Drove. The air swelled. It was too hot to argue. "You know, while back," he started, lighting a cig, "I saw some pictures of Heart Mountain. Looked hot out there."

"It was—in the summer."

"Hotter than this?"

"Much hotter, yah." A pause. "But it was different. It was dry. Today?" kid squinted out the window, "Today's more like when the army sent us to Camp Shelby for training."

"Camp Shelby? Where's that?"

"Mississippi."

"Huh."

"Yah. Just two hours up from the Gulf, in fact. Used to go down to the coast for our amphibious exercises—little town called Biloxi, actually."

Buck stared straight on, casual, "Biloxi, huh?"

"Yep."

"Never been."

Frank said nothing for a long, long time. Then, "I didn't like Mississippi. Too humid. The moisture gets in my chest after a while. Can't hardly breathe without tasting slough water."

"Well, you're not in Mississippi anymore."

"Not much different days like this—especially down at my place."

"And where's that, exactly?"

"Vanport."

10

The stairs were murder. Five flights of them, with each being one of those wide, marble-hard, piano-key steps built for men with too big of shoes and too small of strides. Chandeliers on the landings—but the sensible kind, the *democratic* kind—along with black granite directory plaques lettered in gold. Buck kept on climbing until he found one that read: *Housing Authority of Portland.*

Bingo.

He stopped. Snugged his tie; brushed his sleeves; smoothed down his hair. Then, in like a shot, whole shoulder torquing the knob, "Hiya, miss!" he called out, hurrying into reception.

The secretary's fingers relaxed off the typewriter, "Good afternoon. Something I can help you with, sir?"

"Yah, I think you can, my name's Richard Bennet—Dicky, if you please—and I, uh, had an urgent appointment with Tom—Tom Sackler—is he in today?" He took deep, half-exaggerated breaths and exhales that echoed strangely off the thick glass separating reception from the main authority offices. He could see the clerks working inside. Fish in a tank. Lipless, squinting men typing up forms, marking on forms, gaping at forms, clipping forms to other forms, and generally exuding a frantic, and particularly municipal brand of inscrutability.

"I'm sorry, sir, but Mr. Sackler won't be in today."

"Oh. No?"

"I'm afraid not," the secretary sympathized perfunctorily.

"Shit—oh! Excuse my language, miss."

"That's fine, sir. Maybe I can take a message for you?"

Buck heaved a sigh, "Do you know when he'll be back?"

"I'm sorry, sir, I don't."

"Tomorrow?"

She laced her fingers together and tilted her head, glancing over to the offices, "Maybe I can help you with something. What was your meeting with Mr. Sackler going to be about?"

"It's just, well, I... well, you see, we had a call not too long ago me and him, and, well, this, uh, this business of mine can't wait. It's a mix-up, I guess, a damned—oh, sorry—a *darned* mix-up that's going to get me in some hot water. I really need to speak with him. Do you have a number where he can be reached? Address maybe?"

"No, sorry, but if you let me know what you need, I'm sure we can help."

He nodded—faked a cough to get himself a second to think—but the moment came and went, and he still had jack, so he decided to just press on anyway. "It's, well, I been talking with Tom for a while now about some work we've been doing up by the river, and he was telling me there was some-something we'd need before we could proceed, and that we'd go over it today. Permit or something. Sorry, I don't know the lingo 'round here, miss, and I don't mean to be pushy or nothing, but I really gotta get this figured out today or I'll be up you-know-what creek with only my you-know-what to paddle with."

"You mean the Columbia, presumably?"

He played dumb, faking confusion, "No, no, miss the creek's just a metaphor; an expression."

She faked right back; smiled, purring through a patient little laugh, and said, "Yes, sir, sorry to be unclear, you'd mentioned you were doing work up 'by the river,' and I was just clarifying if you meant the Columbia or the Willamette? As you know, we have a number of different sites, so I could be more helpful if—"

"—You don't know when Tom will be in at all? Did he go someplace or something? I really gotta speak to him, miss. I don't know what kind of crazy form or permit or

132

injunction he had cooking up, but we were supposed to get it solved today. Filed or something, right? Gotta get this put to bed yesterday, I'm sure you understand, miss. I could go to him if I had a notion of where that was, of course."

"And what's the nature of your contract?"

"How's that?"

"What do you do with us, Mr. Bennet? With the authority?"

"I'm a plumber."

"At which site? Columbia Villa? Parkside? Vanport?"

"Vanport. Bingo."

"Alright. And if I can just get a bit more information on the project I can better direct you. Now, how close is the property to the sloughs? Is it near the embankment or more towards the Administrative Center?"

"Embankment."

"And did Mr. Sackler say anything about sandfill or settling concerns?"

"Might've."

"Do you mean to dig up the pipes?"

"Digging. Yah, exactly."

"Well, are you replacing or—"

"—I think I just need to see Mr. Sackler. Sorry, miss, I don't mean to be pushy," he lied. 'Course he did. He *loved* being pushy.

The lady slid out from behind the desk, slow and

smooth and assured, like a summer storm coming on, making his skin prickle. She was pretty, with full cheeks and wheat-stalk eyebrows that were a shade darker than the honey amber of her curls. Freckles hung like twilight stars over the breakers of lace lapping her neckline. Buck could feel himself coming 'round to Karl's way of thinking when it came to getting some secretarial help in the office. "The thing is, Mr. Bennet," she said, "I can maybe go find whatever document you're waiting on if I know what the main issue is. We don't file by client. We file by work order. So, let's try something—I'll say some terms that Mr. Sackler might have used with you, and if one sounds familiar that'll go a long way towards us solving this problem expeditiously for you."

He couldn't help himself. "OK. Shoot."

"Did he say anything about riparian shifting?"

"No."

"What about compression or abscesses?"

"No."

"Liquid soil? Midline access? Bolt crusting?"

"Nope. None of it."

"Anything *related* to erosion?"

"You know, miss, I just can't recall any of it. But you sure do seem to know your stuff."

Lightning in her eyes, the flash unmistakable, "Yes. I do."

"I suppose you pick it up 'round here, huh?"

"That's a way to put it."

Then came the thunder. The door to the offices opened and let loose the roar of clerical work. "Miss Bachinsky?" asked a bespectacled man with high, hunched shoulders. "You know the office is no place for personal visitations."

"Mr. Martins, this is Mr. Richard Bennet, he had an appointment with Mr. Sackler, but I was explaining that Mr. Sackler would not be in today. I was just going to get you."

Martins straightened his jacket. Straightened it again. And straightened it a third time. There was nothing for it. He was too thin a man and in too boxy a jacket. Made him look like a scarecrow. Thin, gray haired, and with a face full of severe, supercilious lines. He cleared his throat with the roll of a snare drum, and held out a hand that was all knuckle. Buck hated him immediately. "I'm Mr. Martins, the Department Director, what can *I* help you with, sir?"

Buck gave the newcomer the same vague, stupid, urgent story. Pretending to be *just* the sort of put-upon rube that these desk-proud pricks really loved to bat around. So, of course, by the end of it, Martins pulled back his pale lips and tried for something human. "Well, now," he said, "I'm sure I can get this sorted for you, Mr. Bennet."

"Please, call me Dicky," Buck said, barely able to keep the loathing out of his voice. Bachinsky clocked it, but Martins stayed oblivious. Buck imagined that kinda split to be pretty common.

"Do you remember the name of the form you need?"

"Nope."

"Was it A 1040-6, maybe? 103-AB?" Buck shook his head, but Martins was undeterred. "Never mind, I'll go look up your name. Wait right over there if you please; I'll just be a few minutes."

Martins slipped back into the office, sealing the cacophony behind him. Buck sat along the far wall of reception. He spread out. Crossed a leg. Ran a hand through his mop and waited. He watched Bachinsky plucking at her typewriter. Few years' experience matching key cadence to mood with Karl had made Buck something of an expert on the sound of agitated typing. Best keep that to himself; best keep up the act and just let things ride.

"Can I smoke in here?" he asked.

"Sure."

He pulled a cig. "Want one?"

"No, thank you."

"I didn't mean to put you in a bind with your boss there," he said, flicking flint towards the office and lighting up.

"Don't worry about it."

"OK."

She looked over. "I can get you an appointment with another inspector, if you'd like."

"You think I'll need to?"

"Yes. Yes, I do."

"What about Mr. Martins? Isn't he off to find my permits for me?"

Nothing. Nothing but typing anyway, one damning stroke after another.

"OK. Fine. I'd take an appointment. Anybody you'd recommend?"

"Well, depends on the job. If you told me anything specific, I'm sure I could think of someone."

"What about Eli Thomayer?"

He expected to get her with that, and he did, but only a little. Turned out she was halfway up the ladder on him already, "That story you told?" she scoffed, "You're not as slick as you think."

"So I hear." He glanced over to all those fishy housing officiants zipping in the tank, "You gonna fetch Martins?"

"How did you know Eli?"

"I don't and I didn't. I'm a PI. How long we got 'till Martins's back?"

She laughed, a real one this time, "Those forms he asked you about? The A 1040-6 and the 103-AB; neither one has anything to do with any part of that yarn you spun. They're about rent delinquency procedures and the regulations for building roads on alluvial deposits, respectively. We have a while, long as you don't do anything fresh."

"Not me, miss. I'm easy as they come." A drag. "Do secretaries always know this much about their offices. Happens I'm in the market."

"I wouldn't know."

"No?"

"I'm not from an agency."

"Oh. My mistake. I thought that's how it worked with you girls."

Her mouth screwed up the littlest bit, "No, *Dicky,* how it works for girls like me is that they go to college, they get their engineering degrees, and so long as there's a war on, they even get to use them. I managed code compliance until the day after VJ Day."

"Tragic how the boys came marching back, wasn't it?"

"If the war had gone on another six months—four even—I'd have made director."

"Wouldn't've lasted."

"No, but the demotion from director is back down to compliance, not compliance down to secretary. There's only so much they can take back before it starts to make them look like fools."

"You sure they know that?"

She sighed, tried typing, gave it up, and bit her lip, the aggrievement faltering in her voice, "You're here about Eli?"

"Yah."

"Eli was a good man. One of the few who really knew his stuff too. Really tried. What happened to him was a tragedy."

"And what was that exactly?"

"The papers said it was drugs."

"Were you two close?"

"Close? No, but we were reasonably well-acquainted as far as colleagues go. He and Tom worked together pretty frequently."

Buck nodded, "I figured."

"Don't look so pleased with yourself."

"Sorry. And how'd they get along—Thomayer and Sackler?"

"They didn't really. But they didn't *not* either, far as I knew."

"They see much of one another outside of work?"

"I wouldn't think so, no."

"And what about you and Thomayer."

"I told you—me and Eli were colleagues. We didn't really socialize, but we were friendly. That's about it."

He held up a knowing hand and went through the usual questions. You ever seen him use? He ever talk about it? You ever find anything? See any marks? How'd he act at work? And otherwise? Buck went through whole script, and Bachinsky had her lines down pat. No, and no, and no, and fine, normal, good. She even hit him with the usual epilogue—the testimonial, the assurance, the all-of-that-what-a-saint stuff with a career conscious spin. But Buck didn't care. Honest. The pearls were for her to clutch, not him. Most folks used something, it was just a matter of degree. Smack's a pretty sheer chute to go tumbling down, but there's always grass, cigs, powder, and pills;

or all that Old Testament kinda crap for the teetotalling traditionalist. Buck himself was boozer—hard pickling in the rye. Not a leg to stand on.

"What's all this got to do with Mr. Sackler?"

"Just wanna ask him a couple questions."

"Is he involved somehow?"

"That's one of 'em, yah."

"Well…" Then her face went tight at the corners, like someone was pulling at a rug that'd been nailed down, and in a flash, she was typing again just as the office door burst open and Martins came back out to join them.

"Sorry, Mr. *Bennet*, you said? Mr. *Richard Bennet*?" he asked.

Buck perked up again, nodding stupidly, "Yes—yes that's right, sir."

"B-E-N-N-E-T?"

"Oh, yah, that's right, but, sorry, sometimes I go by my middle name, which is Francis—Frank sometimes too. I seem to remember introducing myself that way to Mr. Sackler."

"Aha. I see. One moment, Mr. Bennet. I'll check again." He spun on his heels, "Miss Bachinsky, see if the gentleman would take any coffee while he waits, would you?"

Door closed. Roar gone to murmur. The typewriter dead as a stump.

Buck took his time. Smoked. Shifted. Ground a thumb against a forefinger. Waited. Then, "So?"

"You can get your own coffee."

"No. Not that. I'm pretty sure you were about to say something else; something useful about our good buddy Mr. Sackler."

"They say he's on leave."

"For how long?"

"They say two weeks, but they cleaned out his desk yesterday, so, you tell me."

"Huh."

"And," she said, lowering her voice for the first time, "well, it's funny—we were told if the cops come around to direct them to Mr. Martins."

"Martins?"

She nodded.

"Pretty standard, isn't it?"

"No, it's not just if the cops come asking about Thomayer, but it's if they come asking about *Sackler* too."

"And have any of Portland's finest been 'round?"

"No."

"Would you tell Martins if they did?"

She shrugged, "Sure I would. It's my job."

"Lucky for me he didn't say anything about PIs, huh? You got a number for Sackler I could try? Maybe an address?"

"What kind of detective doesn't have a phone book?"

"Maybe he's not home."

She considered that for a moment, "Look," she said,

shaking those amber curls, "I liked Eli. I'm sorry about what happened to him. But if it tracks back that I've given out personal information—especially with them acting as screwy as they are?" She snapped her fingers, "I'm out like *that*. I got a job to think about."

"You're right. It'd be a real shame to lose all this."

"It's temporary."

"You figure?"

She shrugged, "I'm sorry. I have to be careful. I have to be patient. They'll need me again soon enough. Between the Soviets and what's going on in China, there's going to be another big war any day now." With that, her typewriter reared back to life, and their little talk ended. On Buck's way out he laid one of his business cards on the desk.

"Here's hoping."

11

Buck went to Sackler's next. Now was the time. Frank'd said he had to bag it for the day, so Buck'd dropped him at the bus before hitting the authority offices. That Biloxi crack? Kid was crafty. Blunt, maybe, but peering in through the keyhole. Best to lock him out once and for all.

He took his time. Played it out. Rain on the hood, sweat on the seat. The world shimmering, steamy and far off seeming through the windshield. Waiting. Sackler's apartment overlooked the street from the top corner of a brick two-story building on east 12th. It looked empty. No lights. No movement. No nothing.

An hour passed and then he went for it, stopping inside on the landing and listening for a minute. No radios going or pages turning or stews boiling; no arguments, footsteps, or kids yammering—nothing and no one. Clear. So he knelt by the door, first one on the right, and tickled the lock until it gave. He slipped in. Quiet. Closed the door. The place looked like a six o'clock hair cut—drawers open, mangled. Hangers on the bed. Air like a stifled cough.

Yep. Sackler'd legged it for sure.

Buck poked around. Checked the bureau, trash, and cupboards; kicked up the rug and pulled at the bronze wherever it shined from use. He found an old checkbook and flipped through. Dated last year mostly; 'bout half the checks had been made out to 'Lamb of the Mountain Church' for a consistent $30 a month. *Tithing*, he guessed. He went to the pictures, where he found one with two fellas standing in front of a clapboard chapel, hands clasped, heads thrown back in a laugh, the younger holding some kind of glass award stand or something that Buck was just about to go looking for when some gorilla started in on the door—*poundpoundpoundpoundpoundpoundpound*.

Buck pocketed the checkbook and heel-toed over to the peephole.

Huh.

He opened up. "Hey, Frank. I was wondering when you'd show."

"Somehow I doubt that."

"Come in out the hall."

"No way. I'm not going to lose my license on a breaking and entering charge. Not to mention the jail time."

"What are you talking about—jail time?"

"See, it's just a little disappointing, you know? I gave you the chance to come clean—gave you the chance, and you blew me off."

"What'd ya mean?"

"*Biloxi*, Buck? I heard you and Nathans through the window, from out in the alley."

"I knew that 'a man's home is his castle' thing had to be a crock."

"It's not. Only seems that way because you've been caught in a lie."

"Would you come outa the hall, and stop being so goddamn sanctimonious, please?"

"Hey! Hey, you two!" a voice broke in from the bottom of the stairs.

They froze. Turned. "Fuck," Buck muttered, "See what you've done?" He stepped past Frank and out into the hall, "Help ya with something, fellas?"

There was two of them down there. Eyes up, hands ready. Hats. Pinstripes. Black, oily shoes. Square boys; all menace and mean geometry. "You Sackler?" the one on the right growled in between chomps of gum.

"Yep," Buck answered reflexively, "What d—"

They didn't wait to hear the rest.

Thing is, you never *see* a guy pull a pistol. Not if he means to use it anyway. It's a simple motion if you know what you're doing. In the pictures, guys are always waving the damn things around, polishing them, and setting them down on desks to make points. But, most times, there's none of that. If a guy means to blow a nickel through you, he gets right down to business, and if he's smart, he doesn't stop until he's given ya the full dollar.

Big spenders, these boys. They squeezed off a couple right away. Loud as Hell's hail come crashing. Somebody yelled. Plaster exploded overhead. Buck spun, grabbed Frank by the lapels, and heaved him into Sackler's apartment. Tripped doing it. Bent his ankle the wrong way. Hit heavy. Kid went crashing through the door and sent it swinging hard and into the wall. A scream, far off though. Muffled. Maybe. Who knew? Who could tell? Christ, it was loud. Curses. More yelling, downstairs. Few more slugs. Buck half-fell, half-dove against the wall and tore at his pockets. Desperate. Undignified. Clawing for his own piece. *Nope*—he thought, struck dumb in that damn hallway for half a half-second while the slugs whistled past—*no luck there; gun's in the car.* Huh. He staggered up. Firecrackers. Pops. Close whistles. Fingers flexing 'cross chrome. For want of anything to answer back, he tore his hat off and threw it at the bastards. They didn't seem to mind. Traded lead for felt. *Fuck!* He fell again, crawled-rolled-dove into the apartment. Cedar splinters flying. Sulfur stink. Smoke. Steps—rushing—clatter on the stairs. He looked around, grabbed a standing lamp and hurled it down the steps like a harpoon. A grunt, more cursing, and the wall started going to Swiss cheese. Reaching blind, his fingers wrapped around something hefty—it was the glass award stand he'd seen Sackler holding in the picture—but now was not the time for reading, now was the time for chucking like mad, and so he hard-hurled the thing it into the baying jaws of the doorway and listened for the crash, for the scraping, for the cursing, and the shots and the shouts. Frank got in on the idea, stepped up to the mound and pitched something hefty towards home. By the answering yelp, it sounded like a strike. But then, nothing—hard breathing and heart beats, Frank ran to the kitchen, plaster crackling underfoot, waiting, mind blurring—*nothing*.

The kid came back with two knives and handed one to Buck. "They're reloading. Time to fix bayonets."

"What?"

"We have to rush them. It's our only shot. On three. One-two—"

"—No fucking way—"

"—*Three!*"

They burst out into the hall—knives ready for the gun-fight—but found nothing save the spider-silk waft of gun smoke, the shattered jetsam they'd thrown overboard, and a dozen new, revolver-drilled peepholes scattered 'cross the hall. But Buck wasted no time. He tore through the stillness. Full tilt down the steps, twisted ankle starting to swell, swinging that blunt, chipped chicken-boner, more likely to stumble and skewer himself than anyone else. Then, out. Galloping 'cross the street. Key. Lock. A dive. A scramble. And a whipping up with the pistol cocked and ready.

Nobody. Rain. Neighbors cautious behind their curtains.

He hurried back inside, tossing the knife in the bushes, dropping the gun into a pocket, and picking his hat up off the stairs. Bastards had shot a hole through the brim. "Frank? Frank! Frank, where the hell are you? We have to *go.*" he shouted, crossing Sackler's place in what felt like two strides to find the kid on the phone.

On the phone.

On the fucking phone.

"What the hell are you doing?" he asked. But he knew already. It was clear by the kid's cadence and the quick, matter-of-fact way he was speaking into the receiver.

The kid had called the cops.

The *fucking* cops.

He gave his name, Buck's too, and promised they'd be there waiting when the patrol cars pulled up. After he'd hung-up, Buck had some questions of his own, adrenaline boiling in the back of his throat, "Are you stupid? Seriously. Are you the stupidest motherfucker there's ever been, or what?"

Frank didn't answer. "You hit?" he asked instead.

"No."

"Me neither," he looked around, "They still out there?"

"Shit, I don't know. No. No, I don't think so."

"Got your gun?"

Buck flashed it, mind elsewhere, "The cops, Frank? You're shitting me. The fuck were you—"

"—What were we supposed to do? Just drive off after two guys unloaded on us like that?"

"Yes. Yes, we were. Yes, we *exactly, fucking were.*"

"Calm down, Buck, *calm down.* Is this the first time you've been shot at?"

"Don't insult me, kid."

"I don't know what tha—"

"—No, for Christ's sake! No this isn't the first time I've been shot at, but it is the first time I've decided to wait around and see what Johnny Law's take on the whole thing is. Stay here if you want, kid, but I'm out of here." He turned, went down the stairs and to the car, turned the engine over—stopped—killed it, stashed the gun under the seat, went out, up, and back. "You stupid bastard," he said. "You stupid, stupid, *stupid* bastard."

"Thought you were leaving."

"Me too."

The fuzz blew in quick and made a big show of things. By now they had the whole block for an audience. Sirens. Lights. Running and shouting and badges shoved in everybody's faces. They patted Buck and Frank down outside in the rain and left them there on opposite sides of the street. No questions. No answers. Soaked. An hour at least. Then, at the exact moment their lace holes started gurgling up rainwater, they were told to come inside to make their statement. By now it was dark. Sickly light from the lamps. Hall stinking of gunpowder, deodorant, and sweat. Mud, slick on the stairs; glass and plaster grinding to powder underfoot. Back in Sackler's apartment, there was a plainclothes detective waiting for them. He had the look of a greyhound gone to paunch, with sad, azure eyes that never seemed to blink. He looked to be anywhere from thirty to sixty, depending on the light and the fix of his head.

"Howdy, Buck," he said magnanimously, gesturing to a couple empty chairs, "Good to see you."

"You too. Wasn't sure I would again, Behan—not outside *Armstrong's* anyway. McClean told me they'd parked you behind a desk."

"Only mostly."

"Congratulations."

"Hey, thanks. Come sit. How is Pat anyway?"

"Oh, you know, same ole' Pat."

Nodding, "*Hahaha.* Yah. Yah. Who's your friend?"

"Behan, Frank; Frank, Behan."

"Pleasure. What gives, Buck? Karl finally make smart and cut you loose?"

"Nope. We just moved into a new office down by the west precinct, actually. We're neighbors now, you and me."

"Hoh, wow, look at that, really reaching for the big time. Well, that's fine, real fine. Say, how long've my boys here been jerking you around for?"

"Hour and change."

He tutted sympathetically. "Not very courteous. Want some coffee or something? You hungry? How 'bout it? What about you, Frank? I can get something brought in—think I saw a sandwich shop down the block."

"We're all set," Buck answered, chewing on a cigarette, "Let's just get this over with, huh?"

"Nonsense, you boys must be dying for a hot drink and a bit of grub. Hey, Delridge, can you grab us a couple coffees?" he asked to the drowned rat of a patrolman who'd walked them up. The guy nodded wearily, taking his finger from out a bullet hole in the doorframe, and trudging down the stairs. Behan turned to another, the last, "And, you, uh, what's your name?"

Young cop standing in the kitchen. Quick. Eager. Most his gestures looking like some kind of half salute, "Officer Wilson, sir."

"Right, thank you. Listen, Willy, let's get a couple sand-wiches too, from that place on the corner, huh? Least we can do is feed these boys after we've kept 'em for so long. You guys like bacon?"

"Love it."

"Thought so," Behan waved, and the pee-wee patrolman hopped to, no questions asked. Questions were the boss's department. But Behan took his time too. He licked his lips. Unbuttoned his coat. Yawned. Went old. "OK," he said, "Let's have it."

Frank gave him the particulars. House call. Stakeout. Knock-knock, bang-bang. Except, as he told it, they were good little gumshoes until the time the shooting started, whereupon—like true God-fearing, law-abiding agents of righteousness—they had no choice but to enter the Sackler domicile. The rest got told straight. Kid was even pretty convincing. Buck tried to mask his shock.

"Lucky for you two the door wasn't locked," Behan offered after.

Buck, "Yep."

"And even luckier that those fellas couldn't shoot for shit. You get a look at them?"

"Nope."

"I did," Frank said, "They were big guys. Two-hundred pounds or so. One had a broad face and a pinched nose, and the other a scar on his jaw. Both about 5'11—six maybe—and they were dressed upscale, in black jackets and pinstripe pants. One of them had a green ribbon tied around his hat. But they weren't burglars, detective. Whoever they were, they were waiting around to ambush the guy who owns the apartment, they came after us by mistake."

"An ambush, you say? That's exciting."

"Yessir. They opened up the second they thought Buck was Sackler."

"And why would they've thought that?" Behan pondered, hooking one leg over the other, "Hmmm. Alright. So, these mugs of ours were lying in wait—in ambush, like you say—so's they could stick you up and snag the keys. Snatch job gone wrong, am I right?"

Frank glanced over at Buck, "Well, respectfully, detective—no, I don't think you are. There was no stick-up. They just started shooting."

"Must've cased the place beforehand. Lots of nice stuff in here."

"Detective?"

"*Burglars*," Behan marveled at the end of a deep breath, slapping his thigh "Real scourge in this town. Like lightning, there and then gone, am I right? Disappeared. Fact of life, fact of nature; can't very well chase lightning back up into the sky, can we?"

"They *weren't* burglars, detective."

"'Course they were."

"Say, Behan," Buck said, suddenly very, very tired, "Shouldn't you be writing some this down?"

Behan's face changed again, "What's to write? It's a botched snatch job, we agreed, didn't we? And I'm sorry to say boys, but there's not a lot we can do in a case like this. Shame you didn't get much of a look at the guys. A description would've *really* helped. Anything, really. But, hey, like I say, count your blessings—at least you didn't get hurt. Never a given in this world."

Then, like a lot of smart guys, Frank couldn't help but go and do something stupid.

"Those men were here to kill Tom Sackler, detective, and we think it's because he knew something about the death of Eli Thomayer."

Buck shut his eyes. Bit his lip. Slumped.

Bad call, Franky.

Real bad.

But before Behan could say anything, ever-eager Officer Wilson came back in and blurted out, "Where do you want the grub, detective?"

A beat. Another.

Behan smiled. Younger. Amiable again. "Set 'em right here, thank you. And, sorry that I forgot to say earlier—but could you run back and get these boys a couple packs of ketchup?"

"Sure thing. Mustard too, detective?"

"No, Wilson, I think these boys got plenty of that already."

The patrolman gave that a few confused chuckles before setting the sandwiches down and making himself scarce.

"Real go-getter you got there," Buck said once he'd gone.

"He's a rookie. He'll learn," Behan's gaze flicked to Frank, eyes all gone to blue-dark undertow, "What about *him*? *He* gonna learn?"

"He's learning plenty right now."

"That right?"

"Yep. But it's all a bit stale for me. I've known you're a son of a bitch for years."

Behan chuckled to himself, "Well, thanks for your cooperation tonight, fellas. I think we got what we need, and I'll be sure to let you know, personally, if I hear so much as a whisper about this whole business again," he said, slow and dangerous—actual dangerous, none of that puffed-up street-level shit that's all spittle and sneers—*real* dangerous, neck broke in the jail-block dangerous; plain-clothes, slug to the dome, dumped in the river dangerous. He stood to go. But no copper leaves it at that. They always gotta make absolutely sure you feel their boot on your neck. They can't help themselves. It's in their nature. "Bit of advice? Stick to bored housewives, huh, boys? Missing dogs; kids skipping school. Whatever. Just keep your noses clean—next time fellas come for you, they might not miss. Enjoy the sandwiches."

12

Hard not to be a smug bastard in this line. You learn things most don't. Hear things. See things. And when you spend all day turning over rocks like that, it's a professional prerogative to know the many-legged, many-viced creatures of the down-dirt there under. *I told you so*'s just come with the territory.

But there's an art to it, and its main tenet is *don't fall out in front of the fuzz*. No blood in the water; no scent on the wind. Give the pricks nothing. Long as it takes, you keep the acid in the bottle, you take your licks, you give back whatever you can, and when the badges dump you back out onto the street, *then*—and only then—do you level.

Buck'd been ready for that. Good and ready. He'd been mad as hell at Frank and hot to read him the riot act for getting them all tangled like this, but once they were released to their own recognizance and sitting back in the car, engine rattling away, he didn't say anything. Didn't *do* anything. Just sat. Sat, gripped the wheel, and prodded a finger through the new bore hole in his hat. Was all he could muster. His mind was pulp. Each thought soft-ripping like the pages of a phonebook left in the wet. Ink smeared and running. Frank wasn't any better by the looks of it, which made him think of the second of their racket's imperatives—*that pain is wasted on the numb.* Can't learn a thing pounding sand. So, Buck didn't go for it; didn't say a word. Not one goddamned word, mad as he was. And for a while, Frank did the same. Outside, the voices, lights, and silhouettes bled down the glass and into the gutter. The rain came. The windows fogged. And a clattery, tired kind of quiet tightened hard around them.

"Why?" Frank asked suddenly.

"They're cops," Buck grunted.

"But *why*? Why lean on us? Why threaten us like that?"

"'Cause someone told them to. Like always. How's this a surprise to you after what they did to your people?"

"What do they care about Sackler? About Thomayer? Why would that have spooked them like that? Far as they say, it was just an overdose."

"You gonna make me say it again? Christ, I'm tired. My cigarettes are soaked. You got any?"

"It doesn't make sense. It's like they were scrambling.

Like they were overreacting, right? If they'd of just played it straight, we'd have no idea that they knew *something* about all this. Then we'd only have the gunmen, really, and a whole lot of conjecture that doesn't add up to much. Now, well, I don't know what we got exactly, but we got something. It was stupid of them."

"Frank, the cops don't give a shit what we know or don't know; they're not trying to outsmart us, pal—they're playing *their* game, not ours. And their game's simple." Buck reached over, plucked the rye out of the glove compartment, and took a swig. The stuff sizzled all the way down—like he'd licked it straight off the surface of the sun. "Anyway, whatever the why, figure there's no going back. We're in the shit together now, you and me."

"Just needed Jerry to introduce us."

"What?"

"We used to have this saying in my unit that if you didn't like a guy, all you needed was for Jerry to introduce you. It was true too. We had this replacement from Hawaii come in just before we crossed the Arno and I made sergeant—most stuck-up *sansei* you ever seen. Do you know what I mean when I say *sansei*?"

"Nope."

"I'm what we call a *nisei* in Japanese—which means I was born in America, but my parents were born in Japan, which makes them *issei*. And if I have kids, *they* would be *sansei*."

"Japanese's got words for all that, huh?"

"Yessir."

"Can't ya just count?"

"What'd you mean?"

"First generation, second generation, like that? Like normal?"

"It's more than just a family tree type thing, it's cultural, it's... look, for example, a lot of *sansei* guys don't even speak Japanese, right? They take the Americanness of it all as a given, and this *sansei* replacement I'm talking about wasn't just *Sansei,* he was Hawaiian *Sansei*, and it's a whole different deal out there. They weren't interned like we were out here, and there's sometimes a... I don't know... an *attitude* about it—a superiority. And I served with lots of guys from Hawaii and we usually figured it out, but there was just something about this guy in particular. I couldn't stand him. He was always mouthing off; had something against me too it seemed like. But then, the Krauts shelled the line for two days straight, and me and him ended up sharing a foxhole for the duration. And you know what? We talked. We hashed it out. And we were always friendly after that."

"And we're next, that it? Fast friends? Bosom buddies?"

"It's worth a shot."

"OK. OK, fine. Let's give 'er a go," Buck said, nudging Frank with the bottle.

"Oh, no thanks."

"Look, Frank, this foxhole principle of yours is sound and all, but adding in a bit of whiskey is what you army boys might call a force multiplier."

Kid took the hint—took it twice, in fact, "Alright. So, what about you?" he asked clearing the whiskey from his throat, "Did you serve?"

"I was a conchie."

"You're kidding."

"Nope—my number came up and I told 'em I was a preacher. Ended up in alternate service out in Umatilla watching rancher's daughters put the pins into hand grenades until they bounced me out."

"Weren't you worried the draft board would find out?"

"Find what out?"

"That you were lying."

"I wasn't lying. I *am* a preacher. Or, *was* anyway, and it's not the kind of thing with an expiration date, I don't think."

"Well… you…"

"What can I say? That's the beauty of the Pentecostals, Franky boy, they got *zero* oversight of that sorta thing—no popes, no presbyters, no conventions—just between you and the Lord. Ordained when I was nine, if ordination means holding the heads and hooks of one-handed saw men while they flopped 'round in the mud. Mom died when I was three, so it was just Dad and me on the move; traveling all up and down the coast. Astoria to Crescent

City; timber camp to canning wharf; sleeping in pup tents and on the side of the road; all day listening to Dad try and hide his accent behind the tongue of the angels." Buck took a swig and sent the bottle bobbing back 'cross the leather waters between he and Frank, shore to shore, message tucked, "Way I figure it, I did my time. Draft board can kiss my ass. Mud's cold on the coast, and Dad was no peach. He had something in him that didn't react right with the air; some part of him always smoldering, and a man like that can either go out and shoot the president, or he can preach the gospel. He was good. I'll give him that. He would hold out his hand and the whole saw camp or whatever would come and settle right there into his palm. It was a thing to see. *Is*, probably. I haven't heard much recently, but if that ole' bull elephant still has a drop of life in him, he'll be out hollering homilies so loud that even God almighty's liable to straighten in His seat."

"You two don't talk?"

"Hell, Frank, we never *talked*; it's only now I don't hear him neither. He used to send me his bibles after he beat the binding out of 'em, but the last one was… '43 maybe? So it's been a while."

Frank took a pull, "I can't imagine that."

"No?"

"No. I have responsibilities. It's part of being *Nisei*."

"What'd ya mean?"

"My dad's generation—*Issei*, like I said—they built

Japantown out of… out of nothing; they grew a garden out of a crack in the sidewalk, and then," he snapped his fingers, "Just like that, it was gone. Turned into brothels and clubs and pinball parlors. You'd think that would've hit them hardest, but no. My mother was gone by then too, but my father did alright in Heart Mountain. He was used to it in a way, because when he first came to Portland, Burnside *might as well* have been strung with barbed wire. Heart Mountain was just more of the same. Just a bigger, dustier Japantown. It was us who struggled out there; the *Nisei*; the bridge generation; too Japanese for America, and too American to be anything else. So, I joined up."

Buck snorted, "Well, that's one way to show 'em, I guess."

"It's not about them. It's about me."

"Yah, well, if it were about *me*, and they sent *me* to a camp? Humiliated *me* like that? I'd be saying, 'fuck 'em' 'till the cows came home. They wouldn't get a drop of nothin' long as I lived."

"Well, it wasn't you."

"If it were, I'm saying."

The kid cleared his throat, testy, little bit a'slipping-slurry creeping into his voice, "All due respect, but you don't know what you're talking about."

"I don't? Kid, I see things for what they are—I see the kickin' that the pocket watches call a country, and I got no illusions."

"You know, in the spirit of clearing the air, I think I got to say that I've been watching you—and no offense—but you spend a lot of time posturing. You bluster. You play the loudmouth and walk away because you get to—because *you're* not going to wind up in a camp; because for all your railing against the cops, they treat you with kid gloves, because so long as you *look* American, and your name isn't hard for them to pronounce, it's just a little noise coming from inside the house, nothing serious; nothing to answer for. So yah, fuck the law; fuck the draft board; fuck the army and the Whitmores and the Sacklers and the whoevers, and the everyones of the world. Fuck them all. What's the harm? It's just *talk*, right?" As punctuation, Frank snatched the bottle back and took so deep a pull it was like he'd lost a quarter down at the bottom and figured he might catch it with his teeth.

"Was it all talk when I saved your fucking life back there, pal?"

"You didn't save my life."

"I pushed you outa the way when the shooting started."

"We were only there because of you in the first place. Look, in the spirit of—"

"—Christ sake's, Frank, just spit it out."

"Alright. I know that you think I'm stupid, and I know that you were trying to cut me out before."

"I saved your ass *twice,* come to think of it," Buck muttered, ignoring him, "First was with McClean. You know how bad that could've gone had I not been there?"

"You heard something, and you didn't—"

"—Answer me."

"And with Nathans—"

"—Come on, answer me, do you know—"

"—'Course I fucking know! Jesus Christ, Buck, *that's what I'm* fucking *saying!*"

Now, for all the wonders of this modern age—with the atom cracked and penicillin banishing infection the world over—no fella yet had discovered the right way to throw a punch while in the front seat of a '37 Chrysler. Just as well. Would've been dicey after all the booze. So instead, they stewed. Passed and tipped and growled for the sake of it.

"OK," Buck said, "OK, so, maybe heart-to-hearts aren't going to be our thing, huh? So, let's keep it simple; are you gonna drop the case?"

"No."

"Well, me neither, and they'll kill us together same as separate, so we might as well work together."

"That's what I've been doing since the beginning."

"Yah-yah, what a guy."

"I should get home," Frank said, dropping the empty bottle to the floor, "The busses are… I don't where the…"

"Shut up. I'll drive ya."

"No. No thanks, I'll—"

"—Shut up." Buck put the car into gear and drove into the humming darkness towards Vanport—that spit of jumped-up nothing past city limits where the Columbia crept slow and stinking and inevitable. Christ. *Vanport.* Not Vancouver, not Portland, but between. Named on the cheap and built on the cheaper, sitting 'bout a dozen feet below the Columbia River on a couple square miles of reclaimed swampland running along its bank. Buck had been a few times during the war. It'd sprung up basically overnight once the shipyard bigwigs realized they would need a bunch of quick-bin housing if all their new-hired riveters and joiners and welders were going to fill the oceans with warships. And the make-do haste of it showed everywhere back then. Hurry pooling in the gutter-less streets. Smell of sawdust in the air. The acid, back-throat distaste of industry and ambition. Bog-slop up to the ankle of the big, shipyard boots that went tramp-tramp-tramping through the muck. People and lights and people and idling buses and people and tools glinting manic. It wasn't a neighborhood. Wasn't a city neither. It was the dogging end of a firing piston; a big ole' engine working steady, day and night, with tens of thousands of two-bed balsawood berths swinging to the pitch of the drydock's hammer.

But that was then. With no war on to shake the green out the trees, the grand engine had gone quiet. No point anymore. So, lots of folks had up and left, but, then again, lots of others hadn't. Newcomers too—cheap rent being just as good a lure as it was a hook. And word was that Vanport was more swamp than ever now. Nothing but rot, rust, and race mixing; wartime necessity curdling into disrepute. But Buck wasn't so sure. Hard to judge that kind of thing from the car, sealed up behind so much chrome and glass—decline's gotta be waded through to be believed—and anyway the whiskey had blunted him a bit. Even so, here, now, belly-of-the-beast, he wasn't seeing anything more shocking than a couple of stray dogs and kids double-dutching in the bushes.

Though, his standards for vice *had* loosened over the years.

"Wake up, Frank," he said, shaking the kid's shoulder.

He didn't. Groaned a little. Muttered. Buck shuttered the engine, went 'round the other side, and yanked him to his feet. "Come on, fella, rise and shine. Let's go."

"Don't tell Ida," he slurred, slumping like a sack of flour.

"Who's Ida?"

"Ida. *Ida June.*"

"Who's that?"

"Wife."

"You got a wife?"

"*Yep.*"

"Huh. Well, bad news, kid, I'm pretty sure she's going to know you're soused."

"No, no. No-no-no-no. *Don't* tell *her.*"

"OK."

The dead-weight stumble carried them quick down the hall, and Frank was too loud and too fumbling with the keys to recover. Just as he'd started getting somewhere, the door swung open on him and there, squarely, was Mrs. Takahashi, and whoever Buck was expecting to bear a name like that, it wasn't the woman he saw—she was closer to his age than to Frank's; her tight, dark curls done up for the night, but makeup still on. She was black and petite—a full head shorter than Buck—with soft dolloped features and a long neck, dimples like pinwheels spinning curious at the corners of her mouth. She took Frank smooth, ducking under his armpit to take the weight before Buck could say anything, and when she did speak, her voice was as soft and Southern as Spanish Moss, "You must be Mr. Bordell?" she said.

"Mrs. Takahashi?"

"Yessir."

"Pleasure."

"Likewise." She turned to Frank, "My-my, darling, you look fished right out the barrel, don't you?"

Kid tried to straighten; to play the host, gestures limp, pupils the size of dinner plates, "Buck... Ida... Ida... Buck."

She smiled, patting his chest, "Thank you, dear, now let's get you to bed."

"Tell him I'll be by tomorrow," Buck said, "bright and early."

"I will."

"Eight, eight-thirty maybe."

"Alright now."

"We got a meeting with Whitmore at ten o'clock, so…"

"I'll tell him. Good night now, Mr. Bordell."

Then, the door. The flop-alley muffle of the new tenement hallway and he was back outside. Some guys huddled on the corner, their voices cracking like dried cedar; a dog barking through the smoke, and the wheels of his rig starting on their own to bear Buck back towards town. Night was young, and he had another stop to make.

Maddy lived in an apartment under the backend of *Bon*'s. He'd been there before. Used to go quite a bit. For a while, *a lot* even, but that was then. He knocked. Knocked again. Nothing. OK. Fine. He'd wait. Weeknight like it was, it wouldn't be long. Went 'cross the street. Smoked. One. Another. Then, with the clattering swing of the back stair door, he saw the proprietress heading home. But this was Skid Row, and a guy doesn't go jumping from the shadows at a lady like Maddy unless he wants a knife in the belly, so Buck went 'round to the Ukrainian market to buy a stone-cold sack of pierogi and use the phone.

"Hello?"

"Long night in there?"

"Monsieur Sorenson, I told you; if you don't stop calling me here, I will have to alert your wife."

"No, Mads, it's Buck."

"Buck?" A pause. He heard water running. Maddy kept

her phone in the bathroom 'case she needed the inside lock. "What'd you want?"

"Share some grub? I got some of those commie dumplings you like so much."

"You were just in the neighborhood, is that it?"

"Happens that I really was this time. Thought we might break bread."

"And?"

"And have a little chat."

"You're drunk."

"But lucid."

"*Sure.*"

"See for yourself, huh?"

She sighed.

"It's important. Nothing funny. We just gotta talk."

"Do we? Do we ever?"

That was a yes. "See ya in a flash."

He hung up and hoofed it down the block, the dough-balls clacking like a bag of marbles. He could hear music coming through the door; could hear Maddy padding around, ready for him. Still, she made him knock. One of her rules. Always had been.

"Alright," she said answering the door, and sliding out of her heels, "Come inside if it's so damn important." It was the second time a woman had opened the door for him tonight, and it was so far his favorite. Sure, him and Maddy weren't any kind of long-term proposition, but the occasional worked all right he supposed. She lived spare. Harsh lights. Shelves of product. Stone floor. Brick disintegrating in the corners. More like an imports warehouse for perfume and Napolean brandy than a home, even with the singular expense of a big four-poster bed shoved into the corner. As he came in, she slung a glass of gin into his hand. Gin was good; gin meant welcome. For his own part, he handed over the dumplings, and she took them with what was almost a smile. "I'm surprised you remember."

"It wasn't that long ago, Mads."

"Yes, it was."

"Well, it can't all be *escargot* and *fromage*, can it?" he dodged, not wanting to argue; not about this anyway. "Slow night?"

"Eh."

"Any bigshots?"

Maddy passed into the kitchen with Buck following. "You staking out the door or something? Anything I should know about in advance?" she asked, bundling the pierogi in wax paper.

"Nope."

"Better not be. I've had enough ink spilled my way lately. So, what? You just miss me then?"

"Partly."

She snorted, "What's the other part?"

"You might not like it."

"I usually don't."

"Good point."

Twine, looping round the lumps of lard and flour, once-twice-and-tight-for-the-third. "Come on then."

"Thomayer," he answered watching her over the rim of his glass.

She stopped—or, more like, *didn't* stop. Not at all. Not even a little. Going and going and going and going, eyes too eager—eyes too ready—leaping, claws out. "Who?"

"Uh-huh."

"Oh, was that that junkie they found in the alley the other night?"

"Sure was."

"What about him?"

He shrugged, "It's funny, people keep playing dumb on this right up until the time the shooting starts." Their eyes met and he was reminded that Maddy kept a couple pistols in the house herself. One in the bathroom, and the other… well, he couldn't quite recall. Maybe in one of those drawers she'd flung open. They'd always joked she'd plug him one day. But no. Not tonight. All she was rooting around for was another roll of wax paper. Maddy liked to keep her dumplings in the freezer for the morning. Buck figured it was on account of the cathouse hours she kept. 'Course, then again, it could've started as yet another passably continental affectation that, adopted long enough, had become a real part of her. That happens in life—you become the lie. There's no such thing as pretending. Not really. There's only what people do and everything else.

"What shooting is that?" she asked. He swept off his hat and showed her the bullet hole. She snorted again. "Tonight?"

"Yep."

"How come?"

"I was checking up on a friend of Thomayer's who'd split town. Which turned out to be good for him because there were two heavies waiting to take him out. Got me instead; well, got my hat anyway."

Maddy picked a bit of invisible lint from Buck's shoulder. Casual at first. Then not. Just close. Poised. "Missed you by just a couple inches. Shame."

"You know, a guy could take that kind of talk the wrong way."

"So touchy all the sudden. Must've shook you. I thought a man like you was harder to shake."

"Plenty hard."

She tossed her hair, the scent of her crashing like a broadside—smell of cigarettes and Old Rose and sour champagne, "Buck Bordell, *mon Dieu*, you delicate little bird. How surprising could it possibly be for a man in your position? It's a big, loud machine out there, and it isn't pretty, or—*qu'est-que-c'est*—upright. It needs its greasy little secrets staying secret for it to run smooth as it does."

"Your English really is something these days, Mads."

Before, this is where they would have kissed. Grappled. Waddled and tore into the next room, and after, in the black, hungry, dead of the morning they would have eaten those fatty, crackling dumplings over the cast iron, and drank red-black, teeth staining wine and gone again, and again, and again, all before the sun could catch wise. But those days were gone. Maddy stepped away. Beneath those bright lips, her tongue ran slow and thoughtful over her teeth, and she looked him square on. "I'm trying to help," she said.

"I know you are. But help *who*, exactly?"

The gin passed like a whetstone over her face, "You should probably go."

"Who's leaning on you, Mads? I know it's somebody 'cause they're leaning on me too, and it's more than the usual game of footsy this time. Is that why Charlie didn't scoop Thomayer up the other night and chuck him someplace else? Huh? Was there someone else with him? Come on, you can tell me what happened. I know you know something."

"It's late."

"Did the cops pay you a visit already? What'd you see that night? The girls? I know you coached Polly—why?"

Nothing.

"You used to be a better liar, Mads."

"I have to use the powder room."

He watched her go. She'd be ringing upstairs in there;

ringing the body man to come throw Buck out. If she'd wanted him dead, she'd of done it herself; she had the gun and the river nearby, and nobody'd spend much time looking for the town's least liked gumshoe, last seen drunk in Skid Row. Guys disappear. Fact of life. No, she didn't want him dead, this was just to show him she meant business. He thought about cracking the bull with the cast iron moment he saw horn; thought about throwing down then and there, but he left instead—cooler heads and all that. Quick out the door and up, sinking into the shadows of the street and not a moment too soon as the big, lumbering mass of Charlemagne came hot footing it 'round the corner. Message received. Beating dodged. Lucky break.

But sometimes a guy just can't help himself.

"Hey! Hey, Charlie! How ya doing you fat headed fuck, you?"

Without slowing, the big man-shark turned and started right for him.

Shit.

To Buck's surprise, he managed to land the first punch. A good one. Right in the meat of Charlie's ribcage. But, Christ, it was like punching a mattress.

From there, well, things turned.

13

For a few seconds next morning, Buck was sure he'd gone blind.

Then he remembered the wet rag he'd tied 'round his eyes after he'd come home the night before, and when he peeled it off to have his first daytime look at the damage, the shiner underneath wasn't near so bad as he'd feared. He sat up, prodding around. His right ankle had swollen like a balloon, and his ribs ached something fierce. Still, nothing broke. Nothing ripped off. This wasn't the first time he'd gotten a kicking like that. He knew the moves; knew how to get home blurry; how to clean the street out his cuts; and how to taste for broken teeth. Rolling out of bed, he took a couple sore laps 'round the apartment, took a cold shower, had a bit of coffee, couple cigs, bit of butter scratched on toast with salt, and then raced back to the porcelain for an unexpected bit of dry heaving. That done, he felt like a new man—half of one anyway—and half was about as good as he could ever muster these days.

After, he called up the Takahashi's to let him know he'd be on the way. Ida answered, and started right in, "Tell Frank to be ready when I get there. I don't wanna have to wait around all day for him to find his ass."

A pause, then, "Usually—and I don't know about you—but I like to start things with a 'good morning.' Good morning, Mr. Bordell."

"Morning."

"Nice of you to see my husband home last night."

"Don't mention it. Tell Frank to be ready when I get there."

"I surely would, but there's no one here by that name, Mr. Bordell."

"What'd ya mean? Did you kill him or something?"

"Have a good day, Mr. Bordell, thanks for the call."

"Hold on, I—"

She hung up.

Goddammit.

He tried again.

"Hello?"

"It's Buck."

"Yes, Mr. Bordell?"

"Don't tell me Frank went out already. I forgot to tell

him—we got Doreen coming by this morning, and we don't have time to—"

The line went dead. Fuck it. Didn't matter. He'd just head up. But Christ, things were bleak already—sun high, burning like a drip of sap. The smell of it everywhere; of living wood baking dry and some backyard burn bundling smoke down the block. That scratchy, back-of-the-throat kind of air that somehow got worse in the car. Every window down. Drove as fast as he could. One of those hollow days. Buck felt low. Low and sour and blown through. But he had things to do. Hell with it. He drove faster.

Vanport looked different in the day. Long rows of apartment buildings with their siding streaked in discoloration, and dry, tobacco looking tufts of moss growing between the miscut shingles. Cracks everywhere. The cheap sliding off like it always does. A shithole, sure, but the passive kind; the kind borne of neglect rather than malice. There were people here. Schools. Families. Music. Comings. Goings. He'd seen a lot worse.

At the door, Mrs. Takahashi was ready for him this time. She'd changed into a gray and black dress over stockings, with a pair of hornrims pinching her nose, "Good morning, Mr. Bordell."

"Yah, hi," he peered past her, "Your husband ready?"

"He's sleeping."

"I thought, uh… well, could you *wake him up*?"

"I surely could."

She blinked at him.

"OK," he sighed, "OK."

Would you like to come in?"

"Sure. Thank you."

"Would you mind taking off your shoes first?"

"Uh-huh."

He wrestled off his loafers and shuffled in. The apartment was small, with a bedroom, bathroom, and a main room doubling as a kitchen, every inch packed to the gills and careful-stowed. In the corner, cross-legged on the carpet and listening to the Hi Fi, was a bald, older Japanese man. "Hiya," Buck grunted in his direction. Then, to Ida, he asked, "So, where's the man of the hour?"

She chuckled, "See, now, I said to my husband before we moved in; I said 'honey, now don't you think the place is a little too much for us? Between the east wing and the hedge maze and the solarium—our guests will get all turned around.' but he insisted. Willful man, my husband. *Willful.*"

Buck sucked a tooth and took the hint. He found Frank in the bedroom. Somehow, the missus had wrestled him into pajamas. "Frank," Buck barked, "Frank! Wake up, dammit!"

"What? What the—Buck? What're you…"

"Come on, Frank, get up for Christ's sake."

"Shit," the kid swung up into a sitting position. He

blinked. Coughed, "Shit," he said again, "I think I'm going to be sick."

"You're just gonna have to push through. Come on, up, up, up. Let's go. We gotta meet with Whitmore."

"What?"

"Me. You. Whitmore. Ten o'clock."

"Since when?"

"A while. Come on."

Frank stood. Swayed. Groaned, "Wait."

"What?"

"Did you… did you call me Frank?"

"Jesus, pal, you weren't *that* drunk."

"How'd I…did—did you stay the night?"

"No. I dropped you off."

"Shit. What'd you say to Ida?"

"Nothing. I just handed you over and that was that."

"Did you use my name, I mean?"

"As opposed to what?"

"Shit, Buck, I… I told you not to…didn't I?"

"I don't think so."

"I thought I had."

"No."

Radio coming through the wall, clear as day, horns hotter than the morning. "How drunk was I?"

"Pretty drunk."

"How did… how did Ida seem?"

"Polite."

"She's Southern."

"I could tell."

"No, I mean, polite's a given with her. Did she seem annoyed?"

"I don't know. I don't know her." A pause, "But yes. Yes, she did."

"Shit."

"Don't worry, she'll get over it. Everybody gets blotto now and again."

"It's not the drinking. It's the *name*."

"How's that?"

"She hates when people call me 'Frank.'"

"She hates when people call you by your name?"

"'Frank' isn't my name. Not exactly."

"You've lost me."

"I went by 'Frank' in the army. None of our training officers at Camp Shelby were Japanese, and we needed to—whatever, it doesn't matter. I've been going by 'Frank' again since I started this PI stuff. I thought it'd be better for business." A pause, "And other things."

"Huh."

"I don't want to hear it."

"No, no… my partner did the same thing, actually. Kinda. Want me to say something to her?"

"To Ida?"

"Yah."

The kid stopped cold, staring, "No. No, Buck, I don't

think that would help. Just—so long as we're around Ida—do me a favor and call me Sumio, OK?"

"*Su-mee-yo*?"

"Close enough," the kid said, jumping into a pair of slacks before rifling around for a shirt in the closet, where—behind a couple ratty sweaters and a hat box— Buck spotted a big bastard of an automatic rifle leaning in the corner, black and polished.

"Fuck. You weren't kidding about the B-A-R, were ya?"

"I told you, didn't I?" Sumio stepped past, palms pressing hard against his eyelids. "Buck, can you…can you give me a minute? Can you go out and get some tea or something?"

"Thought you didn't want me talking to the missus."

"I won't be long."

The tea was ready for him at the table already. Ida too, "Got any coffee?" Buck asked, tossing down his hat and taking the seat beside the lady.

"Just the matcha, I'm afraid."

"It's green."

"It'll grow on you."

"That's what I'm afraid of."

She chuckled airlessly and Buck turned to the old man sitting cross-legged on the floor, "You like Goodman, do ya?" he asked, voice raised. The codger smiled at the question but said nothing. Back to Ida, "He speak English?"

"Yes, Mr. Bordell—very much so—*otousan* just likes

181

to listen to his records in the morning. He's particular. Sumio is usually working by this hour. I would be too if not for the holiday. Do you like the tea?"

"It's OK."

"I've a weakness for sweet tea, myself, but we try to alternate our comforts, Sumio and I; we try to share them. Tell me, Mr. Bordell, other than that bruise you got there, do you find that the life of a private investigator agrees with you?"

"This was recreational," he said, remembering the shiner.

"I see. And for this vocation, did you come to it naturally or by ambition?"

"Most my ambitions don't last longer than an evening, ma'am."

Another chuckle, "A man for the moment—I see, I see—have you been working long?"

"Fifteen years, give or take."

"Man of some experience, then."

"I 'spose."

"And a bachelor?"

"Yah."

"You'll have to excuse the questions—Sumio may be the one with the license but I'm the snoop in the pair."

"Oh, yah? Well, even so, your husband and I have bungled our way towards some good progress last couple days."

"Have you?"

"Yep."

"So, have you learned who killed Mr. Thomayer, then?"

"Not yet."

"But you know *why* he was killed?"

"No."

The teacup bore the brunt of her sorghum-sweet incredulity. "Sumio tells me that Mr. Thomayer received a call telling him to come up and meet a man around these parts the night he died. Have you considered asking folks up here in Vanport what they may have heard? It's a lively place, Mr. Bordell, one with a lot of ears."

"Kid keeps you pretty apprised of the case's developments, doesn't he?"

"Every great man—as they say."

"Yah, well, at the moment, we're mainly concerning ourselves with finding the guy who made the call in the first place. It's a, uh… a process." Buck glanced around the room, noticing the pictures on the far wall. Most consisted of suit-coated men and pearl-broached women standing on the lawns of grand, southern houses.

"Relations?" he asked her.

"Yes indeed, that one there on the right would be of my great uncle, and the one beside it would be of my grandfather and grandmother. My own parents below. And the house you see there is the one I grew up in in Hattiesburg."

"Ritzy."

"My family did very well. Textiles. I come from a long line of hard workers, you understand."

"Sure." Buck said, finding next a picture of Sumio as a teenager, and his father—the old man now on the carpet—standing together in the middle of a long, dusty, unpaved street. Squat, brown buildings either side. In the distance—far and dark and snow-streaked—a flattop, barren peak. "That from the camp?"

"From Heart Mountain, yessir."

"Strange thing to frame."

"I reckon it's stranger not to."

She smiled; he smiled. She sipped; he sipped. Through the thin walls came the fat sounds of the morning. Not even Benny could push it all out. Engines. Voices. Dogs. Radios. Footsteps. And finally, Sumio scratching at the bedroom knob. Buck sympathized; a man's all thumbs on his climb back out the bottle. But the kid freed himself soon enough and came into the room, kissing Ida on the cheek while she poured him a cup of tea. "Sorry, Juney," he said.

"Don't trouble yourself over it, darling, come and sit with me and Mr. Bordell. We were just having ourselves a fine little chat. Can I get you something? Some of *otousan*'s miso left in the pot?"

"No, thanks, my stomach's not there yet."

"Nonsense—it'll help you settle. I'll fetch you some.

Mr. Bordell? What about you? Can I tempt you with some breakfast?" She outpaced the question, stepping into the kitchen and returning with two small bowls of cloudy soup. "Now, Mr. Bordell, you mentioned that you and Sumio have a meeting with the bereaved sister this morning. The Mrs. Whitmore? What is it that you plan on telling her?"

"Figure we'll tell her there's momentum."

"Momentum. I see," Ida said, her nail skirting 'cross the teal laminate of the table, "You know, Mr. Bordell, when I was at Jackson College they taught us that momentum is the violent meeting of one force upon another, and I can see by the hole in your hat brim and the way it smells of gunpowder, that you and I share a definition of the word."

"I 'spose."

"So, when I venture to use other words—words like *love* and *wrath*—I can count on you to understand me when I say that I love my husband, and that should something befall him on account of this *momentum*, that all the blue oceans of the world will not keep you from my wrath."

"Juney, I was going to tell you—"

"—It's alright, darling, we're all just getting to know one another here, aren't we, Mr. Bordell?"

Buck grinned, lifting his cup, "You know, you were right, Ida. The tea *does* grow on ya."

185

14

Vague or no, it turned out to be a lot for Whitmore to take in.

A madam keeping mum.

A late-night call.

A botched hit.

And the cops covering.

All with Sumio propped up corpselike and Buck's face bruising like a peach. Only stroke of luck was that the kid hadn't vomited in front of Doreen yet—having mostly emptied himself out on the way over. Lot to parse too, with the morning creeping slow like it was; dragging its belly 'cross the floor while the walls stunk of ground-out stogeys and whatever nostril-scorching cleaner they'd used on the floors. Buck had cracked a window, but it hadn't helped.

"So, you know, given the circumstances," he continued, "it might be time for us to reopen the bonus conversation. I don't *have* a going rate for getting shot at, but it seems like it's worth some extra consideration." He glanced at the kid. No doubt Mr. Fair Play disapproved of haggling here, but it was awful hard for him to muster anything too self-righteous sitting there swallowing puke. 'Course, other hand, it's delicate. Even if the purse held out for something extra, if they told Whitmore too much by way of justification, she might get spooked. And there was the husband to consider too—the big shot—and if Whitmore thought something might drag him in, she would definitely bolt. They couldn't have that. Had to be delicate. Very, very delicate.

"Excuse me," Sumio said, springing up and quick-walking it to the bathroom in the hall.

They watched him go. Room rippling behind. "Cig for ya, Doreen?" Buck asked.

"I can hardly breathe as is."

"Downtown living."

"There's no smoking in John's office."

"How 'bout that. Look, I don't mean to be uncouth about the dough, but I think you'd agree that things are likely to keep going a little sideways out here."

"Do you have any proof?"

"How's that?"

"*Proof.* Documents or photographs or something."

"Working on getting a police report."

"Will that help?"

"Probably not in the way you mean."

"The people you're talking to—they're just all so… *seedy*? Jazz men and nightwalkers and the like."

"You expected choir boys?"

"No. But I was hoping for someone or something a little more reputable. What about this…" she cleared her throat pointedly, "this *friend* of Eli's? Mightn't he be lying? Mightn't he have tricked Eli into something?"

"Into what?"

"I don't know."

"He seemed reliable enough."

"*Seemed? Enough?* Don't expect me to pay for conjecture, Buck."

"His story checked out. And the colleague of Eli's he mentioned—Sackler—looks like he skipped town, but we got an idea where he might've gone."

"Where?"

"Church up the mountain. Seems pretty connected up there. Figure they might've taken him in."

"Alright. And… has there been any sign of…" she trailed off, waggling her fine, waifish fingers like the legs of an overturned crab.

"The farm truck? The one with the dent?"

"Yes."

"Maybe. It's like I told ya—the girls at *Bons* got jumpy when I mentioned it. We're looking into it."

Frank returned, face flushed, "Apologies, ma'am."

"Are you feeling ill, Mr. Takahashi?"

"Bit of a bug."

She cooed something sympathetic and turned back to Buck, "I'm afraid more money is out of the question. You have the bonus to look forward to. It will have to account for the extra effort involved."

"Effort's one thing, lead's another."

"All the same."

"OK. Fine," Buck answered, uninterested in drawing things out. Negotiations are like a knife fight—if you don't draw blood right off it all starts to look pretty silly. "The other wrinkle is that folks out there might start connecting dots—if they haven't already—and whoever tried intimidating you a couple days back might try again. My advice? Skip town yourself for a little while. Why don't you and the beau go someplace far for the time being."

"Out of the question. My husband is too important a man at his firm, not to mention we were voted to be among the wavers this year on the Club's float in the Grand Floral Parade. We can't just pick up and leave."

"OK."

She sighed and shifted.

"Alright, Mr. Bordell, you win. Let's try it this way—if you can have things concluded by Memorial Day, I will add another thousand atop what, I think you will agree, is already a healthy supplement to your usual fee."

"What constitutes a conclusion here?"

"More, I suppose."

"More?"

"Yes."

"What'd you mean?"

"I mean *more*. Proof is preferred, but if proof's impossible, an *explanation* would suffice."

"Any ole' explanation, huh?"

"The *truth*, Mr. Bordell—one that you and Mr. Takahashi *agree* upon. Make it make sense to me."

"Memorial Day, huh?" He checked his watch, "Thirty-eight hours from now. That's not a lot of time you're giving us."

"I've been very clear about my desire to wrap this up expeditiously."

"OK. OK, yah, you got a deal," Buck said, sucking a tooth.

Whitmore looked to Frank for cosigning. He grimaced, nodded, and coughed wetly, "We won't let you down," he managed.

"Of course you won't." She stood, "Walk me out, Mr. Bordell? I'd ask you, Mr. Takahashi, but perhaps you should take the morning to rest."

Buck led the way. Got the door. Carried her hat. Attended her like some kinda gentleman. "How's Bertram?" he asked as they dropped into the lobby.

"Fine, I should think."

"You give him my best, yah?"

She stopped dead at the bottom landing. Step below. Eying him. "I can't figure you out, Mr. Bordell."

"No?"

"It's the incessant jestering. This is serious business, you said so yourself."

"I know."

"My John—*Mr. Whitmore*—is an important man; an up and comer."

"You've mentioned."

"We can't have these rumors about Eli, but John can't be implicated in any of this either. It must remain *quiet*. What I'm asking, Mr. Bordell, is for you to tread carefully."

"We'll do our best."

"I'm not worried about Mr. Takahashi." She looked back up the steps, "Though perhaps I should be, seeing the influence you've had on him."

"The influence?"

She eyed him again, plucking back her hat.

"It's a bug, that's all."

"You know, my father used to wake up with bugs like that too—most every morning as a matter of fact. Until, one night in '32, when he got so liquored up that he mistook the streetcar tracks for his pillow. He could have been somebody, too. Instead?" She shrugged.

"I'll keep that in mind."

"Do. And Buck?"

"Yah?"

"I loved my brother—and I want justice for him—but there will be no bonus at all, for you or for Mr. Takahashi, if a word of this gets out. I mean it. Bring whatever you find to me, and me alone. If I get so much as a whiff you're doing otherwise, our agreement is null. People talk, and John can't afford to be in any way associated with all this sordidness and conspiracy."

"Honestly, ma'am, if your hubby's gunning for a seat at the fat cat's table, he'll be laughed outa the room if an estranged brother-in-law is all he's got far as skeletons. Nobody trusts a boy scout."

"What a dreadful thing to say. Why you come recommended, I'll never know."

"Me and you both."

"You'll tell Mr. Takahashi what I've said? Maybe when he's *recovered*?"

"Sure."

Buck got the main door for her too. The noise of the street rolled in; the smell of gas and the stale shuffling of the wind. Doreen squinted into it purposefully and straightened her collar. "You're wrong, by the way. This is the new Portland, Buck; the new America," she said, stepping past, "Respectability is everything."

Buck followed her far as the stoop and lit one up, watching as she made her way down the street. It was frantic today. A tangle of idling trucks, denim overalls, and rising sandbag ziggurats on account of the morning's flood advisory. Buck took it in, mulling. *Respectability*. What crap. Of all the sticks the rich give the scramblers to beat themselves with, *respectability* was the worst. Nothing so capricious; nothing so sneering.

"Well, well, well! If it isn't the boy prince of Columbia Street!" Karl boomed, interrupting Buck's ruminations from a half block away. Jacket. Tie. Hat straight. The whole nine, despite the heat, with only the barest glisten of sweat forming on his brow. He shot up the steps, slapping Buck on the back amiably. "Careful out there, sonny boy, somebody left the oven on."

Buck might've spit, but he hadn't the means. "Hot," he agreed.

"Damn right it's hot." Karl turned to the street, "Look at all these sandbags—reminds me of London after the Krauts started in with the V-2s. Hope the things work better against water than they did against rockets. You waiting on somebody?"

"Nope. Client just left, actually."

"That Skid Row deal? The sister of the junkie?"

"Uh-huh."

"Fools go, partner—fools go! Meant to talk to you about that anyway," he said dragging Buck back inside, "I know I promised you that police report, but my guy's been real squirrelly last couple of days. Don't worry though, I'll get it. I'll run over this afternoon after I get a minute."

"I'd appreciate that, Karl. Things are picking up."

"I bet," he said nodding along, smiling, waving at Dunleavy through the glass of his office, "Say, guess where I'm back from."

"Where?"

"Spent the morning talking with the head of placement down at the secretarial college. Read some resumes. Met some candidates."

"You do seem cheery."

"Don't be jealous. I'll take you next time. You wouldn't believe it down there, pal. All those girls working so hard to impress a fella? I didn't want to leave."

"I'll bet." They started up the stairs. Karl couldn't help but leave him behind. He was all bound today; all two-at-a-time's and on to the next's.

"Come on, don't be blue. We can go tomorrow. You can borrow one of my ties."

"That's OK, Karl. Thanks, though."

"Suit yourself, but I don't want to hear a bunch of noise after I make my pick that she isn't right or isn't your type or something like that—not that you'd have a chance anyway. Now's the time, Buck. Now. Is. The. Time." Reaching the landing, Karl cast his eyes to the office and his grin cracked wider, "You getting some shirts done or something?"

"What?"

"You got a Chinaman in your office."

"That's Sumio. That's the guy."

"*Suh-mee-ya*? The guy? What do you mean *the guy*?"

"The PI. The one with me for the Thomayer case. That's him. I told you—we just got done meeting with the client."

"You're kidding."

"Yep. Good one, right?"

"Thought you said his name was '*Frank*?'" Funny how he said it. Like a curse. Standing. Staring. Stopped in the hall.

"Nickname, I guess. His real name's Sumio, but he goes by Frank on the job."

"Little duplicitous, isn't it?"

"You tell me, *Mr. Stevenson*."

"That's different."

Buck shrugged.

"It is."

"OK."

Karl licked his lips, nodded, and squinted a little as the cheer drained out of him, "Uh-huh. Alright. Did, uh, did Dunleavy see him come in with you?"

"I don't know."

"Did he or didn't he?"

"I don't *know*, Karl."

"Come on, pal, What're you doing here? This kind of thing could seriously hurt our reputation. You can't let folks down here see you working a white man's case with some chink. Folks'll get the wrong idea. Word like that gets out and we're dead in the water, pal. Yesterday's fish."

"Well, good news there—Sumio's Japanese."

"Jesus, Buck, that's worse. Dunleavey's boy just got done dodging Zeros out over the Pacific, you think he's going to be happy about some slant hanging around here in his six o'clock?"

"Kid played for Benson, Karl."

"Who gives a shit? Don't jerk me around here. Not on this. I know we have fun and all that, but this isn't you taking the odd colored case where nobody catches view out in Albina. This is serious."

"We're working a case. We had a meeting. Where were we supposed to go?"

Karl rounded on him, voice low, "Most days it's all I can do—*all I can fucking do*—to pry you off the barstool, but now, with *this*, you've *got* to meet down here at the office? That's a crock of shit, Buck. A crock of shit."

"It's an office, Karl. That's what it's for. Doreen wanted someplace out of the way; someplace discreet—just like it says on the cards."

"Don't start with me about the cards—"

"—Calm down—"

"—And you with the sister? Christ, Buck it's rid—"

The office door opened and Sumio stepped out. In an instant, Karl's smile snapped-to. Voice hailing loud. That's how you could tell with Karl. He always got real loud when he was playing fake, "Hey there! Howdy! You must be Frank! Nice to meet you, I'm Carl Stevenson, Buck's partner."

Sumio came over and they shook. He looked better. Rallying. "It's a pleasure, Mr. Stevenson."

"Likewise, likewise. So, you, uh—you like working with this heel of ours?" one of Karl's big mitts fell heavily on Buck's shoulder, "He can get ornery, sure—likes his laughs, a'course—but he usually does right in the end. He's dependable like that."

"We're making progress on the case."

"I bet. Yah, yah." Karl pointed back to the office, "Well. What'd you think of our little operation here?"

"It's nice."

"Thanks, friend; be even nicer after the remodel; Buck tell you about all that? The remodel?"

"No."

Deep sigh. Nod and a nod and a nod. "Yah, it's just a touchup—just a bit of modernization, you know? It's a pain though, since, after this morning—shit, any time now, eh Buck—we'll have to clear out and go elsewhere for who knows how long while they rework the lights, do some painting, and God knows what else, but we figure it'll be worth the sacrifice. Gotta think long term, you know?"

"Jesus, Karl," Buck muttered.

"Well, I won't keep you, fellas. I got some things to chase down. No rest for the righteous. Good luck and all." He turned, stopped, and offered Sumio another hand, "It was sure swell to meet you, Frank."

They watched the big man take the stairs like an avalanche takes the mountain. "So that's Karl," Buck said.

"Nice guy."

"Yah, he's a gem. You empty yet?"

"Mostly."

"Good, 'cause I got another friend I want you to meet."

15

"You're sure he'll be here?"

"Yep."

A pause. Scratchy. Windless. The dry smell of horseshit wafting through the half-full grandstands of Portland Meadows. The crowd was languid—slouching and roiling and fizzing like a splash of champagne coagulating in the dust. Sumio watched them closely from he and Buck's perch in the upper deck, "What about him? The one coming up on the left side over there?"

"Nope," Buck answered without looking up.

Another pause. More restless than the first.

"But you're *sure* he's coming?"

"Relax, Fra—" Buck stopped himself, glanced over, looked away, cocked back his brim and squinted into the bleary sunlight, "Sorry—Sumio, I mean. Southpaw never misses a race."

Kid grimaced, "Frank is fine. It was fine before and it's fine now."

"You could've told me your real name, ya know? Would've saved you some trouble with the missus."

"Because ours has been such an open and honest partnership."

Kid got him with that one. "Fair enough."

"It's not about you—not about you *specifically*, anyway."

"I get it. Helps with business."

"That isn't the reason."

"That's not what you said earlier."

"Well, OK, yes, the business is part of it—and going by Frank in the army *did* help with our officers, just like I told you—but I did it before the army too. I've done it for a lone time. Using both names helps keep things clear for *me*. It lets me know who I'm talking to."

"I admire it."

"What do you mean?"

Buck pressed back into his seat, settling "I mean, hell, it's a pretty neat setup. Whenever one name stops working for ya, you can always just make up another one and then another and another and another, right? Living like that, you can always just keep moving, one step ahead of whoever's coming up behind. For a while, anyway. For a bit. But you oughtn't rely too much on it, kid, because things have a way of catching up no matter what name you use."

"I'm not running from anything." Sumio swept away his flat cap and ran a hand through his short, dark mop, shaking his head, "It's not an alias, Buck. It's just, you know, the other side of things."

A voice broke in over the PA to announce the next race, and it was, despite the heat, time for the crowd to show something resembling enthusiasm. They obliged—waving, whistling, jostling shoulder to shoulder, and letting out the occasional yelp whenever a hand lingered too long on a sunbaked stretch of railing. The jockeys did their best to reciprocate. Swallowing grit. Ignoring the sweat. Grinning like the thing'd been won already. The horses, though, couldn't help but be a bit more honest about the whole affair. They trudged out one after the other with their heads dipped, hooves dragging. Most reluctant of them all was a slow-plodding, not-so-thoroughbred with the number 47 hanging off its flank.

Buck dug out his last betting slip.

47 to win, it read.

"I'm shit at this," he said, tossing the slip aside. Still, Sumio waited for the official results to gloat.

"You seem to like the longshots," he said.

"Isn't that supposed to be the fun of this whole thing?"

"I think most of these folks would say that the fun is the *winning.*"

"That what you say?"

Philosophical. Antsy. Still hungover. All three at once, "I say we need to go find Sackler."

"We will. Don't worry. But we also need to see what we can find out about how Thomayer ended up at *Bons*, and since Maddy and her girls won't tell us, this is our best bet. Speaking of bets—why don't I hurry down and place a couple more since we're waiting anyway?"

But Sumio didn't take the bait. Instead, he swatted a fly dead on his pantleg and allowed Buck to infer the rest.

"OK. Fine. If you're in such a hurry, let's do it then."

"Do what?"

"Go talk to Southpaw."

"What?"

"You heard me."

"He's here?"

"He's *been* here, pal," Buck said, standing and tugging at his shirt to unstick it from the sweat, "I just wanted to wait until it looked like he'd won one before going to talk with him. Catch him in a better mood."

"Is that necessary?"

"Couldn't hurt."

Sumio shot up, peering down the risers as the crowd settled back into its sweltering, post-race daze. "Which one is he?"

"See that lanky bastard down on the end? The one drowning in fabric? That's Southpaw. But don't let the dandy getup fool ya—our boy was the state light heavyweight runner-up three times over. Never clinched it, though. Big fights always had the habit of going south on him. Hence the name. It's a joke. Get it?" A long drag. "But the jokes on them, because by the time it came out that Southpaw'd been taking dives in those big-time fights, he'd already made a fat wad over the years betting against himself. That's how me and Karl met him. Was us who used to place the bets for him."

"That's illegal."

"You don't say. Anyway, after the fight game went bust, Southpaw dabbled in bird-dogging for a while, but PI work wasn't proactive enough for him. He preferred something a bit more direct. So, instead of spending all his time following people to their respective vices, he got the bright idea to go straight where the action was happening and take snapshots of whoever came along looking to partake. He takes pictures all over town, him and his little minions. For a fee, any negative in his collection can disappear, or, for an even bigger fee, any mister, missus, or bored busybody can peruse the lot at their leisure. First come, first served."

"So, he blackmails people," Sumio summarized neatly, if imperfectly.

"Sure."

"And your friends with a man like that?"

"Figure of speech," Buck said, starting down the stairs. As he and Sumio worked their way through the crowd, the next slate of horses started off, thundering down the stretch, dusting the grandstands in a fresh layer of grit and busted betting slips. And poor Southpaw's horse must've tripped straight out the gate, because he spent most of the race turned around, haranguing a pair of toadies until the pair of them scuttled off to place a fresh set of bets. Once they'd gone, Buck and Sumio slid into their places. Leaning forward, hands together, Buck asked, "What's the matter, pal? Ya get some bum tips or something?"

Southpaw turned. He was gangly and broad-shouldered, with a big, jowly, pockmarked face and cuts of cauliflower for ears. He wore a bright burgundy suit, a striped boater's hat, glasses on the end of his nose, emerald cufflinks, a loosely hanging paisley scarf, and a big, square ring on each of his long fingers, like some kind of beanpole Caligula, lazing in the cheap seats, "Haven't seen you at the track for a while, Buck," he said.

"Been busy."

"Don't suppose you've stopped by to pay what you owe?"

"'Fraid not."

"You know what, good for you." Southpaw turned back to the track, "Lot of guys wouldn't have the gall to show their face someplace where they owe people that kind of money, but to each their own. So, what is it then? What brings you by?"

"Wanted to see if you—"

But Southpaw waggled one of his jeweled fingers under Buck's nose at the sound of the PA kicking on and made a big show of hanging on its every crackling word. Not that Southpaw actually cared about who'd sired who and all that bullshit—he just wasn't the kind of prick to let any jab go untaken, conversational or otherwise. Eventually though, the track announcer exhausted his knowledge of equine family history and Southpaw deigned the conversation continue, "You were saying, Buck?"

Buck smiled, unperturbed, "You get Sunday's shots from Skid yet?"

"I did."

"Got 'em on ya?"

Southpaw grinned right back, threw one long leg atop the other, and lifted a pantleg to reveal some kind of cross between a bandolier and ankle holster that was fully stocked with date-scribbled rolls of film. He plucked free the one labeled '5/21' and, pinching it between his fingers, flicked it so hard with one of his gauntleted rings that Buck thought he might've cracked the plastic. Then, pleased as punch, he said, "I sure do, Buckaroo. I *sure* do."

A long, lock-jawed game of chicken commenced between them then. One minute. Another. Could've kept going too, but Sumio started making sounds like he was going to butt in on the negotiations, so Buck was forced to cede the ground. "How much you want for it?" he asked.

Smug. Smirking, "For you, Buck? Not a cent."

"Bullshit."

"No, no. No bullshit. All's I'd ask is a favor."

Again. Stronger this time. "*Bullshit.*"

Southpaw turned to Sumio, setting the canister on the seat beside him. "You're—what—the client?"

"We work together," Sumio answered.

"No shit?" A glance, back and again. "Well, even better. Maybe you can talk some sense into our mutual friend. We can help each other, me and you. Sometimes there's just no getting through to Bordell over there." Southpaw extended a massive, jewel encrusted hand, "What'd you say your name was?"

"Frank."

They shook. Southpaw withdrew his hand and adjusted his glasses. Tugged his shirtsleeves. Scratched his jaw. "Tell me, Frank—do you pay your debts? You do, right? It's what makes a man, isn't it? Win, lose, or draw, a man's always gotta be good for it, yah?"

"What's the favor?" Sumio asked icily instead of answering.

"Peas in a pod, you two." Southpaw said with a laugh and jabbed his scalp back towards Buck, "Ask Bordell what I want. He knows damn well."

To his credit, the kid didn't ask. Didn't even flinch.

"How much for the roll?" Buck asked instead, reaching into his pocket, "Will ten do it?"

"Ten what? Fucking Spanish doubloons? 'Cause I know you don't mean dollars."

"Twenty-five, then."

"*Twenty-five*?" Southpaw whipped around, and flashed a sneer before catching himself, and slipping back into his sour geniality. "Twenty-five," he said recovering, "is *a quarter* what we could've gotten out of that lawyer. You owe me a c-note just for *that*, let alone the canister. But I don't want the money. All's I want is a favor. Just a little one. Quick call, that's all. Or, hell, I'm feeling generous, you can even just tell *me* where the whore went, and I'll call the guy myself."

"Come on, Sumio. Let's—"

Just then—with the gates loaded and the starting pistol cocked—Southpaw's toadies came up the steps. Except, now there were three of them. The new addition being that moon-face'd guy Buck'd tussled with over at the pinball parlor couple nights back.

Off went the starting pistol.

Down went the gates.

And with the hoofbeats shaking the risers, up sprang Moon-Face, hollering "That's him! That's the guy!" as he came on, blade in hand.

Buck squared up, only half-ready to catch a bleeding, but Moon-Face picked the wrong route up through the grandstand by trying to shove his way past Sumio. The kid saw him coming and hooked him 'round the ankle as he passed, sending Moon-Face toppling ass-over-teakettle down onto Southpaw. Flailing as he went, losing hold of his knife—the blade skittering away somewhere 'cross the risers. And bad as that was for him, it got worse once he'd sprawled out on top of Southpaw. In a burst of pure instinct, the boxer started peppering the poor toady with a flurry of shots to the kidneys before realization passed through him like a shot and he snapped to, dispensing apologies to the ruffled punters in each cardinal direction. But by then, Buck and Sumio were long gone. They'd bolted straight off, and even with Buck's bum foot, they were in the car and driving before anybody'd even thought to scrape Moon-Face up off the floor.

"Well," Buck said once they'd reached the highway, "say what you will, but Southpaw's got some loyal guys working for him. Not that they get much for it." He looked over. Kid was giving him a hard look. "What?"

"Have you ever considered," Sumio asked, "that if everywhere you go somebody's got it out for you, that it might be time to change your approach a little?"

Buck snorted, "Hey, don't blame that on me. You saw for yourself—Southpaw's an asshole."

"And the other guy? The guy with the knife?"

"I don't know. Just one of his guys. What's it matter?"

"What's it matter? He tried to stab you."

"Come on. He wasn't gonna stab me; he was just gonna

wave it around in my face a little. Really, you're the one who escalated the whole thing. Nobody asked you to throw the poor bastard down the stairs."

"I've seen people get stabbed, Buck. He was *going* to stab you."

"Yah, yah, yah. My hero."

"Is it always like this with you?"

"What'd you mean?"

"Everywhere we go, someone has a problem with you, or you with them. How do you work like that? Doesn't it just get exhausting?"

"OK. First of all, if you're running in this profession and everybody likes you, it means you're doing something wrong."

"I accept that. But that's not what I'm saying; what I'm saying is that it's been *every single person* we've—"

"—And *second*, I don't think you wanna be taking Southpaw's side in this whole spat without knowing the particulars."

"Alright, so tell me the particulars, then."

"You wanna know the history there? Sure. No problem. Anything to wipe that look off your face," Buck said, easing off the accelerator, patting 'round for his cigs, "I told you—me and Southpaw used to work together. Couple years back, some big shot lawyer checking up on his fiancé happens upon a picture of her in bed with another man in Southpaw's stash. Guy goes ballistic. Southpaw tells him about me, and he hires me to take a couple more pictures just to confirm things. So, I do, and I follow the gal around a bit too. Pretty quickly I figure out that she's fixing to leave town with her new guy. I even get a shot of them together with their suitcases boarding the train at Union Station. That's it, I figure. Case closed. She's legged it, so now everybody moves on. It's a blow, sure, but that's how it goes sometimes, right?

"Oh no. Not in this case. 'Cause once I tell the lawyer his missus has run out on him and isn't coming back, he *really* loses it. He comes by, goes all lawyery on me, and starts making threats. He wants to know where she went. Where? Where? Where? He keeps asking, right? Well, lot like *you* can tell when a fella's gonna stab another fella, *I* can tell when a rich prick is fixing to make trouble, so, I blank him. Box him out. I'd of lied from the jump about the platform picture, only I'd told Southpaw, and Southpaw'd told the guy, so they were both tryin' to squeeze it outa me.

"But I keep on stonewallin' him. Give my condolences. My heartfelt bromides. All that shit but not a thing besides. Like I'm gonna get pushed around by some vest-coat wearing son of bitch? Anyway… it turns into a big mess. Guy makes a bunch of noise like he was gonna sue and the whole time Southpaw's acting like he doesn't get it. He's leaning on me harder and harder, trying to get me to spill; to just tell the guy where the missus had landed and be done with it, but if I'd of done that, there's no doubt in my mind he would've followed. And I've been doing this job too long to think that a trip like that would've ended well. So, there ya go. That's the story. Still think I'm the prick in it?"

Instead of answering, Sumio reached into his jacket and, like a magic trick, pulled out the '5/21' film canister Buck'd last seen well out of reach beside Southpaw. Somehow the kid'd snagged it in the fracas. Sumio screwed off the lid, unspooled the crackling gossamer string of negatives, and, holding them up to the sun, started squinting his way through the panels one by one.

Buck stared.

Looked ahead.

Took a curve. Then another.

Shifted gears. Lit one. Smoked it. Rolled his neck. The houses were thinning out now, with fields and pastureland springing up in the gaps between as the road stretched eastward. "Pretty slick," Buck said as it all rolled by, "But Southpaw'll notice the canister is missing, if he hasn't already. Not gonna be happy when he does."

Sumio shrugged, "Well... if he was just going to use it to blackmail people anyway..." He shrugged again.

That got Buck. Really did. The idiotic simplicity of it; the clear mindedness. Kinda thing Buck couldn't help but admire, really, so he grabbed the kid's shoulder and gave it a good-natured wrench, saying, "Jesus, Sumio, you're gonna have to watch yourself out here, pal, or people are gonna start taking notice."

But the kid was curiously limp as Buck batted him around. His attention elsewhere.

"That's it," he said.

"What is?"

Sumio handed over the strip of film with a particular panel folded and pinched between his fingers.

It took a minute for Buck to realize what he was seeing—the image was small and the details hard to make out at first, especially since he had to switch his focus back and forth between the tiny, washed out image and the highway frequent enough to keep them outa the ditch—but glance by glance, Buck started to make out a light colored pickup with a couple dark creases of dented shadow on the door, and, most telling of all, a half-dome of wiring arched over the truck bed. People-shaped blurs hurrying on the edges of the frame. *Bon Vivants* clear in the background.

"Huh."

"That's it," Sumio said again, "That's the truck. Just like Mrs. Whitmore described. Which tells us that whoever tried breaking into the Whitmore house was also hanging around Skid Row the night Eli died there. That can't be coincidence. And whoever they are, they're connected to the cops somehow—connected enough to get them to cover things up when the hit on Sackler went sideways. But still, why the hit? Why the break in?"

Buck didn't know. But the kid was right. The truck *did* look exactly like Doreen had described. He'd just assumed that the 'chicken wire' she'd been ranting about had meant that the truck they were looking for was some kind of farm rig—one strung up for livestock or maintenance or something—but the wiring in the back didn't make sense for anything like that. What it *did* make sense for, Buck had no idea, but at least now the local poultry farmers were exonerated. The rest though? For that they needed Sackler.

16

It wasn't much of a sermon. A slog through the Book of Numbers, so aimless and interminable that even the Israelites would've balked, while the congregation listened in a sweaty stupor, supplying just enough *amens* to scare off the coroner. They were three dozen in all. Buck had counted, twice, twice more, and twice again. Faces were hard to see from this far back—mostly thinning scalps and pious profiles—but he saw nothing to match Sackler's picture. Then, thank Christ, the thing ended. The pastor met the congregation at the door. He shook hands. Patted shoulders. Talked politics. And kissed cheeks chastely. It hadn't ever been that way with Dad after a sermon. Preaching was a lonely business for the old man. It ended neither clean nor congenial. His services kept on—on and on and on—until the Walls of Jericho lay crumbled at his feet, the language of the angels had enlivened his tongue. and he'd kicked up so much holy hallelujah that the ground was slick with it. You could see it in the martyred bibles he sent. Torn and burnt. Nothing like the green-spined, gold-lettered wholesaler's copies tucked into the pews here, all mannered and pristine.

Buck waited until the last stragglers had gone scurrying for their cars like lizards for the shade. The pastor met him warmly, "Welcome to Lamb of the Mountain, brother, awful glad to see a new face around here—awful glad! I trust you found the service to your liking?"

"Truly a balm to the spirit. Thanks for having me."

"No trouble at all, son." They shook and the pastor's eyes fell on the bible slung under Buck's arm, "Now I know that's not one of ours you got there—I respect a man who gets such use out of the Good Book. It's for reading first and foremost, after all. Don't do nobody no good up on the shelf," the preacher said. He was thin. Suspendered. Spectacled. Half-leaned back in his stance, rumble in his voice, and with a face rough as a pine knot. "A family bible, I assume?" he asked.

"Yes, sir."

"Passed one loving hand to the next? Through the many generations?"

"Yes, sir."

"Very fine. Very Christian. Your mother's?"

"Dad's actually—until such time as he went to his reward. He was a man of, uh, *profound* devotion."

"So, it would seem. May I?" The pastor took the bible delicately, nodding his approval at the dog-eared passages and penciled marginalia. Still perusing, he continued, "So, what brings you out this morning, brother? Passing through? Heading up to Timothy Lake for the trout? I was up there at the lake Wednesday, and Lord wasn't it a blessing to be out on the cool water."

Buck feigned uncertainty, "No, no; no, sir, nothing so recreational. I, uh, well… In fact, I'm up here to see you specifically."

"To see *me*, you say?"

"Yes. I was hoping…" Buck fidgeted. Glanced. Swallowed and shuffled like he was trying to kick his way through the good Lord's carpeting. No trout for him, but a bit of bait all the same. "It's just, I've heard lots about you. Lots."

"Well, I'm sure I'll be happy to help however I can, Mr.—?"

"—Stevenson. Carl Stevenson."

"Pleasure, Mr. Stevenson, name's Bradley. How might I be of service?"

"Well, it's about a friend of mine; a friend of *ours* really. Member of your church, as a matter of fact."

"That right?"

"It is."

A long, long pause.

"Look, sir, can I come clean with you?"

"It's truth that shames the devil, son."

"I'm just not one for obfuscation, you understand?"

"I do."

"I'm worried about a friend, that's all. Got this note saying he was gonna leave town; gonna find somewhere safe. And me and some others, well, sir, we figure that he might've come to you for that safety."

"It's a shepherd's duty to mind his flock," Bradley said affecting the kind of knowing smugness that men often mistake for spiritual depth. Buck hated him. Hated the type. Wanted to piss in his gas tank.

But he smiled instead, nice and wide, "I knew you'd understand."

"I do, son, I do. And this friend of yours, how'd you say you knew him?"

"We're both members of the Glisan Street branch of the Men's Chapter and Verse Society of Portland."

"Chapter and verse, you say?"

"Yes, sir."

"And Portland, you say? I reckon the godly have their hands full down there."

"Like you wouldn't believe, pastor, but we do our best."

Another all-knowing nod, "It's the communists, son. They're taking this country straight to hell. We used to know what to do with them—like how the Legionnaires handled those Bolsheviks back in '19—but not anymore. Things being as they are, there's hardly a spot left in this once great nation of ours not under the yoke of socialism. It's that damn Roosevelt, son." He shook his head, "Only 'deal' that man ever made was with the devil. You went for Dewey in the primary last week, I hope?"

"Yes, sir. All the C and H boys did," Buck answered, clueless on the name.

"Good, he's the one to take out Truman. Best shot, I reckon, though he could be tougher."

"Tom says the same thing."

"Tom, you say?" Bradley asked, suppressing a twitch, the red menace forgotten.

Buck leaned in, "Yes. That's our friend. The one I mentioned. Tom *Sackler*."

"A good man."

"Yes, sir."

"A good Christian."

"Yes, sir—a rock for us in the society."

Bradley cleared his throat, "No doubt, son, no doubt. It's just that I hadn't heard him speak of your… *particular* association. But then again, I'm not surprised to hear that Tom might have looked to buttress his faith down in that Sodom. But you say… you say he's gone… missing, was it?"

"Left town, I said. Very sudden. Got me and the boys worried for him."

"I see. Well, son, I'd love to help but I just *don't know*

where he might've gone, if—that is—that's even your question for me. I'd love to help, if I only could. But I can't, you understand, though you seem like a fine, fine friend of his—and if I *were* to see him, I'd certainly say as much. Give the message… as it were."

"You would?"

"I sure would, son."

The heat pressed and the grasshoppers buzzed. Buck squinted up into the sunlight and then, as if slowly catching on, "Oh! I… right… ah, if you were to see Tom, maybe you could tell him I tried to come up and give him my bible—I know how much it'd mean to him to have it, and to know a brother Christian was thinking of him in his time of hardship."

Bradley looked down at the ratty old book in his hands, "You want to give Tom your bible?"

"Yes, sir."

"Your *family* bible?"

Buck nodded.

"That's very generous."

"He'd do the same for me."

"I reckon that's right. Listen, why don't *I* hold on to this and if Tom passes through—*when* he passes through more like—I can give it to him then."

"You think he'll do that?"

"I do, son, I do. In fact, might be that it finds him quickest this way, assuming that's alright with you."

Buck smiled, "I'm sure you're right about that. It's only…"

"Yes?"

"I… well… I'm considering things, pastor, and I wouldn't want Tom to get the feeling that the other C and H boys aren't thinking of him just as much as I am. I wouldn't want to take sole credit for the gesture, you understand?"

"Of course not."

"So, maybe—if you see him, that is, a'course—maybe you can just tell him it's from 'his friends at the society' and not me specifically? Could you do that, pastor?"

"I certainly could. Be glad to."

"Bless you, pastor."

"And you, son."

They went back and forth like that a couple times—trading benedictions—until Buck cut things off and walked back to the road. He was slow about it. Waved from the mailbox on the corner, taking care that Bradley got a good, long look at him as he walked down Sandy's main drag and back towards the highway. At the block, he gave Sumio the signal—the kid having borrowed his car—and kept on. Walked to one of those roadside diners sprung up all along Highway 26 that catered to canvas heavy sportsmen and rusted out chassis. Had some lunch, some pie, and some coffee. He called *Bons* twice and Karl after but got nothing. He mulled. Small-talked. Waited.

Even got so damn bored that he picked up some left behind edition of the town rag—the *Sandy Post-Gazette*—stocked as it was with more mountainside moralizing and whispers of decline downstream. A cesspool that-a-way if you believed it; all degeneracy, crime, mongrelism, and corruption. Portland, lost to the wolves. Upsetting stuff, really. Just terrible.

Then, sometime after his third cup and ninth smoke, Sumio pulled up. Buck dropped a couple dollars for the spread and hurried out to meet him. "Got ya a slice of pie," he said, leaning in through the driver side window and handing Sumio the slice wrapped in wax paper.

"Really?"

"Yah. Thought you might be hungry after this morning."

"I am. Thanks."

"Don't mention it. So? Where'd he go?"

"What flavor?"

"Marionberry."

"How did you know I like marionberry?"

"Everybody likes marionberry, for Christ's sake. What about Bradley? He take the bait or what?"

"Looks like."

Buck rapped the hood triumphantly, "And you thought it wouldn't work?"

"I didn't say that."

"I didn't *say* that you said it, I said that you *thought* it. Hop out, I'm driving."

Next, they were roaring down the old-growth artery of 26 as it ran up and over Mount Hood. Hood, from Portland, is a postcard kinda mountain—sharp and white, jutting like a solitary fang out the gummy Cascade Range. But here in the foothills it was all mastication; all bends and rises and close in chomps of timber. The woods. The jungle. The eradicating green.

The kid took out a notebook and read back the particulars—Bradley'd come about seven minutes after Buck had signaled; pulled out of the church and kept on east out of town. Sumio'd followed him all the way to the next town over, where he pulled off and took a quick turn up a long, narrow driveway with a 'No Trespassing' sign nailed to one of the Doug firs.

"You didn't see him get out?" Buck asked.

"No. I didn't want to risk getting spotted, so I parked off the road a bit further down and doubled back on foot. About ten minutes later I saw him drive out again."

"Sackler with him?"

"No," the kid said, glancing down at the pie, "You didn't happen to grab a fork, did you?"

"Sure, right here in my pocket next to the ice cream. 'Fraid you're gonna have to rough it." Sumio didn't need the encouragement, not with that morning's miso splattered for the crows back on Fifth Street. Kid was starving. While he chewed, Buck asked again, "So'd ya see Sackler or not?"

Sumio shook his head, bear-scooping up a final bite.

"Well, he's there. Trust me. Bradley was making the ole' *ichthys* eyes at me like you wouldn't believe."

"The what?"

"Never mind."

They drove on. Roads tight as thread 'round the mountain's spool; the touch-close country a howling, snapping blur of trees and chrome. Sumio pointed out the driveway as they cruised by. It was nothing really. A gap of tread marked in clay and a shot blasted sign. They parked 'round the bend, same as Sumio'd done, and walk it in. Kid was right—sound of an unfamiliar engine might send Sackler into the bush, and if he made that dive before they could spot the leaves rippling, there'd be no going after.

"Don't suppose you got that cannon of yours strapped somewhere, do ya?"

"No. You?"

"Right here," Buck said, reaching under the seat and grabbing his revolver. They went on. The air thick with the smell of baking pine, the dry needles crackling underfoot. The driveway was longer than they'd guessed. Narrower too. The low-down ferns coated in a fine layer of road dust while the sloppy, uncut hang of the blackberry vines told them there hadn't been too much in the way of traffic since spring. They slowed up. Went quiet. And after another five minutes or so they came upon three abandoned cabins. They were old, half century or more, half-swallowed in understory; their gutters swinging, porch stairs buckled, and the rightmost charred by some recent fire. But no movement; no people.

Soldier Boy didn't like the approach, "We should flank. Cut through the underbrush, use the trees for cover so we can get close and come up around the back. If he's armed, we'd be walking straight down the barrel going up the drive like that," he said, so they doubled back to pick, crouch, scratch, tear, and wrestle their way wide right and through the brush, slow and quiet as a pair of elephants. Still, if Sackler heard them coming he didn't take any potshots.

"OK," Buck whispered, tangled in foliage, "Now what?"

"Well, if it were me, I'd post up in the center there. Best line of sight; best chance to fire and maneuver; and it's got the best fallback option."

"It's a hidey-hole, Sumio, not an SS bunker. The guy's likely to bolt more than anything else. I bet he's in that rightmost one. Straight out that backdoor and your gone into the trees."

"I think middle."

"OK. Sure. Fine. Whatever. Middle it is. It's a crapshoot anyhow." Buck rolled his shoulders, "You ready?"

The kid nodded. Buck too. Ready as ready gets.

They went for it. Dashing through the new-grown green of spring towards the cabin. Sumio was first through the door. Then Buck, his bum foot slowing him some.

They spread out. Stomped around. Shouldered into walls. Made a hell of a racket. Found nothing. No cot. No cans. No bible. Not a goddamned thing, save for what had long, long ago gone gray, dirty, and forgotten.

"*Shit*, Frank!"

"Next one! *Go, go, go!*"

Sprinting now. Full bore. Full as it got, anyway. Sumio vaulted down the broken stairs, and Buck tried following, but he botched the landing and went down hard. As he staggered up, something tugged at the corner of his eye, stopping him in his tracks.

There, off left, standing in the drive, slack-jawed and staring, was Sackler.

"Don't run!" Buck hollered, "Damnit! *Don't you fucking run*! Just stay right th—"

Guy didn't listen. Tried to leg it. But Sumio was quicker, even with the hangover, and had him tackled before he could make the bushes. They rolled around for a while. Bit of flailing. Couple smacks and an errant elbow. Bloody nose. No big deal. Buck hobbled over, "Calm down for Christ's sake!" he said, "Ya hear me, you stupid prick? I said, *calm down!*"

Guy didn't listen to that either. He grunted and huffed and snarled and took big, heaping bites outa the duff, dry as baking powder. But Sumio managed to get a knee between his shoulders and a grip 'round his collar which helped a little. Still, the guy's face was buried. Gasping.

Spitting up leaves. Hiccupping half-breaths like a stalled-out motor. Belly trying to push its way to China. Voice muffled, "*Please don't* … please *don't! I swear—swear to God—I'm gone... gone... let me go, and I promise you'll never... never see me again! I won't talk; won't say a word!* Never! I'll leave right away—tonight! *I swear-I swear-I swear! Just* don't kill me!"

"Relax, would ya, pal?" Buck said, dropping onto his haunches and into the guy's peripheral. "Nobody's here to kill ya."

"*I swear to* God, mister! I swear, I—" He stopped cold, realizing. "Wait. Wait. You're not—not here to...to—?"

"—To kill ya? Nope."

"Then... then what..."

"We wanna talk."

"Talk?"

"Yah. Talk."

"About what?"

"Eli Thomayer."

"I didn't have *anything* to do with that."

"That why you ran?"

"How was I supposed to know who you were? People are trying to kill me."

"We know. We met 'em," Buck said, flicking his hat brim, "But lucky for you, they ain't us."

"Who are you guys anyway?"

"PIs."

"Working for who?"

"Not gonna happen," Buck said, popping in a cigarette and shaking his head genially. Sackler lay there for a while, limp as a fish on the brick. Eyes popped. Mouth agape.

"How'd you find me?"

Buck fished the chipped glass out of his pocket and read what was left of the engraving, "'*To Thomas J. Sackler on behalf of the Lamb of the Mountain Church, for upstanding fellowship and yadda-yadda-yadda.*'" He pocketed it again, tutting, "Seems you're a model Christian, Tommy boy. A prize winner."

"I told you; I didn't have any part in what they did to Eli."

Sumio edged in, "But you called him the night he died. You asked him to come out to Vanport. Why?"

"It was just supposed to be a talk. That's what he told me it'd be—a talk! That's all."

"Who's he?"

"The director over at the authority—Martins. You gotta believe me. He *lied* to me. I had no idea about the guys and the car and the any of it! I got ambushed, same as Eli."

"Martins, huh? Didn't seem the type to me."

"You know him?"

"Kinda. What about the cops? Where do they come in?"

"Cops? What cops?"

"Must-a been after," Buck said to himself, sucking a tooth and looking back towards the cabins.

"*What cops?*" Sackler grunted into the dirt.

"We'll get there. First, be straight with me now—if we let you up, you gonna settle down?"

"Yes."

"Ya sure?"

"*Yes.*"

"'Cause we won't be so delicate next time. My partner here'll kick the ever-loving shit outa ya if you try to run again." Sumio glared at Buck when he said that. He didn't like threats, especially when they were being made on his behalf. Liked to be professional; liked to be legal and moral and upright. Yah, yah. Buck'd heard it. And he'd even believed it before the kid'd lied to Behan, stolen the canister from Southpaw, and started throttling Sackler like some cowboy bucking at the Roundup. "But, other end, we can be as friendly as you want us to be, pal. Friendlier even. What'd ya say we all take ourselves inside, brew a couple cups of coffee, and hash this thing out, huh? How 'bout it? Ya got any java in that hidey-hole of yours back there?"

Sulking, "Yah."

"'Course you do."

"I… I tell you what I know and then you'll go?"

"Bingo."

"OK. OK, fine."

Slowly, Sumio let his weight off Sackler, keeping hold of the guy's collar just in case. They came up awkward, like a ventriloquist and his dummy. Buck dusted Sackler off—patting around extra in case of a pistol—then, satisfied, he slipped one of his cards into the guy's shirt pocket. Karl'd been right. The things were pretty handy. Sackler glanced at it, moodily straightening his loose flannel and undershirt, hiking up his flaking leather belt, and cuffing at the new coat of brown on his boots. His face was narrow and his eyes too heavy for their lids. His hair was brown and unwashed looking even before the tussling; his cheeks flushed. Buck led the way him and back to the cabin, going slow to hide his bum ankle. He checked things out inside. But the place was pretty sparse. Cot in the front room with Dad's bible on it as well as a sheet, a pillow, and an old suitcase with a razor and a basin of milky water on the side, while the kitchen had a couple second-hand pans, gutted cans, and one of those army surplus stoves. Buck pocketed the razor and flipped through the linens. "No booby traps, eh, Tommy? No guns? No blades besides the Gillette here? Nothing stashed? Speak now and all that!" he yelled to the peeling wallpaper. Sackler hollered back a couple assurances that were convincing enough, but Buck still gave the place another once-over anyway. That done, he started a little water on the stove and sounded the all clear for Sumio to frog-march the guy in. "Why'd you call Eli the night he died?" the kid asked again.

"Because Martins told me to."

"Why didn't Martins call himself?"

"He and Eli weren't speaking. Eli wouldn't have trusted him."

229

"Why not?"

"Look, Eli never played the politics, alright? And with the war over, Vanport's been nothing *but* politics. The authority never wanted it in the first place, and now everybody wants it gone—department heads, city hall, the real estate people, the developers—*everybody*."

"Why?"

"I think I chipped a tooth."

"*Why*?"

"You serious? It's half blacks up there. Mexicans too. And, uh, *others*." Sackler said, glancing at Sumio. "And it's not just them. The whites are trash too. Hobos and Okies. Or, you know, that's the thinking downtown anyway."

"And is that *your* thinking, Mr. Sackler?"

"I keep my head down."

"But not Thomayer?"

"He couldn't just leave something alone. He needed to *fix* things. He would get something stuck in his craw and just keep at it. On and on and on. So, when he submitted that first failing safety report and Martins ignored it, he just couldn't let it go. Things got ugly."

"How ugly?"

"Arguing at first. Shouting. Then threats. Martins threatened to fire Eli, and Eli threatened to take everything to the papers if he did. He said he'd made carbon copies of everything; said he had months' worth of documented negligence on the authority's part. It got to be where Eli and Martins couldn't hardly be in the same building without a fight. And then, well, with the rain and the snowmelt and everything, it really came to a head."

Buck leaned in the kitchen doorway, one eye on the stove, "Why didn't Thomayer—you know, what's it called—*appeal* or something?"

"Appeal? Appeal to who? They were stonewalling him all up the chain. I told him it wasn't going to go anywhere; I told him that he needed to drop the whole thing if he knew what's good for him, but it's like I said, he wouldn't listen."

"And if he felt so strongly, why didn't he just go to the papers in the first place?"

"He thought he had more power inside the authority as an inspector than outside as an agitator. Or, that's what he said to me, anyway. But if you want to know what I think—I think it played to his ego to be the dissident, you know? The lone voice. He was like that. He'd grandstand."

"I 'spose from down in the mud, everything looks like grandstanding."

"What the hell's that supposed to mean?"

"Nothing. Let's take it back to those reports or whatever."

"Here I am helping you guys, and—"

"—And we're appreciative. Now the reports. What were they?"

"They were about the levee," Sackler muttered.

That got Sumio. He straightened like a rail. "The levee in Vanport? The one with the tracks on top?" he asked.

"Yah—the levee that's not a levee—exactly."

"What'd you mean?"

"I mean everybody calls it a levee and everybody thinks it's a levee—on account of how it's high and it's between Vanport and the river on the west side—but it isn't a levee, not in the technical sense. It's a berm, built by the railroad, and it's chock full of fill."

Buck again, "Levee? Berm? What's the difference? Dirt's dirt, ain't it?"

"No. Not at all. A levee is flood infrastructure. It's built and maintained specifically to resist the pressures of moving water, and a berm—this berm at least—is just hard-pack, and just because it *looks* solid doesn't mean it has the right features or composition to keep water out, particularly in the case of a flood—and I don't know if you fellas have been listening to the radio, but the flood's coming."

"And because Thomayer knew all that, they killed him?"

"*I* was told it was supposed to be a talk. I told you that already."

"That a yes?"

Sackler scowled, "I assume. I wasn't there. But Martins all but told me so after."

"You expect us to believe some middle manager wrestled a guy to the ground and injected him with a lethal dose of heroin?"

"Not Martins himself, but I think I saw the guys."

Sumio again, "Start over from the beginning and be as exact as possible."

Some they knew already. The ask from Martins. The call. The meeting spot and time. But then Sackler started in on the new stuff, "I asked Eli to meet me on the southwest corner of the berm, on the water side, down by where it meets that railroad bridge crossing the slough where there's some privacy. Martins had told me he wanted to meet Eli there and talk things over—settle things. But then, next day, Martins calls me into his office and says that Eli never showed... but the way he said it... it was weird. If you know Martins, you know that whatever idea he's got in his head is because someone else put it there, and I knew he'd been taking calls after hours in his office. So, I got a bad feeling and looked for the complaints Eli had been filing and they were all gone. Martins had tried to scrub the archive, but he doesn't understand the filing system, so he only scooped up the survey memos that Eli had put together, not any of the safety reports or the work order logs—and then I heard about the heroin and everything, and I just got a bad, bad feeling that they'd done something, and that if they had, they might consider doing it to me next, and if that happened I'd need some insurance. I stayed late the next day and boxed up some of the files they'd missed—the originals, on account of Eli having the carbons—and put them in the Attaché here," he kicked the case beside him, "And, sure enough, on the way home that night I noticed some guys following me."

"Were they driving?" Buck asked.

"Yah."

"What kinda rig?"

"A truck."

"Color?"

"White."

"Notice anything else about it?"

"What do you mean?"

"Dents? Chicken wire?"

"I don't know. Maybe."

Sumio pulled out the film canister and worked his way through the roll until he reached the relevant panel, "Was *this* the truck you saw?"

"Yah. Yah, it was. How did you—"

Buck again, taking the length of film from Sumio and stowing it away, "Never mind that. Keep going."

"That's it really, I saw the guys, got spooked, and got out of town soon as I could."

"So, you took all this on a hunch?" Buck asked, kicking the Attaché, "Just for safety?"

"Yah."

"You haven't called anybody?"

"I called Pastor Bradley."

"And?"

"And nobody. That's it."

"Doesn't that kinda defeat the purpose?"

"I don't know what you mean."

"If the purpose of taking those reports was to keep Martins or whoever from coming after you in the first place, it doesn't look like that's worked so well, has it? So, at this point you might-as-well hand it over to somebody who can use it to nail the bastards to the wall."

"Like *you*, you mean?"

"Bingo."

"Or the papers," Sumio offered.

Buck shot him a glare, "Sure," he said unenthusiastically, "And we'd be happy to play courier if that's what you want. *We* might even pay *you* for the trouble."

"How much?" Sackler asked a bit too quick for a guy trying to sound guileless.

"Couple hundred, maybe? We'd have to see."

"What if I say no?"

"Well, that'd confuse me. And in my confusion, I might start getting crazy thoughts—like that you maybe didn't take these reports on account of insurance; that maybe the purpose was a little closer to blackmail. And hey, I figure, fuck 'em, what do I care? But it might change the nature of *our* negotiations a bit." Through the quiet, they could hear the water starting to boil in the kitchen. Buck smiled, "Coffee's ready. Got any mugs, Tom?"

"I'll get them."

"Hold up." Buck gave the kitchen another check. Cabinets. Drawers. Lock on the window, "OK. Go ahead.

Sumio and I are going to take a look at this case of yours."
Sackler brushed by while Sumio started picking through
the case. Buck watched from the doorway, glancing
between the two. "What'd we got, pal?"

Pages. Picking. Reading.

He craned to see, "Sumio?"

All at once, the sounds started stacking quick in the
kitchen. Steps. Creaks. A cupboard. And on top it all, the
unmistakable slide of a shotgun.

"Fuck."

In an instant, he and Sumio were all motion—both
rushing for the far end of the get clear. "*Out! Outoutout-
out!*" Buck started moving just as the spot of wall he'd been
leaning against exploded into so many rotten splinters.
Another slide. Another blast, clear now, chasing. Birdshot
skittering. They ran. Wood underfoot then gravel then
grass. Buck turned and saw Sackler standing on the porch,
leveling some old grouse gun he'd probably borrowed from
the pastor. Blunderbuss like that wasn't good for anything
past thirty yards. Still, Buck'd left his ruler at home, and
it's hard to count paces when you got two barrels rearing
up on you.

"Who keeps a shotgun in with the Folgers?" Buck
asked later, once the dust had settled and him and Sumio
were back in the cabin. They'd come through without a
scratch—long as you didn't count the brambles they'd
dove into that'd torn them all to shit—but Sackler hadn't
followed that far, and by the time they crawled back out

236

the foliage, he'd legged it. Gone. Him and the suitcase. Kid took it on the chin, parsing fresh abandon from the old, while Buck found the hole in the drywall where Sackler must've hid the soup-maker.

"I can't believe it."

"How was I supposed to know he had something stashed?"

Kid squatted, checking under the cot, "No... I mean about the levee... I can't believe they'd just... they're going to get people *killed*. We've got to tell somebody."

"You'll call Ida from the diner—put her and pops up in a hotel for a while."

"No. I mean we have a responsibility to tell somebody who can do something."

"We can't do that."

"Why not?"

He pivoted, "Who would we tell, exactly? The cops? The mayor? The papers?"

"The papers."

"How do you think that'll go, kid? You think we can just show up screaming about some conspiracy and make the front page? We got no evidence. They'll laugh us out the building. Not to mention all the ink *they* spill tryin' to wash away Vanport all on their own. Even if they believe us, they won't care. But if we can make 'em too greedy to care, we might be in business—I'm still waiting on the police report from Karl, and it strikes me that if Thomayer had something like *ten times* the fatal amount of heroin in

237

his system, no amount of ineptitude misses by that wide a margin—it'll go a long way towards proving somebody stuck him. And think about what Sackler said about Martins. I met the guy. He's an office manager. Do you really think he has the kinda juice to get the PPD covering his tracks for him? No way. Somebody with a lot more clout is pulling the strings here, pal—*somebodies*, most likely. We only have half a story here, and we have to be smart about how we put the other half together if we're trying to get anybody to care."

"There's no time."

"There's time. We got a lead on the truck now, don't we? How many trucks are there like that? Why don't we try doubling-back and seeing if anybody—"

"—I saw the reports, Buck."

"You saw 'em for a *minute*, Sumio. So what? You're an engineer now?"

Sumio stared, "You're worried about the bonus, aren't you? Still? After what we just heard?"

"It's a bad plan, pal. Plain and simple. We can't rush this."

"We have to do something."

"And we will, but just take a beat, OK? Think this through. Two g's is serious money, and it all goes up in smoke if we show up to the papers with nothing but our dicks in our hands. What's the problem with taking things to Whitmore first, huh? See what she has to say; let her decide."

"Let her decide? You can't be serious. She'll bury it."

"We don't know that. I'm sure we can convince her to take things public. But it's gotta be her call. Who knows? It might help to have her in our corner."

"We can't wait that long, Buck. We can't take the chance."

"We have to."

Sumio drew a long, even breath and shook his head at the floor, "I knew you'd do this."

"It's a lot of cash to light on fire, kid, and—"

"—I asked you not to call me that—"

"—Acting like you are, I'll call you whatever the fuck I wa—"

"—Buck, I'm not going to—"

"—Listen! Listen, OK? It's a lot of cash—more'n enough to get you outa that shithole you're in now and into someplace where they can't fuck with you. This is America, pal; this is how it works—you make the money so you can tell 'em all to go to hell or so you can move on and keep moving—that's the *deal*. Or maybe it's good to have an excuse ready in the pocket, huh? Something or someone to blame when shit goes sideways?"

Sumio looked straight at him then. Long time. Funny how his face went, "Good luck with the bonus, Buck—I hope it all works out for you."

"Fuck you, kid."

17

After the kid stormed off, Buck'd meant to find a phone and call Whitmore, but somehow—even though there was a lot of money waiting on the other end of that line—he missed 'em all on his way down the mountain. He tried Nathans' boardinghouse up in Albina, but one of the jumpsuits told him nobody'd heard any kind of root-a-toot-toot through the walls since yesterday morning. No sign of him; no clue where he'd gone. Which didn't matter, because even before he'd gone to ground, Nathans'd made it more than clear that he wasn't about to stick his neck out over all this. And, hell, even with his part of the story, without any of those reports Sackler had spirited away, all they had for proof was a couple of rumors and a grainy picture of a pickup—none of which was likely to make front page news no matter how well they spun it.

Buck drove back over to the westside and parked outside of the office, and even though there was a perfectly good phone up there too, he found himself hoofing it over to *Spindelman's* instead, only stopping once he reached the box office, where he stood sweating buckets, hands in his pockets, eyes glued to the marquee.

The name '*Spindelman's*' itself was spelled out in golden, five-foot-tall lettering, each bolted to the wall and adorned with a half-dozen high-watt bulbs, while that night's acts were written out in smaller, interchangeable panels that were presently being updated by a trio of workmen on ladders. One of 'em must've told Rachel he was out there gawking, 'cause she came out after a while, moving like she was trying to outrun the black feather boa trailing off her shoulders, "Gee, sailor," she said, sidling beside him, brow arched, "you're like a bad penny."

"Hiya, Rach."

"Hiya."

"Says you got Barbara Stanwyck in tonight."

"That's right. Fella up outa LA. He does a phenomenal Stanwyck. Guy's a riot. But you'll have to wait, sailor, we don't open for another couple of hours."

"Nice sign you got there," Buck said after a while.

She turned to follow his eyes upward, "We like it."

"Must've been expensive."

She chuckled, "I hate to spoil whatever glamorous illusions you may be harboring, Buck, but nothing about a music hall is what you might call cheap."

241

"I guess a music hall operates a little different than a revival tent, huh?"

"A little, I suppose."

"Not like you can just wipe the chalk off the board and keep moving."

The holiday weekend pushed in around them. Sunlight and laughter and nickel-polished hurry. You could smell the river when the wind'd let ya, but mostly it was just hot dogs and pomade.

"You know," Buck continued, lighting one, "Me and Dad had ourselves a nice sign too down in Lincoln City for a while. You know Lincoln City?"

"No."

"Lucky you. Anyway, winter of '30 Dad had something in his chest and a hell of a cough hanging on, so we finagled ourselves into a little shack by a lake out that way—Devils Lake, they call it." Buck laughed ruefully, "Dad didn't have much of a sense of humor about that when he found out, but by that point, he couldn't do much more'n rack his lungs and moan. All winter we stuck there tight as a tick. Holes in the wall, leaks in the roof, mice bold as brass, and the old man cocooned in the corner, muttering 'bout Job and listening for whales all night. After a while, I got it in my mind that we needed that collection plate to go walking or we were gonna starve, so I hiked down to the logging camp in Kernville and ran a circuit for a couple days. I was no Dad, but a fifteen year-old spitting gospel is a bit of a novelty out there, so I did good enough to think—hell—why not keep things going? Take care of the old man; buy some blankets and some wool; get us through. Couple weeks later, I got a good deal on a sign out off the highway—*Bordell Family Revivals*," Buck recited, sweeping his hand up at the *Spindelman's* marquee as if reading from there, "Not as nice as yours, a'course, but it was pretty slick for Kernville—at least until two weeks later when a couple fellas spotted it from the road and came 'round asking for Dad. When I told 'em he wasn't there they kicked the shit outa me."

"Why?"

"Don't know. Won't ever know. But knowing Dad, I'm sure he did something to deserve it—man hates sin the way only a real sinner can. Point is, I understood the virtues of the chalkboard better after that. There and gone; easy to move, easy to clean. Dad knew that it's the putting down roots that gets you in the end. Once his chest cleared up, we were off again, and I was in Portland by the summer."

"That's a sad story, sailor."

"But you've heard sadder."

"'Course I have. But you're right," she said, the irony flattening in her voice for the first time, "A sign like that's a *real* headache, but, then again, so's a backbone, and in my experience, the bastards find you whatever you do—it's your friends the sign is for."

"I prefer when it's me doing the preaching."

"You sure? Sounds like you got a habit of getting your head kicked in." She eyed him, tapping the spot on her face where his shiner had started throbbing again, "Looks like, too."

"Slings and arrows," he said.

"You know, I asked around about you after our *kibbitz* the other night."

"You did, huh?"

"Know what I heard?"

He shrugged and she laughed airily, stepping away.

"I heard you were alright."

"Yah?"

"Yah. Loud. Prickly. But alright far as a gumshoe goes."

"You believe it?"

Now it was her turn to shrug and his to laugh. He was surprised how bitter it sounded.

"Yah, well, don't believe everything you hear," he said, leaning towards the black, trampled gum of the sidewalk and stubbing out. "Look, we're friends aren't we, Rach?"

"Nope."

"OK, not friends, but peers, right?"

Cock of an eyebrow, tilt of a head.

"Well, whatever we are, I need a favor," Buck said to Rachel's complete and utter lack of surprise. But whatever glib little barb she had ready for him stayed swallowed as he unspooled the roll of photonegatives from his pocket and lassoed her interest with the delicate, gossamer cord of them, threading along, searching and searching, "I'm guessing that when you were asking around about me, you did a bit of due diligence on Thomayer too?"

"Here I was thinking this was just a pleasant little chat—"

"—And I'm guessing you know now that he was one of your regulars?"

"Sure."

"And that he hung around with the acts? The musicians?"

"Mmhmm."

"*And* that he was involved with that horn player of yours Nathans?"

"I'm not going to—"

"—Here's what you don't know—Eli Thomayer was murdered for what he knew about a plan to sabotage some embankment over in Vanport. I don't know the technical details of it all—it's something to do with the wrong types of dirt or something—but the point is, with the rivers rising like they are, Vanport is liable to get swept away. Wiped out. Thomayer was trying to stop it, so they killed him."

"They?"

"Not sure who exactly, but whoever they are they've got serious pull. Enough to have the PPD at their beck and call. Nathans tell you 'bout the phone call that night?

The one where Eli talked to somebody named Sackler? Well, it turns out Sackler worked with Thomayer over at the housing authority and that somebody used him to lure out Eli. But he started to get the feeling that whoever bumped off Thomayer might do the same to him, so he skipped town. Which was smart, 'cause when we went by his apartment a couple goons were waiting for him and opened up on us by mistake." Buck flicked the bullet hole in his brim. "Then, when my associate called the cops—"

Rachel made a face.

"I know," Buck said, "I know. He's an idealist or something. Anyway, the cops chalked the whole thing up to a burglary gone wrong and then tried backing us off the case entirely with more than the usual bit of insistence."

"But you didn't."

Buck handed her the negatives, the tasseled ends fluttering either side of where his thumb marked the panel in question, "Ever seen this truck before? It keeps popping up and we think whoever's driving it might've been the ones who killed Thomayer, among other things."

Rachel didn't answer, her eyes ricocheting from off the image and onto him, the street, the traffic, and every plain-faced scowler making their way up the block before she carefully respooled the film and handed it back, "Shouldn't you be out chasing down this Sackler character instead of bothering me?"

"Tried."

"Alright. So—what—now you're stumped and you're gonna take it out on me and my trumpet player?"

"No. I just need to talk to him. That's all."

"Seems like you've talked plenty already"

Buck took a drag. "Just tell Nathans I'll be 'round tonight. Please."

She laughed. "I'll tell him, but I'm also going to tell him about this conspiracy of yours and all the rest, and I can't promise he'll stick around once I do."

"Fair enough. But when you do, maybe mention that not everybody has the benefit of being up on that stage like he does."

Buck thought that'd be the end of it; thought she'd turn and *click-clack-click* away as quick as her wingtips'd carry her. But she lingered on the sidewalk, listing with the heavy ballast of hesitation that no one, not even her, could bear casually. She shook it soon enough. But it'd been there. It was like looking in a mirror. "You know, it's not just the lights and the panels that make that sign up there cost so much, sailor. What'd I tell you the other day? What'd I tell you? I told you that you PI boys love to go around making *your* questions somebody *else's* problems; love to stumble around until somebody kicks you in the ass, points you in the right direction, and says, 'that'a'way! Go get 'em.'" Then, all at once, she was off down 10th street, like a shot, making it damn-near halfway up the block before Buck even realized he was supposed to be following.

"Alright. I'll bite," Rachel said once Buck'd caught up, "I'll let you rope me into all this *mishigas*, but the least you can do is give me some kind of certainty that my helping you is going to get you somewhere."

"Can't."

"You don't make it easy on a girl, you know that, don't you, sailor?"

"Just trying to be square with ya."

"And the tail?"

"Tail?"

Suddenly, she double-timed it straight across the tangled traffic of SW Park and darted into Nordstrom's department store. Buck scrambled after. Inside, he lost her twice, once among the crowd of slip-clad mannequins in the entryway, and then again when an overzealous perfume girl spritzed him right in the eyes with one of Paris's finest fragrances. But he found her again just in time for the both of them to pile in shoulder-to-shoulder behind the clattering Koa slats of the ladies' changing room. Slowly, he knelt down to look out through the narrow gap between the door and the carpeting to see a ruby-red pair of men's 13's striding right towards them. Buck jumped up onto the bench and hauled Rachel up after him. Wrestled off his jacket. Rolled his shoulders.

Primed himself like a rusty old Jack-in-the-box, ready for another spring.

They heard the soft, padding footsteps outside. Searching. Tentative.

A shadow passing through the slats.

The handle rattled.

Froze.

Again.

Footsteps. Away this time. Quiet after.

Slowly, Buck relaxed. "Friend of yours?" he asked.

"You kidding? Fifteen years and I've never seen any vice boy break a sweat like that. This one's on you."

"No way. I'm fresh off Hood. I only swung by Nathans' for a minute before parking over at the…oh… huh… shit. I must've picked him up over at the office."

"Got any clue who he might be?"

"Nope."

Rachel hopped off the bench and patted her pixie mop back into place in the mirror. "Well, ruminate on the go, would you, sailor? I really got to get back, and we've got a stop to make before I do."

They slipped out of the changing room and took what Buck at first assumed was just the long way out. But instead, Rachel led him up to the second floor and over to one of the long plate glass windows that looked down onto the bustling brickwork of Pioneer Courthouse Square. It was hectic down there. Caught amidst dual and dueling preparatory fervors. First for that weekend's Memorial Day festivities and second for the annual Rose Festival which would begin shortly thereafter. The festival being a multi-week civic spasm of contests, picnics, and genteel merriment which culminated in the well-to-dos puttering up and down the city's boulevards in rose-covered floats at the head of the so-called Grand Floral Parade. So, in addition to the solemnity of the 48 star-spangled wind-socks strung between the square's white-stone columns, its center was occupied by three pickup trucks midway through their transformation into parade floats. Beside them, a sign detailing how any of the passing hoy polloi could buy himself a cheap, felt rose to pin onto one of their sculpted chicken wire frames and bring them that much closer to completion—one for a nickel, six for a quarter.

"Look familiar?" Rachel asked.

They did. 'Course they did. But Buck unspooled the film all over again just to be sure. Pressing the panels against the glass and transporting the frozen, washed-out image of the truck onto the sunny, living brickwork beside its three doppelgangers, muttering, "That's a new one."

"I'll bet. You're welcome, by the way."

"Thanks, Rach."

"Don't mention it," she said, spinning on her heels and tossing both the words and a length of dangling boa over her shoulder as she made for the stairs, "It's been a hoot—really has—but I think it's best if we split here. You take care of yourself out there, sailor!"

"See ya, Rach."

When she'd gone, Buck headed over to the square. Up close, he could see that the wiring on each of the floats would, once fleshed out by a couple thousand five-cent roses, depict the three high holy totems so dear to a city spiritually born along the Oregon Trail—a bald eagle, an ox, and a covered wagon. Buck gave the attendant fifteen cents and pinned a rose on each, scanning, as he did, the prominently displayed list of sponsoring organizations until one in particular jumped out at him.

"Hey, buddy?" he asked the attendant, "How's a fella go about joining *The Portlandia Club*, anyway?"

18

Buck found the note taped to the door. One word: *Arm-strong's*.

He plucked it free and pushed past, jimmying the lock into Karl's office, and helping himself to some bottom drawer bottle that tasted like burnt licorice. He tossed the crumpled note onto the desk and let it blossom back into legibility. *Armstrong's*, huh? It'd be stupid of him to go there. That was the belly of the beast; mouth of the lion. Sure, the brass boys spent too much on shoe polish to blow his brains out *inside* where it might make a mess, but there were plenty of places nearby where a guy could go facedown and not be found for days, if ever.

Stupid to go. Real stupid.

He drank.

Oh, well.

It was quieter than he'd expected. Couple mid-shift sprinters fresh off the blocks. Little stuffy; little hot, with Karl perusing a stack of papers at the bar, fingertips black. He turned at the sound of the door, "Hey-hey! Was wondering if you'd make it. Catch any flak coming in?" he asked.

"A little."

"Yah, I heard you chipping on Mitch out there. What's so hard about playing nice, eh, buddy?" He waved himself off, "Ah, well, never mind, you come along more often and things like that will straighten out. Gotta know to be known—isn't that what they say?"

"Something like that."

"You see this?" Karl asked, rapping the stack of papers with his knuckles, "Water, water everywhere, you know? More than they know what to do with. Makes you glad we got ourselves a second-floor office, don't it?"

"Still drinking in a basement."

Karl chuckled, half-listening as he ordered them up a couple of fresh slugs. "So, where is he?"

"Who?"

"That new buddy of yours. Peas in a pod you two, eh? You got him waiting outside or something?"

"Nope."

The bartender brought the whiskeys for Karl, and a glare for Buck. "Hard to be sure these days. You been doing alright, pal? You've seemed, I don't know, *off*."

"Off how?"

253

"I don't know, just off. If I had a better word, I'd use it."

"OK."

"Distracted, maybe. Yah. *Distracted*."

"Been workin'?"

"Yah, I know—maybe that's the problem." He downed the brown and hailed for another, sighing, "Look, I wanted to apologize for getting a little hot under the collar with you back at the office, I know it was just a mistake, a one-time thing, and, uh, well, hell, you get the message, right?"

"Message?"

"We just can't have that kind of thing, you know? We've got to be selective with how we present the business, right? I get it—I really do—this downtown scene is new for you, and I know you got your issues with it, and I'm sure this Frank guy is great, real peach of a man, all that, sure, but this isn't Albina, Buck, and the folks down here have plenty of options for snoop work. It's make or break like *that*, pal." He snapped two of his big, ink-stained fingers, "So whatever we can do to make folks feel most *comfortable*, well, we should do it, right? And what's going to make folks most *comfortable* is if they see us working cases with people they recognize, they understand, and, uh, well, that they trust. Right? *Their* people. You know what I'm saying? That's the game, pal; that's the deal."

"Uh-huh."

"Yah-yah. You get it; you got it, we're good." Karl said, turning gleeful, "Hey, uh, I tell you how that Montgomery

Park thing ended? Turns out, what the office jockeys were really fighting about was which one of them studs was going to get to mount the company mare, if you catch me, and for the better part of the year my guy wasn't too happy that there hadn't been any champagne for second place. That's how it all started. And, as it happens, I'm currently sympathetic to the jilted romantics of the world, so I applied myself above with the usual diligence, and it turns out our derby winner—the guy *not* signing my checks—had a second little side piece with a foreign name—I'm not sure on the pronunciation but I think it's a little something like *embezzlement*. So, that's all my guy needs, right? More than he could have even hoped for. But I don't stop there. I sweeten it for him, you know? Finesse a little; give him some advice—tell him how to play it, and, lo and behold, he's top of the ticket. Winner-winner, you know?"

"How'd ya mean?"

"Well, right words to the right people and he got himself that office he wanted, and a fancy title to boot. That made him happy. Yes sir, so happy he put a week's charge on top of it all to show his gratitude. What? You didn't think you were the only one bringing in the bonus checks around here, did you? Anyway, my gain is your gain. Same with the whiskey, eh, Bucko? So, drink up."

"That's swell, Karl."

"Isn't it? Isn't it swell?"

"I said it was, didn't I?"

Karl threw an arm around Buck, pulling him half off stool, "Come on, come on, come on, pally boy, don't be jealous! I know you got wrong-footed on this case of yours, but we'll get you on the right stuff soon. It'll happen for you quicker than you think—*easier* too. Hell, Buck, what've I been telling you? Most of it's just about playing nice down here. Do that and the rest just… comes. Then, you know, it'll be you calling the shots."

"Play nice, huh?"

"Yah, pal. Easy."

"I can do that. I can play nice. I can parade my own little pissant around the office and dig his dirt for him and show the badges I'm a trusty pair of hands for a favor. I can do that, *pal*, I can do that *real* easy."

The big man blinked, but not with his eyes. It was the smirk that faltered; the tone that was half horseplay and half condescension; the solid set of that fjord-cut jaw now askew. It was suddenly off. All of it. Off, and starting to stink. Karl drew back his arm just in time to snatch his next whiskey as it arrived, "Alright. Never mind then. Thought you'd get a kick out of that story, that's all; didn't know you'd be pickled so soon."

"I'm not."

"No? Congrats."

Buck rolled the bottom edge of his glass along the grooves of the bar and looked around. He started to notice things. Like how nobody else in there was talking or ordering or reading. Place was a quiet little box hanging from the high wire. "You left the note, Karl. I only came down 'cause I saw it, and 'cause I wanted to ask about that favor you promised me."

"What favor?"

"The one about Thomayer. You said you'd get me the notes any of the beat boys took at the scene or afterwards; said you'd get me the full coroner's report, remember? You said you'd have it by today."

Playing casual, "I did."

"And?"

Shrug like a landslide, "Sorry, pal. It isn't happening."

"No?"

"Meant to tell you. It's my guy down there, I don't know, he couldn't get it done."

"You ask him why?"

"No. I try not push what isn't going to move, you know? Present company excluded."

"'Course."

He shrugged again, "You know how it is, Buck, these things happen. No rhyme or reason. And, you know... maybe it's not such a bad thing to hit a dead end on this one. I got to tell you, I think this junkie goose-chase case of yours is a loser."

"You've mentioned that."

"Well, I'm mentioning it again. Don't be a smart ass,

Buck, I'm trying to talk to you. I know you like to be, you know, *the guy*; the guy who says 'to hell' with everybody and goes anyway, but this one's a crock of shit and don't pretend you don't know it. It's not your fault. You took a chance here and it didn't pay off. It's time to admit you got suckered in on this one. Don't be stubborn. I know you're smart enough to see things for what they are by now. And it's a mess; a headache; something you got roped into under false pretenses. It happens, right? It just happens. They know that. You took a leap of faith, that's great, it's admirable and generous and all that shit, but the ground's coming up fast, bud, and pride's a bad reason not to pull the chute—not while there's still time."

"Still time, huh? Before what?"

Karl shook his head, tipping back the whiskey, "Before you make a fool of yourself, that's what. Before word gets around."

"And *they know that*, Karl? Who's *they*, huh?"

"What?"

"Who's they? This is a junkie case, isn't it? Who else might there be?"

"*They*, Buck, Christ sake's, *they*. The system—the world, the universe, the laws of fucking gravity—I don't know, it's a figure of speech, bud. And anyway, don't for one second pretend that's not how you see every case that comes across your desk. Because you got some monumental chip on your shoulder and you can't help but make things messy, can you?"

"What's so messy?"

"Are you kidding? Why don't you shut the hell up before you say something you're going to regret."

"No."

"Alright. What's messy? Your fucking face for one. The cuts? The bruises? You been by a mirror recently? You look like shit."

"Uh-huh."

"You're tired. You're drunk."

Buck glanced around the bar again. The tableau of a midday swill-house, frozen in disinterest, had cracked into something hard and menacing. He turned back. Shook his head, "So how'd it go down, Karl? You get a call? Or'd they buttonhole ya down at the precinct when you went over for the report? Was this little come-to-Jesus we're having Behan's idea? One last heart-to-heart before they gotta get serious on me, huh?"

"Settle down."

"You expect me to believe it's just a coincidence that you can't get the reports, and that you call me here, and that you lean on me like this all right after Sumio and I got shouldered by the cops last night? That all just happenstance, is it? That the universe too? The world? The laws of *fucking gravity*?"

"I come to you as a friend, worried about you, and you hit me with a bunch of paranoid bullshit? You really do need a break, pal."

"I told you, Karl, don't play dumb—you're no damn good at it."

The big man lifted the whiskey to his lips with a snapping, full-shouldered jerk and held it there. He laughed after, short and sharp and straight to the ribs. "*Don't play dumb*, he says—you first, Buck. *You. First.* You spend all this time bitching at me, night and day, and you don't got a fucking clue—without me, you're on your own; all you got is some looney broad and a Jap for a lapdog. And you know as well as I do, Buck, that isn't shit in this town. I'm on your side, you stupid fuck. I cover for you; I keep you in the game. Don't you get that? Without me, you're done—you're *fucked*."

"None of this has anything to do with you, Karl. Stay out of it."

"Of course, it has to do with me. I *vouched* for you."

"Well, thanks for that. You've been a real pal."

"And you've been a real prick, Buck. When this goes bad, don't say I didn't try, because I tried."

Buck looked over his shoulder. Counted 'em at their tables. Four high-cuts. Dead sober. Lumps in their jackets. Eyes like marbles, "So how bad's it gonna go?"

"That depends."

"On?"

"On if you walk away or if you and me go up together and tell them everything you and the Jap've got. If we do that, they're willing to be magnanimous about it, far as your concerned."

"What about the kid?"

The big man sneered into his glass, "Nope."

"The kid's clueless, Karl. He doesn't know anything. There's no reason to go after him, it's all me."

"Doesn't matter. Their minds are made up."

Buck's initial, knee-jerk reaction to the ultimatum was efficient, direct, and monosyllabic. But—being a thoughtful guy—he gave himself the benefit of a few moments' careful introspection, just to be sure. Which didn't turn out to change things in the least but was good practice as far as these things went.

"No," he said.

"*No*? What'd you mean? What's that mean? *No*?"

"It means fuck them."

"You're making a mistake, pal."

"Yah, well, you tell Behan thanks for me, huh, Karl?"

"Tell him yourself."

It was a raw couple seconds then. Kind that grinds your teeth to powder. Buck sat, bracing for the sound of upended chairs; for the rush; for the crunch of a pocket cannon cocking against his dome; for the tangling shouts and the short, simple answer. But the mooks didn't come for him after all. So, slow as anyone had ever done anything, he slid off the stool and straightened his collar. Nothing. Got his hat. Not a cough. Not a flinch. Only movement was Karl reaching over to snatch his next whiskey and down it joylessly. Then, much, much less slowly, Buck hurried up the stairs and out to the street.

There, waiting, was Behan. He was leaning against a cruiser, arms crossed. He smiled, waited for a moment, and asked, "Carl coming?"

"No."

The smile widened, "Alright then."

Buck looked the street up and down. Busy here. Behan followed his eyes, and then came over, continuing, "Don't worry. It won't happen here. It'll happen later. This was a real chance, Bordell, and you blew it. You—"

But Buck didn't let him finish whatever speech he'd had prepped.

Instead, he head-butted the bastard hard as he could right between the eyes. Walloped him. Left him dazed. Both 'em, really. But even as Buck couldn't manage much more than a kind of limping gallop getaway, and even though his head was swimming, he was still fast enough down the block to get clear. Behind, Behan stood stupid, wiping thick, long licks of red onto his sleeves, and yelling after, "You're a fucking dead man, Bordell! A *fucking* dead man!"

19

"Hello?"

"Sumio, listen, it's Buck, don't hang up. Ya there? OK. OK, good. Couple things—one, Doreen's truck? *The* truck? It was meant for the Grand Floral Parade. That's what the wiring is for. It was meant to look like a covered wagon once it was decked out. It's one of the ones they use for fundraising down in Pioneer Courthouse Square; for the rose pinning; so, whoever's been taking it out for joyrides must be connected to one of the sponsoring organizations. I made a list. There aren't many. Just a handful. But, for my money, I think somebody at the Portlandia Club might have it out for the Whitmores. Second, it looks like Behan and his boys are getting serious, so we gotta get serious back—no more tantrums. Come meet me under the *White*

Satin Sugar sign downtown at eleven o'clock. That's the big, bright one down by the river. Come on. I need your help here. We can still chase this thing down, huh?"

The line buzzed back empty.

"Sumio? You there?"

"Sumio is out, Mr. Buck."

"Who's this?"

"Aito. His father."

"Is Ida there?"

"Regrettably, my daughter-in-law is also out, Mr. Buck, but I will give to them your message when they return."

"Just Sumio. Tell him eleven o'clock, under the sugar sign—the big one with all the lights," Buck said before hitching the receiver. He'd called from a payphone outside the *Hotel Treves*—one of them dog-ass, half-dollar joints off Burnside where he'd just gotten himself a room—but he didn't hang around. Instead, he went up to Nicolai Street and cracked peanuts in the union hall 'till the Stevies asked to see his card; he moved on; moved careful; holed up in the empty bucket of the hitch yards where he could kill an hour without witnesses; where he could stomp out cigs and nickname bricks; where he could check the chambers of his shooter like a station agent anxious on an engine; where he could mull; where he could spit; and where he could watch the twilight wick away to neon. Quarter to ten, he made for the river and slipped into one of the sandbag-buttressed doorways directly beneath the blazing lights of the *White Satin Sugar* sign, where it was dark and where he had a good view of the street, the river, the bridge, and, bang on the hour, of Mrs. Ida June Takahashi coming straight his way. Reluctantly, he waved her down and she joined him in the shadows, sand crunching underfoot as they stood shoulder to shoulder, backs to the wall and eyes to the river.

"What're you doing here, Ida?" he asked.

"I got your message."

"That wasn't for you."

"Grandaddy didn't become the richest man in Hattiesburg—black or white—by grandmama sitting on her hands."

"Hell's that supposed to mean?"

"It means too bad."

"Where's Sumio?"

"By now? Troutdale? Gresham, maybe? It's a long way down the mountain from where you left him."

"I didn't *leave* him. He threw a fit and walked off."

She shifted, sand crackling, voice crisp, "He was upset when he called. He said you were going to drop the case."

"That why you're here? Come to give me a piece of your mind?"

"He said that you don't care if the berm fails or if people die, so long as you get your bonus. More the point, Mr. Bordell, he said that we couldn't count on you anymore—if we ever could at all."

"He said all that, huh?"

"He did."

Buck fished for his cigs and sat on the lip of the sand-bags, "Want one?"

"I quit."

"Look, it was a misunderstanding. I didn't say to drop the case—what I said was, that we needed to be careful; that we needed to be smart. Patient. It wasn't what he wanted to hear. He wants to go to the papers? OK. Fine. But with *what*? Us two spinning yarn won't be near enough."

"I understand that you have a witness."

"You mean the trumpet player?" Buck shook his head, "Fat chance there. He ain't talking to the papers, and even if he did, all that gets us is the midnight phone call, and that's nothing on its own. If we had proof of what the authority was up to with the berm and that Thomayer was threatening to take it public, maybe—*maybe*—that would be enough to get the papers interested, but without Sackler and his documents we got nothing—no proof that the authority had any reason to want Thomayer dead, much less that they had anything to do it."

"What if someone saw something."

"Saw what?"

"Saw them *take* Mr. Thomayer."

"Who? Where?"

"I'll tell you. But I need an answer first."

"To what?"

"To my question."

"Remind me."

She turned, "Was Sumio right, Mr. Bordell? Can we count on you, or can't we?"

"*Jesus.*"

"I'm afraid I need an answer."

"You and everybody else."

"What do you mean?"

"*I mean*, Ida, that you're not the first person to ask me that today."

"The police?"

"Bingo."

"And?"

"And? *And*? Hell, Ida, don't insult me—I told them to go fuck themselves."

While she considered that, the milk-gray river looped a first and feinting finger up through the slips of the seawall. "That works for me—it might not for Sumio, but..." she shrugged, dropping beside him on the sandbags, "His name's Malcolm. He's an acquaintance of mine over in Vanport. He lives out by the berm. On the night Mr. Thomayer was killed, he says he heard men arguing and that he saw one of them wrestled into a car. He says he was close when it happened. He says that he heard things."

"He did, did he?"

"Yessir."

"And he just came up and told you this?"

"No. I asked around after you and Sumio left this morning."

Buck lit one, "Grandmama must be proud."

"She is. Very much."

"Will this friend of yours talk to the papers?"

"I mean to ask him."

"Good. I'll come too. I'll get my rig and meet you up there."

"We'll go together."

"Nope. Too dangerous. Remember how I said I told the cops to go fuck themselves? Well, on account of that, I had to ditch the car, and they'll have had somebody watching it since. That's why I wanted Sumio to come down in the first place."

"So, what is it that you propose we do?"

"*We*? Forget it, Ida."

"I commend what I presume to be your sense of chivalry, Mr. Bordell, but the waters rising outside Vanport, and we haven't the time—if anyone asks, I will attest that it took *hours* to wear you down, so that we may now— quickly, if you please—move right along to the part where I save your ass."

Buck grinned, "Works for me."

Fifteen minutes later, he watched from the corner as Ida hurried down SW 5th, nervous and obvious, stopping at his car, hesitating and glancing and fumbling with the keys, only to get in, fire up the engine, and sit idling, which gave Buck plenty of time to spot the black Buick hardtop five cars back readying to follow. He went for it wide, on the far sidewalk, hat low, pace casual. He saw that the driver was alone, with both hands on the wheel and the window down. Buck pulled his piece and came diagonal, approach slipped between the mirror's angle and the driver's peripheral, steps lost to the purring of the engine. He burst through the window, pinning the driver's arm, and sticking the pistol into his ear, "Move and I will blow your fucking head off," he said. Then, squinting into the cab, "Oh. Hey, Pat."

"Hey, Buck."

"Still doing Behan's dirty work, huh?"

"Pays the bills. Who's the darkie?"

"Nobody."

"Nobody's nobody to us, you know that." McClean said, his cheek brushing against the pistol, "'Cept you, Buck. 'Cept you."

"Give me the keys."

"Fuck you. You think I'm afraid of some conchie playing tough guy?"

Buck cocked the pistol.

A slow second.

"Take 'em," the copper grunted.

He did, reaching past slow and careful, shuttering the engine and drawing back,

Then, the sound of a car horn from up the street. His. Over and over and over—

"*Sh*—"

Instinct took Buck at the knees, and he dropped. Then, from just behind where his ear had been, a gunshot, the crack of glass, voice and blur and the hard, rising edges of the street. Buck scrambled to his feet and started running. Ida was ready for him, having nosed the car into the street and flung open the back seat door. He dove for it, barely touching leather before she'd slammed the gas and left his legs kicking at empty air. It was all he could do to hold on. He dragged himself up to the back window where he saw that damned rookie of McClean's standing plain and open, leveling his shooter for a second go—but before he took the shot, Ida took the corner, and they were clear and off and racing 'cross the river. Halfway over the bridge, Buck chucked McClean's keys into the dark water below and crawled up to the passenger seat. "Nice work on the horn," he said.

Ida kept one eye on him, and one on the mirror, saying, "That man would've killed you—shot you like a dog in the street."

"Told you, didn't I? They'll try for us any place and any way they can. That's why I told Sumio that you two oughta get outa Vanport for a while—not that you'll listen."

"It is our home, Mr. Bordell."

"Well find a new one. Christ's sake, Ida, we're talking about a shoebox here."

"It's not so easy."

"I thought you came from money."

"I do."

"So, use it."

"What do you have against Vanport?"

"Nothing."

"It sounds like something."

"Well, it isn't. It's just that it's a big, damn country, and there's no sense dying over any piece in particular."

She looked at him, eyes bright with the passing of headlights, "I believe I'll have one of those cigarettes after all, if you please."

"Fine."

He lit her one and passed it over, but she didn't smoke it. She just let it burn between her fingers, down and down, "What has Sumio told you about me, Mr. Bordell?"

"Nothing, really."

"Did he tell you I'm a teacher?"

"No. He's cagey with me."

"Professional," she corrected.

"Whatever."

"Well, I *am* a teacher. One who graduated from a very fine teaching institution in Mississippi, but do you know how many schools in Oregon would hire me?"

"Not many, I'm guessing."

"One—Mr. Bordell—one, and it happens to be in Vanport. And as for a house?" She shook her head, "Vanport is… not ideal. No, sir. But for some of us, Mr.

Bordell, it is not, as you say, '*a big, damn country*' out there, with plenty of hinterland to run off into."

Wind in.

Hum out.

Road slipping by in big, long, white tallies, keeping score. Night came bubbling in like a hole in the boat. They heard laughter off behind a rotten fence. A siren. Cats in the alley. They drove on quiet for a while.

"A teacher, huh?" Buck asked eventually.

"Yessir."

"Which grade?"

Hands slow on the wheel, slow and smooth and flicking the cigarette free of ash, "Third."

"You like it?"

"Very much. I don't have much patience for cynicism, Mr. Bordell, and children that age are wonderfully uncynical."

"Think they got any working at the *Journal*?"

"People need to know about this. With the press involved it'll be a scandal, and they'll have to back down, whoever they are. But even if they don't, if we can just get *something* in the papers to sound the alarm people will see it for themselves and be able get out of Vanport while there's still time. Maybe it would even force the authority to evacuate or refortify the berm. Whatever the case, we need to wake people up to the danger."

"And if nobody bites?"

"Then we'll insist."

"Gonna go kick down doors, are we? Raise hell? Stand on Burnside with a couple sandwich boards hanging off us?" Buck said, digging the meat of his palm into the side of his head, thinking maybe a bit of pressure might snuff out the ringing in his ear, "Christ, Ida, I see why you and Frank get along—you got a lot of spunk for a schoolteacher."

She laughed at that, night whirling like a zoetrope, "I suspect that that's as close to a compliment as men like you come, Mr. Bordell."

"I suspect you're right."

"That's all fine by me. I'm used to it." She looked over, "You know, my uncle used to have an old pointer by the name of Big Oat, and Big Oat was just like you, the kind of dog that you could give just about anything—prime cuts, fresh bedding, or bones to gnaw—but no matter what you did, if that dog was in the house and idle, he was just about the meanest creature you've ever seen. He scared the daylights out of just about everybody, but not me. Me and him always got along just fine because I knew Big Oat wasn't looking for pampering, and he certainly wasn't looking for friends. What Big Oat was looking for was turkeys. It was all he knew how to do; all he knew how to be."

"That's me, huh?"

"Yessir."

"Maybe. But by the way you been talking, I figure you got a bit of bite yourself."

"Oh, I do. Of course I do. But I try to keep it in proportion."

"For the kids?"

She shrugged, "For them. For Sumio. For me. Too much of that can burn right through you if you let it. Can and will."

"It's useful though—spite, I mean."

"Yessir. Yes, it is. That's the trouble."

It was a different kind of bustle when they pulled into Vanport—one of flashlights up top embankments and crowds on corners. Nerves in the air. They found Sumio on the far side, out front the last, long row of apartments, his back to the street and his eyes on the berm. At the sound of the car, he turned.

"Buck," he said.

"Sumio."

A long moment passed.

Then another.

"Look—"

"—Come on," Ida said, cutting between them and heading up the walk, "Malcolm's waiting."

20

"I'm thinking Sacramento," Malcolm said as he worked a couple sausages on the stovetop. "Land's cheap out that way, I hear. Been thinking of tagging south anyhow. Been saving. Reckon I can set myself up nice down there after Vanport gets swept off."

"None of that now, Malcolm."

"Man's gotta have himself a plan, Miss Ida—that's all. Reckon you should have one too."

"That's why we're here bothering you."

Guy turned back to his sausages, brown and crackling. He was a beanpole. Adam's apple sticking out his throat like one of them shale-cold calderas bumping up outa Sisters; arms ropey and bent like wisteria in winter. His grin was empty, as if strung up with fishing line and nothing had been biting. Buck and Sumio were behind him, plugging up the doorway, while Ida sat at the kitchen table next to a carefully lain out rail porter's uniform. Apartment was the same as the Takahashi place only spare, only quiet, only dark.

"I got a buddy riding Shasta in and outa Sac. He says it's better tips, better schedules, better whole way 'round. Do that a while, get my feet planted, and get a sense. Done it before—couple times, plenty since Chicago—don't scare me none. Sure you don't want no sausages, Miss Ida?"

"No, thank you."

"How 'bout you, Sumio? You hungry?"

Sumio then, "I'm alright."

"And your friend there?"

"He's fine."

Malcolm shrugged, "I hear they grow rice down there. That'd be fine. I know something 'bout that. Maybe get me some peaches too, some pears. Whole set up. Yessir, that'd work fine. But I ain't picky neither. I'll tend whatever grows. Work like a mule, work hard, you hear? I don't mind none of that long as it's *my* bed I'm making—mine and nobody else's. 'Cept when you and Sumio come to visit, of course. Wouldn't that be something? All us down there together? Me put up like that? Peaches for the table, rice for the bowl, yessir."

"It sounds lovely."

"Don't it?" He looked over his shoulder, straight at

Buck, "But I reckon you fellas aren't here for daydreaming. Reckon you wanna hear me talk 'bout the other night?"

Ida, shifting, crossing her legs and braiding her fingers, "If you would, Malcolm."

"Lot of good it'll do." He rolled the sausages onto a plate and rested his hip on the countertop, quartering the links with a fork. "Well, as you folks know, I porter for the Southern Pacific Railroad—Cascade line to San Fran—and we hit Portland 'round about nine thirty when we're making schedule. So, 'round that time I start turning over cabins, doing my checks, and getting things neat before I can clock out, which means I'm gone by eleven if I'm lucky. Way back, I like to get off a stop or two early and walk home over 'cross the slough bridge—the one just out here that spits you straight onto the berm. It's quicker that way. Quieter too on account of the bridge being a rail bridge—quieter most nights anyway. Last Sunday I was headed home that way at the usual time when I see a car parked half into the brush—like somebody was trying to hide it, even though it's all kinds of dark down that way already."

"What kind of car?" Buck asked.

Malcolm took a bite, scratching his cheek and squinting at the ceiling, "A Rolls Royce. Real nice. I'd just come up on it 'round about the time I heard some fellas talking, so I ducked into the bushes."

"Why?"

Another bite, "I've had some trouble out that way a time

or two, so if I hear folks coming, I just let them pass on by."

"Could you hear what they were talking about?"

"Not really. But all the time they were coming up their voices sounded normal like—just two fellas talking—and then," He snapped his fingers and popped his tongue, "*bam*, pair of headlights come on, and there was suddenly another car, parked and facing our way a little ways down the road. I was deep enough into the bushes that nobody saw me, but these two boys coming on were all lit up."

"What'd they look like?"

"One of 'em was real slick looking—had one of those big, college boy rings and a nice suit—and the other... I don't know, just your everyday kind of white boy in flannel—no offense."

"None taken," Buck said, handing over Thomayer's picture, "This the guy?"

"Yessir, that's him. Mr. Slick grabbed that fella there the moment the lights came and held him so two of his friends—mean looking types—could come over and drag him back to their car."

"Just like that?"

"Yessir."

"Anybody say anything?" Sumio asked.

"Shouted some. Argued. It was hard to make out. They were all of them talking over each other, and they had that fella in the picture gagged up pretty quick. They took his keys, too."

"What'd you mean?"

"Mr. Slick took your guy's keys off him and took 'em back across the slough, while the others drove off. Just me and the night for a long while before I reckoned it was safe to make a run for it 'cross the bridge."

"You remember much about the Rolls?" Buck asked.

"Got the plate number if you want it."

"What?"

Malcolm stepped out the kitchen and back again, handing Sumio a notecard. Kid flashed it Buck's way.

$$Sep - Oregon - 47$$
$$262 - 799$$

"You're sure on the numbers?"

"Yessir. Thought I should tip folks off. That's why for I mentioned it to Ida June in the first place, so's she could look out for a Rolls with that plate and keep clear—not like a Rolls don't stand out good enough all on its own 'round here."

"What about the other car? You get anything on it?"

"Nope."

"Could it've been a truck? One with chicken wire in the back? A *white* truck? Dents in the door?"

"Could've been the *Spirit of St. Louis*, for all I saw."

Sumio pocketed the notecard, "How much has Ida told you about what we're dealing with here?"

"Some, I guess. Enough."

"Did she tell you we're going to the papers?"

"She did not."

"Sacramento sounds lovely, but do you think you can stick around a while, Malcolm?" Ida asked, "We need you to tell the papers what you've told us. It connects things, and it's the only way anybody's going to listen. You know I wouldn't ask if it weren't for real, but I'm honor-bound to tell you that there's people trying to stop this from getting out, and you've seen with your own eyes how far they'll go. It's a favor, Malcolm, and a big one."

Next minute might as well've been an hour, their host suddenly and entirely consumed with a couple water spots on the kitchen ceiling, "Alright, Miss Ida, alright. I reckon them peach trees can wait a little while."

Buck figured he wasn't needed for the details, so he went out for a cig, but Sumio followed, hot on his heels—pace tetchy, expression neutral. Wind was heavy outside, swollen and stinking and kicking down 'round their ankles. "Got another wartime parable for me?" Buck asked, chomping on a cig, "Maybe it'll take this time."

"Fresh out."

"OK, let's try this then—no more homilies, no more sermons—spite and leather from here out, us to them. Let's make Big Oat proud and kick the bastards hard and keep right-on kicking."

"Big Oat?"

"Ask your missus."

Sumio considered. Sky overhead cut by the swinging of the lights up on the berm. Air stinking. Water high. Night uneasy. "Alright."

"Yah?"

"Yah."

"Good."

"But this is about more than your pride, Buck, and I need to know you understand that."

"What'd you mean?"

"This is about protecting Vanport—Ida's home, my father's home, *my* home; It's about what's right, not about getting one over on Behan or whoever else."

"I know that."

"Do you?"

"Yes."

"Prove it."

"How the hell am I supposed to do that?"

Kid shrugged.

"We're in the same goddamned boat, aren't we, Sumio? Long as we're both rowing in the same direction, what's it matter the why?"

"Because I'm not rowing just to row, Buck. It's not just anger for me. *I'm* rowing to reach shore, and shore for me is stopping them from wiping Vanport off the map. But maybe shore for you comes once you've gotten payback on Behan, or finagled your bonus, or lost interest or nerve or whatever, and maybe that means you stop rowing *right* when I need you most. I can't have that. Not now. So, if we're going together, Buck, I need to know I can count on you the whole way across."

"OK."

"*OK*, what?"

"OK, I hear you, for Christ's sake. Look, I know it don't seem like much to you, but spite hasn't let me down yet and it burns my ass when these sons of bitches figure they get to say who lives where and who gets what. There's too much space for that—too goddamned much—and I like me an underdog."

Kid nodded, sighed, and nodded again, mulling.

Then, as the quiet started looking like it might tear at the seams, Buck decided to pull out all the stops, "I know it doesn't help with anything," he said, "but I *did* break Behan's nose earlier today."

"Yah?"

"Yah. Headbutted him right on the button."

A smile stole 'cross Sumio's face.

"We good?" Buck asked.

"Yah."

"Yah?"

"Yah."

"Good, 'cause we got business to get to."

21

The knob turned like the tensing of a muscle.

Buck checked his watch. *1:04.*

He stowed the ticklers and pressed himself flat to the wall. Waited. Shook his bum foot to wake it up. Cracked his knuckles. Pulled his collar. Waited. Watched for shoe polish. Watched for chrome. Watched for any settling interest among the boys emptying a truck 'cross the street.

Then he waited some more. Checked. *1:05.*

Shit.

A fire engine passed, its lone, bloodshot eye spinning towards the river, washing rouge over the brick grout. Buck pulled his hat down and watched it speed past the felt, on towards Burnside; to the river; to the big, black, Willamette chewing its way up the banks; biting deep into the side-lying country. The air smelt of clay. Of damp. When Buck and Sumio had crossed over the Steel, they could taste the mud from the bridge, close as it was, while the radio had stacked its bulletins like more sandbags.

Water over the east bank and rising, they'd said.

To 2nd now.

To 3rd.

East Grand a canal. Cleanest it's been in decades.

Suddenly, the sound of commotion from through the door. Buck pressed his ear. The voices on the other side were muffled but laughing and hooting and shouting-orange. Not yet.

1:08.

"Where is Mr. Tanaka?"

Buck jolted, cracking open the door, sharpening the sound.

"*Get* your *fucking* hands off me… hey! **Where… *where is Mr. Tanaka*?**"

"Goddamned Jap!"

"What's he—"

"—Throw… before we have—"

"What'd I tell y—"

"—Shut your pig mouth! ***Where is Mr. Tanaka?*** This is *his* store, isn't it? Where is he then? You goddamned vultures—"

Buck slipped into the back hallway and moved towards the bar. The door to Maddy's office was closed. Mads

284

usually locked herself behind it on Sunday evenings to go over the champagne and brandy tabs before the second shifters rolled out. Sparse in the bar. Peeled off galoshes, ripped napkins, and only the hot wake of commotion breathing life. Buck hurried for the stairs, grabbing a greasy highball glass and taking a long, dry, face-covering sip from it as he rounded the foyer and through the crowd of gawkers gathered in the doorway. Up. Two at a time. He glanced back. Charlemagne stood in the doorway, distracted and flanked by two dead-drunk looky-loos, shouting towards the street, "—I swear to god you Jap bastard, if I see you again, I'll—"

Buck made the landing and hurried to the front corner room. No card in the stack. Lucky. He didn't knock. "Sue, I just need five minutes of—" He stopped. Confused. It was Sue's room. Sue's night. But it wasn't Sue he found in there. It was Maddy. He almost didn't recognize her. It'd been so long since he'd seen her surprised. She shot up, hand hovering over the boudoir switch.

"Sue?" Buck asked for want of something else to say.

"Sick," Maddy answered for want of the same.

"No tally tonight?"

"Was over talking to Jane and I heard shouting in the street." She squinted at his bruises, "Charlie give you that?"

"Uh-huh."

"Just now?"

"Last night."

"What the hell are you doing here, Buck?"

"Save it, Maddy. Help or don't, but don't do that."

"I *did* help. I told you to butt out."

"Can't."

"This one's different, Buck, this one's—"

"—Yah, yah, Mads, I know, and I know you're getting the lean and hard, but I was hoping—for old time's sake— we could have one chat that doesn't end with you siccing Charlie on me."

She eyed him coldly, "He see you?"

"Nope."

"Close the door."

He did. "Hand off the switch."

"No."

"Fine."

Laughter. Creaks. Clinking glass. All dull and far.

"You look like hell, Buck."

"Yah."

"Behan came asking about you today."

"How'd his nose look?"

"A lot like yours, as a matter of fact, only fresh."

"*Ha.*"

"It's not funny, Buck. Not to me. If that bastard finds out we've been talking like this, I'll have a lot worse than a busted nose coming my way."

"He doesn't have to know I heard anything from you."

"But he will. You leave tracks."

"Bullshit."

Contemptuous, "*Please*, Buck—we're each of us only afforded *so much* credit on our delusions."

"Nobody has to find out anything."

"Except whoever you're going to tell, right?"

"Fine. You're right. But this isn't some horseshit affair you're sweeping under the rug this time, Maddy. If you keep whatever you know secret people will die."

"Which people?"

"People out in Vanport."

"Vanport? *Mon dieu*," she said, her voice low and casual, dropping like a stone, "What's Vanport got to do with me? With anything?"

"The dead guy—Thomayer, the one they dumped on your doorstep—he was trying to get the word out on a bad berm they were covering up. They're sabotaging the place, hoping it'll flood and wash Vanport off the map."

"Isn't that what we're *all* hoping for?"

"It's wrong, Mads."

Her mouth screwed up tight. "Wrong?"

"Water rising like it is, they'll—"

"—Don't you lecture me on what's *wrong*, Bordell," she snarled, "Water's rising all the time in this country. It never stops. It's only suckers who tie themselves to something so heavy as *what's right*. Not me. What do I care about family disputes and moral crusades? I got a business to keep afloat."

Huh.

"Family disputes, Mads? Which family?"

She laughed bitter, smiled hard, glared, shifted, shook—all of it too slow by a hair—finger worming towards the boudoir.

"Which family?" he asked again.

"Shut up."

"Who was it, Mads? Who was with Thomayer that night? A woman?"

"You used to be reliable—in a backwards kind of way, maybe, but I didn't need much, did I? Where was your right and wrong then? Where was that when it was me and you?"

"You misremember. It was you who cut me out."

"I'm *asking* you, Buck. Please. Leave it."

"They weren't subtle, were they, Mads? Just rolled up and dumped the bastard? You think that's a one-time thing? You think whoever did that doesn't know *exactly* what they were doing? They could've chosen anywhere in town—anywhere—but they chose here. You think it's an accident it made the papers? Come on, Mads, they're after you as much as anyone. Why cover for them?"

"Because that's how you survive, Buck. That is how you survive."

"It doesn't have to be. We can get them. We can. All's I need is a name. We know it was someone with pull; somebody big time. Just tell me who and I'm out the window and nobody's the wiser."

If he hadn't known Maddy well as he did, he might've mistaken the sudden hang-dog slump of her shoulders and the doleful little shiver that followed as some late-breaking pang of sympathy for him; some embodiment of their time together—the minutes and the days and the years.

But he *did* know her. So, when he saw it, he was already making for the door.

"There's easier ways to send you out the window, Buck," she said, flipping the boudoir switch. Buck tore out the room, racing for the stairs with Charlemagne halfway up and rising. Fucker was quick. Quicker than you'd imagine for a man of his size. But all that muscle and mass didn't play so well on the climb. Buck hollered, "Hiya, Charlie!" and hard-planted a heel on the big man's chest, knocking him back and through the banister. He fell ten feet, hit heavy, groaned, rolled to a knee, cursed, fumbled up his revolver, and waved the thing limply in front of his face as if gunpowder were a smelling salt. But Buck hadn't done much better. He'd kicked with his good leg, sure, but the bad had given way in the effort, so he fell too, thumping his jaw on half the steps of the stairway. First breath rising was ragged. Arms shaking. Felt like he'd lost a tooth—bit off some cheek too maybe—but now wasn't the time for inventory. He got up, spit the iron, and quick-timed it past the confusion and through the streets until he got to *Spindelman's*.

Thing was though, he didn't see Sumio anywhere.

"We gotta quit meeting like this, sailor," Rachel said, falling in beside him, dragging him over to the bar, and nudging him down onto an open stool, "What chewed *you* up so bad?"

"Couple things, actually."

"You want some ice or something?"

"I'm OK."

"You don't look it."

"Won't argue with ya there. Look, I'd love to chat, Rach, but I'm looking for somebody. You seen a Japanese fella come through here in the last half-hour or so?"

"You mean, Frank?"

"How'd you—"

"—Sure, I saw him, I fixed him up with a ticket. He's in now watching the show."

Buck stared, head foggy, tongue tallying teeth, "*What*?"

"It's a can't miss act tonight and he said he was a friend of yours, so I figured I'd take care of him."

"That... wasn't the... it was *Frank*—Japanese fella, mustache? You're sure?"

"Yep. I'm telling you, you'll wanna get in there too— folks've been hanging around here *all day* waiting for the show to start." Above the bar, waist-up, she was casual, friendly, smiling big for the backrow, but under the bar where no one could see, she was digging a wing-tipped toe into his shin. "So how 'bout it? Take me up on a little hospitality?"

"I—"

"—Thought so. Now get in there, enjoy yourself, and we can all meet back here after for a drink, how 'bout that? Here's your ticket," she said, pressing something into his hand and leaving faster than he could blink. He looked at it, expecting a ticket. It wasn't. It was his business card; the one he'd given her days earlier. On its face, six new words written in hasty script:

Dorothy's back.
Ditch him.
Backstage after.

Buck beelined it for the theater. Head down. Hobbling slow. Jaw swelling like he was growing a melon in his gums. He paused at the theater door and looked back.

Bulky. All shoulders and sharp stride, wearing a pair of red shoes, following, faking like he was reading a playbill, bulge under his left lapel.

Shit.

Buck slipped into the theater. Some guy on stage was saying something to the crowd. A wave of laughter, a disembodied introduction, *composer, ragtime, with me,* a tinny, wavering breath into the horns and they were off. Loud and jaunty. The backstage door was too far, Buck'd never make it before Dorothy spotted him, not with the bum leg. Instead, he jumped into an open seat in the middle row and slumped down. The band hit gear. Through the tangle of knees and collars and fine-curled hair, he saw a shape hustle by.

He waited.

Rubbed his cheek.

Nodded to the older woman pretending not to notice him.

Then, he raised his head just over the next row to see a man's silhouette standing beside the stage, scanning the crowd through the spill of the stage lights.

Down again.

"Psst. Sir?"

Buck waved her off.

"Psst. Excuse me, sir?"

He edged up again. The silhouette was gone. "Lost a quarter," he said, tipping his hat to the woman and wriggling out into the aisle. He made for the backstage door in the far corner. Rachel was waiting on the other side, hands on her hips. She leaned past to lock the door, yelling to be heard, "How many hints did you need, sailor? Didn't I tell you about PIs? Dumb as dishwater, every one."

"Where's Sumio?"

"Who?"

"*Frank*?"

"Come on."

They went deeper. Backstage proper. Plain balsa and painted faces; wigs and grease and sequence floating in the thundercloud. Brass—music like from the inside of your skull. Rachel pointed to a ladder and mouthed: *Up*. So, he climbed and wound up alone on the light rigger's gangplank, high over the stage. He looked out and from his perch he could see the first few rows of the audience. Not a red shoe among them. He sat, legs dangling in the high-tempo air, sore jaw pressed to the cool iron of the handrail.

Then, two numbers later, a tap on the shoulder made him jump so bad he damn-near went hurtling down into the percussion section. It was Sumio.

"How'd it go at Bons?" he yelled into Buck's ear.

"Mads slipped up—said something about this being a *family* affair."

"Her and Thomayer?"

Buck shook his head. Just then, Rachel climbed up, lugging a couple of bandstand blazers and an old carpet bag under her arm. She ignored Buck's questions and set to work on them right away—new jackets, new ties, boater's caps, and even chalked on a couple layers of makeup to cover Buck's bruises. When the music waned, she finally said, "Dorothy's waiting for you in the lobby, and he's got a couple of badges with him. I can't delay them all night. Go out back with the band. I'll give him and his friends the runaround tour, might buy you a couple minutes. Best I can do."

"We owe ya, Rach."

"Naw—it's my name on the sign, ain't it?"

It went smooth. Just the way Rach'd laid it out. Buck and Sumio fell in with the bandstand as they marched out the back door after the performance and spilled out onto 11th Ave under a cloud of fresh exhale and chatter. Down on the corner, there might've been some heavy leaning on light post—he looked the part right enough, shoulders set like a mousetrap—but after a long stare he kicked off the pole and disappeared 'round the block.

"Buck—look."

"I saw him. I couldn't tell for sure, but I think we're good."

"No, over there, it's Nathans."

Buck turned to see him breaking from the pack and heading south. "Shit. I got him."

"No. I'll talk to him. I'll bus back up to Vanport after."

"Let me pay your fare," Buck said, pressing his pistol into Sumio's palm. "Eyes up out there, huh? Don't miss your stop."

They parted. And as Buck went up Yamhill, slow to hide his gait, past the unblinking storefronts and the gray brick hotels, he started to think about what Maddy had said, and Ida and Sackler too; started to think about who could show up at the wrong end of a midnight phone call looking so much like salvation that Thomayer wouldn't sense the knife until it was square in his back; about who could know enough to clean out Thomayer's desk at home, but still need to break the lock; about who could land so heavy that the Martins and the Behans of the world would hop to, but that Sackler wouldn't even know; about how Eli could've just disappeared, but someone *wanted* him found outside *Bon's*; and about how Mrs. Doreen Whitmore had been saying since the beginning that her husband had wanted all this just to go away.

So, he gave the roaches another hour in his room at the *Treves* and drove east. Went the long way on account of the river—threading a thin asphalt needle between the rising river and the sinking backrooms further up.

He was faltering by the time he pulled up outside the Whitmore place. Tired. Chewed up. He got out. Checked the card. Blinked, and checked again.

Huh.

832-182.

Same as the Rolls in the drive.

22

Jesus.

He tried to stand. Too sore; too stiff—couldn't manage it. Tottered back down. Sighed. Tried again

Jesus.

It'd been a while since he'd slept rough. He'd remembered how soft a pine root cradle could look but forgotten how fast the ground hardened 'round 'bout three. 'Course, he hadn't planned to bed down with the headstones, it was just that when he'd gone back to the *Hotel Treves*, the lamp was off in his room. He'd left it on before. Thought he had, anyway. Might've been him. Didn't matter. Couldn't chance it. So, he drove down to the Ross Island Bridge with the idea of sleeping under the span, but there were too many firetrucks—with their butterfly lights flash-flapping outside the cab all night—so he doubled back east, to the cemetery where he'd first heard about the case. Cemeteries were good for tramps—quiet, dark, and the neighbors never hassled ya. After a bit, he walked down to Belmont, got himself some joe, and threw a nickel into the phone.

"Terwilliger Answering Service, good morning and to whom am I speaking?"

"Buck Bordell," he croaked.

"Do you have an account number?"

He gave it.

"Thank you, Mr. Bordell, would you like to hear your messages?"

"Yah."

"From when, sir? From last call?"

"From yesterday. Anything past noon."

"Yes sir… thank you, sir. Yes, I have two messages I can read back for you. The first came in at one thirty-six PM from a Mr. Raul Hernandez. The message is as follows: '*Down day estas? La chow-ta es acki.*' End of message," she said hesitating for half a second at the Spanish.

"OK. Next please."

"The other came in last night at nine twenty-one PM and is from a Mr. Thomas Sackler. The message is as follows: 'I reconsidered your offer. Bring $1,000 to Multnomah Falls by one o'clock tomorrow, and we'll do business.' End of message."

"You're shittin' me."

"Excuse me, sir?"

"Nothing. Never mind. Thank you. Thank you, that's all, or, no, hold on a second—"

"—I'm here, sir."

"Earlier… when you… when did you last get a call from me?"

"Hold please… my records show your most recent call came in last night, sir. There's a note here saying you last called at ten twenty-two yesterday evening."

"And you gave both those messages to… me?"

"That would be the usual procedure, sir."

"Shit. OK. Thanks."

He spent another nickel to call the service back, except this time he gave them Karl's name. But Behan and his boys evidently weren't the right breed of stupid to leave messages, so he packed up and hit Vanport just as the bureaucratic storm clouds were breaking up overhead. On every post and door and windshield the Housing Authority had left a flyer that made oblique mention to the rising waters before ending with three fully capitalized promises and a final admonishment:

REMEMBER:
DIKES ARE SAFE AT PRESENT
YOU WILL BE WARNED IF NECESSARY
YOU WILL HAVE TIME TO LEAVE
DON'T GET EXCITED

Sumio came out just as Buck finished reading. "They moved the horses," he said.

"What?"

"Over at the Downs—they moved the horses to higher ground. And I heard the authority is moving their files out of the administrative center even though they've had guys up on the berm since dawn telling residents it's safe to stay. They're going to get people killed, Buck. We have to hurry. Who knows how much time we've got. We'll need to split up. I can take the *Oregonian* if you take the *Journal.* We'll meet on Grant after and see if—"

"—Sackler wants to play ball."

The kid sighed. Hands on his hips. Eyes shut. "How do you know?"

"He left me a message. He wants us to buy the reports off him."

"How much?"

"A thousand."

"I don't have that. Not even close."

"Me neither, but it's negotiation, and we'll be persistent. Hell, maybe you can tackle him again."

"Where is he?"

"Wants to meet over at Multnomah Falls."

"When? Today?"

"Couple hours. Catch is, Karl's caught wise, and that means Behan has too. Might be a trap; might get messy."

"How do you know?"

"Me and Karl share an answering service."

"You should get a secretary."

"So I hear. What'd ya think?"

"If he's got the proof we need there in black and white, I say we go—trap or no."

"Yep, good, come on, let's do it then. You got my piece?"

"I gave it to Ida."

"Really?"

"Yes."

"Why?"

"I thought that—"

"—Never mind. It'll probably do more good with her, anyway. But I think we should—"

He didn't finish. Didn't need to. Kid walked straight into the apartment and came back carrying a thick coat bundled 'round something long, heavy, and high caliber.

Sumio pointed to the Housing Authority building as they cruised by on their way outa of Vanport, and it was just like he'd said, with its doors thrown open and a steady stream of plundering clerks moving in and out. Whatever wasn't nailed down had been dragged out into the street or loaded into the back of a waiting truck. Files most of all. Box after box of them. And by the looks of it, they weren't leaving so much as a scrap behind.

From there Buck and Sumio made for the highway, its length between Vanport and the falls stretching like a couple dozen miles of taut ribbon along the southern bank of the Columbia. Officially, it was closed, but they'd veered 'round the barriers and took it anyway, the river wide beside them, its banks jumped and pines drowning; the asphalt going next. Buck asked Sumio about Nathans, but the kid hadn't gotten much. Same story, and all this business was too much for him to stick his neck out over. Nobody could argue that.

Half hour later, they pulled into the empty lot beside the river-stone structure of Multnomah Lodge, and looked beyond to the spout of the falls, its black rock basin roiling with thin mist and fat, splattering spittle, while the stone bridge built at the basin's edge stood slick and dark and solid like the lone buttress of a buried cathedral. Buck and Sumio split up. Hurried. The kid took the lodge and Buck the trail to the bridge. There was no one around. A pulp-beaten kind of silence where it was impossible to hear a step, a voice, or an anything for the thunder of the falling of the water. Buck looked up the cliff, looked back, looked around, stood, waited, and took the rising corner. No one. Nothing. Mud and wind and nodding green. He went on—soaked within the pink side of a minute—reached the bridge's middle and drank the tempest.

Checked his watch.

10:46.

Looked up again.

Saw it.

Saw *him*.

A man.

A man, *falling*.

Strange how quiet.

Guy was clawing at the mist as he fell, desperate, to gather enough droplets to cushion the drop.

But no chance of that.

Down and down, quick as quick. Screaming, probably, but silent anyhow.

Same as when he hit, body landing like a sodden rag.

Dead.

The water didn't even blush.

Buck's eyes traced the body's arc back up the heights to see the lean figure of Behan and a couple others looking down, but it was another long, long second before he realized they weren't *just* looking—they were shooting too. He dropped behind the bridge's railing as the mist thickened into lead. Flicks of it. Hollow little pops. Cracks and sparks and whistling near misses.

Paper too.

Reams of it.

Falling all around, damp and heavy.

Buck dragged one sheet over with his heel. Ripped Housing Authority letterhead; ink illegible—Sackler's proof, dead as he was.

Shit.

Buck risked a glance. There were two rifles he could see up there, but it must've been more. He was pinned.

Time was—days maybe, or, shit, *years* more like—he would've chanced the run, and maybe even would have made it, but he was all banged up—wit-slow and stretched stupid. They'd get him for sure if he tried anything like that. 'Course, they wouldn't content themselves to just wait on the skeet shoot either; there'd be a couple fellas already hoofing it his way down the switchbacks.

Shit.

The world drew tight, the air brittle, and the bullets tracing the outline of his cover. He wished he had his gun, but, really, that wouldn't've mattered. He was drenched. Sopping. A panicky little flame rioted in his chest, but the runoff chill had wormed so deep into him that he didn't know if he could even *pull* a trigger, much less keep an arm steady enough so's some tippy-top, look-down bastard took one between the eyes. Couldn't run. Couldn't shoot. It was even money between Sumio's backup and the avalanche coming his way.

Any minute now. One or the other. Any minute.

The next shot he heard was different. On instinct, his eyes snapped shut, his ears filled with sawdust, and his joints turned to jelly. He could tell the shot had come from close, but that's all. It might as well have come from inside his own skull for as much as he could make out on the right or the left of it, the up or the down.

And then, slowly, he realized three things.

First, that he wasn't dead.

Second, that the *shot* wasn't just *a* shot, it was a rolling purr of cannon fire.

And last, that firing from the trees off to his left, wasn't some downtown thug, but was Sumio Takahashi, and in his hands, that big, bawling, beautiful BAR.

Fuck!

The blood rushed back into Buck all at once, and he went half-stumbling, half-diving towards the safety of the bridge's left end, towards the wide embrace of the trees, towards cover, towards the delicious, muddy, mossy, sweet-sick smell of life dragged ragged up outa the earth and into his buried nostrils. "**Holy shit**!" he yelled, flopping onto his back.

Sumio answered with one spattering volley, then another.

"Holy *fucking* shit!" Turning, "**Sumio**! Sumio, listen! Sackler's dead! They threw him off the falls!"

"What?"

"**Sackler's dead! They threw him off the *fucking* falls!**"

"**The files? The proof?**"

"**Gone!**"

A branch burst between them. One of the down-trail triggermen finally having loped into view on the far side of the bridge. Sumio spun, the B-A-R jumping in his hands, shredding green, "**Get the car!**"

Buck went fast as he could, sure that a slug would land right between his shoulders on the way, but he reached the rig unscathed, slammed it into reverse, and went hot-skipping backwards up the trail, horn blaring. Behan's boys managed to put one through the back window and another couple through the roof before Sumio had jumped in and they'd floored it back to the highway. For the first mile they were clear, they traded nothing but ragged breaths and dull-eyed looks.

"*Jesus*."

"They... they threw him off the falls?"

"Yep."

"Jesus."

"I know."

"Alright," Sumio said, "Alright."

"Yah?"

"Alright—here it is. We get back to Vanport. We hunker down and call the papers. We write everything down—*everything*—and we send it out. We *make them* listen." He fished Thomayer's address book out of his jacket, "We got a lot of it already. We will make copies. Get signatures. We will tell them about all the witnesses we got; we will walk them through. They'll go for it. We'll tell them about this morning, and about how Sackler told us Thomayer knew about the coverup and was threatening to take his reports to the papers, and about what you heard from that secretary at the authority, and about Mrs. Whitmore getting hassled, and about what Malcolm heard, and about how Thomayer told Lou that he was afraid he wouldn't come back from the meeting that night in Vanport. It's too much to ignore. They'll have to print it, we just got to secure a perimeter and hold out until we get them interested. It'll work. It will."

"*Huh.*"

"What?"

"That's right. Lou said… said that Thomayer was afraid he might not come back that night."

"He did."

"But Lou didn't know why."

"Not exactly."

"And at the time, neither did we. But now we know that it's because Eli suspected Martins or somebody might try to take him out. So, what's our guy do? He squirrels away all those reports and documents and everything as a hedge, thinking that if he's got that, that the authority can't make a move on him without it all landing in the papers—but a maneuver like that only works if he's got somebody else in reserve; somebody capable of *sending* all that proof if he gets bumped off."

Sumio, catching on, "Who're we missing? I've been through that book of his a thousand—"

Kid stopped.

"Who?" Buck pressed, "*Who?*"

"The record."

"What?"

"*The record.* Remember what Thomayer told Lou? He

told Lou to play the Calloway record if he didn't come back—not just play *something*, but that record *specially*."

"Shit."

"You figure he—"

"—*Shit*," Buck hollered, slapping the wheel, "It was there! Right there! That son of a bitch!"

23

They were at Thomayer's for less than a minute. Just long enough to shoulder the door, grab the shit, and get out. It'd been right there the whole time; just sitting there in the Calloway record sleeve—a few dozen pages of delay, double-talk, and failed inspections—proof that the authority had been ignoring the danger to the berm—and then they were out again, hauling ass for Vanport while Sumio rocketed between outrage and excitement with each new page. He read some bits. Intoned. Thundered. But pretty quick he realized Buck wasn't interested in the line-by-line, so he traded prose for predictions, "Those bastards. Those *fucking* bastards," he said, and then, "But with this…I can't believe it. It's all here. I can't believe it.

We can nail the authority to the wall with this—this and what Malcolm'll tell the papers—we can nail those sons of bitches."

"Proof is only half the game here, pal."

"I know."

"Yah?"

"Yah, but come on—"

"—No, no, really. Games not over. It's still a longshot getting this in print. No matter what we got there, we can't assume the papers'll print anything the downtown crowd don't wanna read over breakfast."

"Maybe, but I don't think so. I think this is going to work, and I think you do too."

"We'll see."

Kid bit his lip, turning and turning, "It will. We just have to get back, dig in, and make the calls. Somebody'll bite. Somebody'll print. They'll *have* to."

It was a good plan—best they could do anyway—too bad it went straight off the skids the moment they showed up in Vanport. Ida was supposed to be back by then, but she wasn't, and the old man hadn't heard squat. Odds were, she was out warning people. But who? The neighbors? Friends scattered all over? And where? The Extension Center? Her school? Some place halfway 'cross Vanport? Sumio had plenty of guesses but nothing certain. But the soldier in him hadn't gone anywhere since the morning's shooting, and so he was quick to cook up a plan of reconnaissance and objectives and maneuvers—he'd range out to any the haunts he knew about, while Buck would keep lookout from the bird's eye of the berm top.

"Take the rig," Buck said, chucking him the keys.

"Thanks." He went for the door, "Buck?"

"Yah?"

"Be smart."

"Too late, pal."

He hurried off. It was strange going. People weren't panicking, exactly, but some kind of corner had been turned, and the place was emptier than Buck had ever seen it; all but given over to the boot and wader-clad holdouts who stood on the corners trading tools and tips and downtown promises. Voices muffled by the spongy sink of the grass; roads clear. He looked for Ida among the back-turned, berm-top silhouettes, but he didn't see her on the way up, and once he reached the top, it was hard to look at anything but the river. Or. No. Whatever this was, it wasn't a river anymore. A river is glassy, and purposeful; a line on a map ridden by a dead man's name; silver conquered under steel; a thing you could always outclimb or outrun. What was here now was something else—a burst-up gullet swollen from too much rain, too much heat, too much sweat and spit and blood and all of it down from the gutters of a thousand miles and more, risen, stinking, brown-gray, and just inches from crawling over the lip of the berm and flooding into Vanport.

"You're a real son of a bitch for making me do this, you know."

He turned.

It was Karl.

Karl and a pistol.

Karl and a pistol and a look of boundless self-pity.

He sighed.

"You haven't done anything yet, Karl. There's still—"

But before Buck could finish, the pistol went off and buried a slug in his stomach. Staggered him. Took his wind; took his balance. His gaze dropped to where the hollow sprig of nothing had been slipped into him, and the stain spreading in its wake. Strange how numb he felt, how empty. His hands were moving on their own, clamping down on the hole but doing nothing to close it up; nothing to stop the blood from flowing sticky and warm between his fingers. Through and through and through and through.

Then time caught up with itself. People screamed. People scrambled. The pain came then—came like hell.

"For Christ's sake, Karl, you shot me?"

The big man seemed just as surprised, his mouth hanging open, but before he could give any kind of answer, the ground went strange on them. Buck thought it was just him at first. He'd never been shot before. Didn't know what was normal; thought maybe feeling like the soil was giving way underfoot was just part of it. But then came a noise from behind so loud and low that it dragged his rioting attention back along with it, and when he turned to follow it, he saw the berm starting to crumble some twenty yards off—first as a dry-dirt slide on the Vanport side, and then as a full-on collapse within the space of a single pedal-down second. The water poured in. Fanning out. Rushing. Shallow at its edge, but fat behind—fat as the whole goddamned Columbia, and free to follow.

Fast as all that went, the patience of the pistol brought Buck back around, swaying and staggering and spitting and waiting on another twitch of the big man's finger. Wasn't dignified, but then, nothing is when it comes to dying.

"I had to," Karl offered.

Buck straightened and sagged and straightened again, "We could'a beat it."

"We, Buck? *We*? There is no fucking *we*."

Karl raised the pistol, but before he could do any more than that, somebody put a bullet in his ear, and the big man was dead before he hit the ground.

Buck stared at the heap of him. Brain scrambled. Numb and boneless.

Huh.

Suddenly, Ida was there, pawing at him, "Buck? Buck? Are you alright? Lord, you're bleeding."

Blinking, "He dead?"

"I think so," she said, then, "Yes."

Buck lumbered over to the fast-cooling lump of what had once been his partner, "Shit."

"Do you know him?"

"'Course," he said through gritted teeth, "He's my partner—*was*, anyway."

"But he shot… Never mind. We have to get out of here. *Otousan* is back at home. We have to get him, and have to… wait… wait, where's Sumio?"

"Out looking for you."

"Where?"

"Dunno."

"We have to find him."

Buck nodded, trying not to retch.

Then they hurried. Best they could manage anyway. The water had reached the first apartments and buckled a few outright; even as it was pouring past and fast and wide and through. Buck and Ida tried to stay out of its way but there was no out of the way down where they were, and even though they saw the water coming, and it was shallow, and they were braced, when it hit, it hit like a slap and knocked them on their asses. But they got up and kept on, chancing the whitewater sluicegates new-sprung in the space between the buildings. Buck went down again. Ida too maybe. He didn't see. It was all he could do to haul himself back up this time, and when he did, she was only a few steps off. His hat was gone. Jacket too. World muffled. There were other people now. Yelling and pointing and wading. Turning keys of stuttering engines while shapes barreled in and out of slanting doorways. Kids on shoulders. Hands and knees. Hurry. Voices. Down the block, some torn-off apartment went floating by, slow and serene.

"Ida."

Her grip tightened. Dragging at him. His shoulder wrenching in its socket.

"Ida."

"What?"

"You gotta go."

"Enough of that, Mr. Bordell."

"No. No really."

"Hush up."

"No, Ida—"

"—Mr. Bordell, *be quiet*! Chivalry is *damn* annoying at a time like this."

"It's *not* chivalry, Ida, for Christ's sake. I'm… I'm losing gas." He spit. "You need to find Sumio, load up the old man, and come back."

"Come back?"

"And get me, yah."

"You'll… you'll be alright?"

The long whine of a siren answered for him.

"This road here? The one we're on now?" Ida said, stomping on the brown water, "This is Victory Boulevard; *keep* on this road, you hear? If we can't make it back, it'll take you out of Vanport, but if we can we'll look for you down Victory, alright?"

"OK."

"But we will come back."

"I know."

"We will."

"Got it."

"This road right here, you under—"

"—I got it, Ida. Now get going, goddamnit!"

And she did, rushing through the water and the crowd and the bobbing debris before reaching a hiccup of slight high ground about a hundred yards ahead. This far from the breach, the water had slowed for the moment, and most people could stay ahead of it, but then, most people hadn't had their ticket punched with a half-dollar slug of American-made slow-down, so Buck cut himself some slack and kept going best he could. Least he had momentum. Was moving. Had his wits. Not like the stupefied bastards he saw here and there, standing with their eyes panicky and feet planted. Lucky for them, Buck was happy to lend 'em a kick in the ass to get 'em unstuck, and if a kick didn't work, whatever hoarse words he could muster, and if that didn't work either, he doubled right back to the kicking until some mix of the two got the fella moving. Some tried to return the favor once they'd come to, but Buck shoved 'em off. Nice of 'em and all—a nice gesture—but no amount of shoulder tugging was gonna shift Buck into anything higher than first.

So, he was alone mostly.

Alone, and with the water getting higher.

Faster. Louder. Meaner.

Who knew why it'd sped up again. Maybe the breach had widened, or the berm had gone altogether, or somebody'd left the bath running, but either way it was soon going to be more 'bout swimming now than it was 'bout wading, and the only thing he did worse than wade was swim. Still, it was something to do. If he stopped, he'd pass out, or—God forbid—start getting philosophical over his floating face-down on what'd been dry land ten minutes before, and getting philosophical was the kind of a thing a fella did just before he kicked it, and Buck didn't plan on kicking it, so he swam by Christ; swam and pushed and swung heavy, with all the dignity of a cat in the wash, same as ever, same as always.

Up ahead was a bridge over one of the long-swallowed slough lines, where a car had just stopped halfway across, engine rattling and water pouring out its undercarriage.

No. Not a car.

A truck.

A white one.

Dented. Couple big ones in the door.

And with a strange wrapping arch of chicken wire stretched over the goddamned truck bed.

Made Buck laugh—laugh and laugh—and reach for the cigs he didn't have. "Well, come on then," he muttered, "Come on. Come on."

The siren. The water. The sun glinting off the shuddering, waiting hood.

Again, "Come on. Come on. Come on, then. Come on! Come-on-come-on-come-on, *come on*, you sons of bitches! *Come on!*"

And they did—revving and skidding—but in the wrong direction, with a couple fresh B-A-R punched holes in that sun-washed hood to go with the dents, hightailing it through the shallows and out of sight.

Sumio next, hurrying over, and Ida after, while Buck swayed where he stood, still laughing—laughing and laughing—before pitching headfirst into the silence of the water.

24

"Before we bring up our final speaker for the day, I wanted to take a minute and thank some of the folks who've made all this possible. First and foremost, a special thanks to the Pittock family, not only for the use of these wonderful grounds—and on so *stunning* a day no less, golly, Edward, how'd you manage that—but for their many, *many* years of generous sponsorship to the Club. And thanks to Frank and Chuck and all the rest of the boys in the political engagement committee for organizing such a fantastic roster of speakers—with a special thank you to Mr. Plunkett here on behalf of councilor Lee—let's give him and all our speakers a hand, folks!" A ripple of applause passed through the crowd. "Let's see, who else? Well, Johanna and David from the Krogh Foundation, of course, for so generously lending us a last-minute replacement for our entry into the Grand Floral Parade! You're a couple of live-savers, you two! Oh, Stephan, as well, over at *Schultz's Roses*. Our friend Seth over with the Chamber of Commerce, and Ms. May from the Eastside Improvement Society, the Rosarians, as always, and *Crawley's* for the catering. Who'd I miss? Ed, is there anybody?"

"Just *yourself*, John!" a voice shouted back, prompting another bout of applause.

The speaker beamed, waving them off. He was handsome and clean cut, pleated and parted and pruned as precisely as the roses of the garden, "Alright, folks, alright. But seriously everybody, thanks for coming out today, and for giving so generously. Now I'll stop yapping away and turn things over to our final speaker. So, let's give a big, Portlandia Club welcome to our esteemed guest—Dr. Richard Paulson of the state planning office! Doctor, if you please?"

There were about two hundred people on the lawn, dressed in linen, gathered polite and proper and in lazy, wicker rows 'round the sweeping granite steps of Pittock Mansion, high in the hills above town. John welcomed the doctor with a pose for the camera and then moved off—slow as not to spill his julep—towards the far edge the garden. From there, behind a shale-rock wall and a hole somebody'd punched through the trees, a guy could see the mountain, the rivers, and just about the entire city stretching below.

Clear. Peaceful. Dignified.

"Ya know if there's a shitter I can use 'round here, pal?" Buck asked sidling up alongside, "Caught some lead in the gut last week—plays hell with the plumbing."

"There are restrooms inside just past the foyer," John answered.

"Uh-huh. Say, don't we know each other?"

"I don't think so, no."

"Sure we do. John, right? John *Whitmore*?"

"That's right."

"Thought so."

"And you are?"

"Ah, come on now, really?"

"Sorry."

"Buck Bordell, I'm a friend of your wife's. Friend of your brother-in-law's too, as a matter of fact—much as anyone can be friends with a dead man."

John's smirk stiffened, but a waiter came rushing to his aid, "I told you once already, *sir*," he hissed at Buck, "this is a closed event. I saw you loitering around the cars earlier, and if you don't leave immediately, I'm going to have to—"

"—It's alright, Jack."

"Are... are you certain, Mr. Whitmore?"

"Yes. In fact, could you get my friend here a glass of the '21?"

The waiter looked ready to blow a gasket, but he thought better of it, and instead winced his way through something vaguely hospitable before turning about-face and scurrying into the house, never to return. Buck went for his cigs, enjoying the view of town while John feigned interest in his tweed-clad successor, now beginning his remarks from the steps. "So, where's the missus?" Buck asked, "I figure Doreen wouldn't miss a thing like this."

"She's at home."

"Really?"

"Yes."

"Funny, 'cause that's where I been calling."

"The doctor says she needs her rest—calls included."

"Sick, is it?"

"Yes."

"*That* sick?"

"We have the baby to consider."

"Must be a hell of a bug. Wonder if it's the same one they got going 'round the newsrooms downtown—been hell getting any of those boys on the line too."

"If it's newsmen you're looking for, Mr. Bordell, you're in luck. We have just shy of the entire *Oregonian* editorial staff here today. I'd be happy to introduce you."

Buck shrugged, hands in his pockets, rocking on his heels. Then, the voice of Dr. Paulson echoing off the granite and moving like a dozer 'cross the crowd, "*Now, ladies and gentlemen, what we at the state know is that for a city such as Portland to meet its 20th century potential, it must unshackle itself from 19th century thinking and harness the transformative promise of the automobile. We can think of the modern city, ladies and gentlemen, as a heart, and for a heart to beat clean and prosperous, spacious arteries are required, and what are highways if not such arteries? Our plan, then, recommends the construction of two major highways through the Portland metropolitan area, the first of which would pass through Albina to provide ready commercial and commuter access to stimulate not only the business district but the riverfront industrial areas as well…"*

"Speaking of rigs," Buck said to John, "Lotta nice ones out front. Must be frustrating."

"Frustrating?"

"Yah."

"Why might that be?"

"Fella spends all that money on a flashy Rolls, only to come up here and be one of a dozen. You know what you oughta do? You oughta take a car like that down 'round Vanport where folks'd remember *every detail*. Really appreciate it, ya know?"

"Taking my car anywhere *near* Vanport would be difficult now—things being as they are. The water was how high there last they measured—what was it—fifteen feet? Sixteen?"

"Wait a while. It'll go down."

"And what of Vanport will be left when it does, I wonder?"

Buck smiled and said nothing, resisting the urge to smack the son of a bitch in the mouth.

"It's a tragedy, of course. But I'm sure that you've heard that a generous portion of today's proceeds are dedicated to the cleanup efforts. Our organization has been intimately involved down there. In fact, key members of the club are scheduled to discuss the Vanport situation as well as some other items with President Truman when he arrives tomorrow."

"*Key members*, ya say?"

"Yes."

"So not you?"

Whitmore sipped his julep, "Everyone has a role."

"Yes sir, and yours is bag man, and Rolls or no, bag men don't meet presidents. Makes 'em easier to cut loose."

"You know, Mr. Bordell, it seems that you are positively *obsessed* with personal aggrandizement. Though, I suppose I should suspect as much from a man in your position. Some of us have wider concerns—causes we believe in. I trust my associates to communicate our shared position to the White House."

"Which is?"

"That Vanport was a *mistake*, and one that we must never repeat."

The good doctor again, "*It is of course true that these highways would mean substantial urban redevelopment, and that means that some homes will be torn down, but our studies suggest that such revitalization will actually be to the city's long-term benefit rather than its detriment, given that the neighborhoods in question are blighted beyond salvaging and are places with deeply suppressed property values, as well as hampered commercial prospects. Creation through destruction, then, ladies and gentlemen. For inspiration there, we need look no farther than New York in this century and Paris in the last to...*"

"You're a weed, Mr. Bordell."

"Huh?"

John cleared his throat, "I say, you're a weed—just like the rest of them. And what the weed sees as cruelty to the weed, the gardener knows is kindness to the garden."

"And what about Eli?"

"Better he be remembered as a whoremongering junkie than a queer, I should think." His eyes narrowed, "We're building a respectable city, Mr. Bordell. And we don't mean to abide the flesh peddlers any more than we do the deviants and dope fiends."

"You think it's that easy?"

"Easy? No. Just inevitable."

"What about the truck?"

"The what?"

"The parade truck—the white one with the dents—you know, *the truck.*"

"I don't know what you're talking about."

"No?"

"No."

"OK."

"What'd you think coming here was going to achieve? Did you think you'd intimidate me? Or are you planning on making some petty public spectacle of yourself? Go ahead. Now's your moment. See how far it gets you."

"No, thanks. I just came to give you something."

"Keep it."

"Sure. No problem," Buck said, fishing a folder out of his jacket, "But since *you* hired me, I gotta at least *show* you my summary of services. It's a licensing thing, and I happen to be a stickler."

"I didn't hire you, my wife did."

"Check's in your name."

Whitmore snatched at the folder, but Buck held on for a couple seconds before letting John wrestle it free and fling it into the trees. Poor guy spilled his julep in the effort. "The money's nothing to me. Keep it. It's nothing compared to what's coming my way."

"Hell, pal, you took the words right outa my mouth."

25

As a wave of applause rose to wash Dr. Paulson from his perch, Buck followed one of the jacketed waiters into the kitchen and on through to the dripping mahogany of the Pittock Mansion foyer. From there, he called the tip line desk over at the *Portland Journal* and told them everything; he told them how the Housing Authority, along with the fine, upstanding officers of the PPD and whoever else, had sabotaged the flood infrastructure of Vanport, and then murdered an inspector by the name of Eli Thomayer to keep it quiet; he told them how it'd all gotten so far out of control; how he was guilt-ridden, burdened, and hunting for absolution here. And then, when he'd finished spilling his guts, and the girl on the other end asked if he'd like to leave a name with the message, he said, "You bet—my name is John W. Whitmore, and you tell your bosses I'll come down to put all this in writing at their earliest convenience."

After, he drove down the twists and turns of the pine-choked road to where Sumio was waiting for the pick up. He hopped in, swatting at his dusty pants and pocketing the film from out the camera hanging loose 'round his neck. It was a while before either of them spoke. "Well?" Buck asked eventually.

"I got about twenty shots of you two talking."

"Any of him holding the folder?"

"A couple, I think. We'll see how they turn out."

"Good. When they come through, we'll mail 'em to the authority. That'll be more than enough to get people panicking."

"What about the reports? Did you get them into the car alright?"

"Yep. Had some pissant running interference in the parking lot on the way in, but I gave him the slip long enough to get everything stashed. Anybody who searches John's Rolls for more than a minute'll find the whole shebang."

"It's not enough."

"Sure it is. They killed Sackler over a whole hell of a lot less."

"No, I mean, it's not enough to *answer* for Vanport. It's not justice."

Buck considered that, rooting around for his cigs. He shrugged, "Maybe not, but it makes for one less son of a bitch out there."

"It's not enough," Sumio said again.

It was slow going back through downtown—with knee-deep water far as fourth street, and half the bridges still closed—but nothing serious. Meanwhile, Vanport was just *gone*. Things had been chaotic since. People missing. People dead. It would've been easy for Buck and the Takahashis to have slipped away—after all, Ida had plenty of family back east, while out towards Reno Buck had, well, if not a friend exactly, someone who owed him a favor at least.

But instead, Buck and Sumio had jumped right into their cross-town-tour of slamming doors. All the proof they had? All the witnesses and names and specifics? None of the papers would touch it. Sure, a couple hacks played along here and there—listened, nodded, took notes, and even skimmed the reports, but that was as far as it'd ever gone. No prints; no promises. It got to Sumio after a while. Turned out, his skin was plenty thick when it came to shootouts and pig-eyed fuckwits, but there was something about sad-eyed men in bowties crying crocodiles tears that he just couldn't stand. So instead of waiting 'till the kid snapped and stuck some poor bastard's head into the presses, Buck'd suggested they tack into a more Old Testament kind of direction. Make some calls. Stash some papers. See what sticks.

"Only if we warn Doreen," he'd said, "She deserves to know."

And he held firm on that. Even if it meant John getting tipped off before the hair-triggers came knocking on his door. Didn't matter. Wouldn't budge. Professional integrity and all that. And—even though he knew better than to say it—Buck knew the kid was holding out hope that Doreen might catch a case of conscience and help them get the story out. So, with Mr. Whitmore stashed up at Pittock, rubbing elbows with the other muckity-mucks, Buck and Sumio went beelining for the missus, hats in one hand, guns in the other.

But there was no ambush waiting. No white, wire-wrapped trucks skidding 'round corners, no gunmen, no McClean, no Behan, no nothing but a fierce, bright day and the *rat-tat-tat* of the neighbor's sprinkler.

Still, they didn't linger out in the open. Pulled straight into the drive, popped the lock in a flash and went in lickedy. At first, it seemed like no one was home—shades drawn, motes dead in the air—but then the faint sound of music came bleeding through the ceiling. They went after, climbing to the upstairs hall where they saw Doreen sitting on the floor of the nursery. She was dressed for company—buttoned and broached—with a pride of blue, painted lions grinning from off the walls all around. Her hat beside her. Her eyes down. White gloves picking through the stack of type-dense housing authority reports piled neatly on her lap. Calloway crackling on the Hi-Fi.

They watched her like that for a long, long moment until Sumio said, "Mrs. Whitmore?"

She didn't look up. Didn't answer.

Sharper, "Mrs. Whitmore?"

She jumped a little, mouth pursed, voice thick and far off sounding, "What?"

"We need to talk."

"Mr. Takahashi… Buck… what're you… you can't be here."

"You weren't answering the phone," Buck said.

"I've been out. Busy."

"John said you were sick."

She blinked back, expression empty, "You… you talked to John? Why? When?"

"About an hour ago, up at Pittock."

"After I gave you *explicit* instructions not to? What were you thinking?"

Sumio again, "I'm sorry, Doreen, but there's no time." He nodded to the stack of pages, "How much of that have you read?"

"I'd like you both to leave—now, please. After the dis-

330

respect you've shown me, I won't be needing your *services* any longer."

Buck glanced at Sumio, expecting him to high tail it down the stairs, but the kid didn't budge this time. "You want us to leave?" he asked instead.

"Yes. Now, please."

"Quit the case? Just like that?"

"You should be ashamed of yourselves for taking it in the first place; for taking advantage of my grief and my confusion like you did."

"So, you've read them. Then you know why we're here, Doreen. You know *exactly* why."

"Mr. Takahashi, I haven't a clue why you're—"

"—John killed Eli, Doreen," Buck said, "Maybe he didn't stick the needle in himself, but it was him that done it all the same."

"*What?*"

"Where'd ya get those reports? They were in the record Eli gave you, weren't they? The one he gave you as *peace offering* couple weeks back?"

"I don't see what that has to do with—"

"—But it wasn't you who first played the record, was it? It was John."

"He… I can't remember…" She looked over suddenly, as if snapping awake, "John *did not* kill Eli, Mr. Bordell! What a despicable accusation!"

"It's the truth."

"How vile. How absolutely—"

"—Doreen, listen to me," Sumio said, "You have those reports because Eli wanted you to have them in case something happened to him, and something *did* happen to him, Doreen. He was murdered."

She stared back, mouth moving, no words.

He dropped to his haunches, "Your brother was trying to stop what happened to Vanport. He was trying to do the right thing, and they killed him for it. We've seen the reports; we know how bad they are. We have another set of copies your brother made and have been trying to get the word out on our own, but you *know* people, Doreen. You can make the difference. You can open doors Buck and I can't. If you help us, we can *do* something about this—for Eli and for Vanport both."

"Eli is dead, Mr. Takahashi."

"But it's not too late to get him justice."

Doreen sprung up and crossed to the Hi Fi, dumping the papers from her lap, "I don't know what you're talking about."

"I know this puts you in an impossible situation, but now you know the truth and you—"

"—Truth? What truth, Mr. Takahashi? All I hear is a baseless, and might I say, *shameful* accusation."

Sumio straightened, exhaling even, "Where was John the night Eli died?"

"How dare you interrogate me in my own home."

"Where, Doreen?"

Too fast, "Here."

"No. He wasn't. Not all night, anyway. He was up in Vanport. We have a witness who saw him there with Eli; someone who saw John lure your brother into an ambush and stand aside while he was dragged off, held down, injected with a lethal dose of heroin, and left to die on the sidewalk."

"My husband was here. All night. You hear me, Mr. Takahashi? He. Was. *Here*."

"You knew something was going on, remember? In the beginning, you were *certain* that—"

"—I was grieving. I was confused. You took advantage."

He reached over picked up one of the scattered pages, "So all this is what? A coincidence?"

She rounded on them, seething, but when she spoke, something in her voice hit the air stone dead when she said, "It doesn't matter."

"Please, Doreen, there are *bodies* in the water. Are you really going to sit here and help these bastards bury the truth your brother died for?"

"Whatever happened to my brother—"

"—*Murdered*, Doreen; he was murdered for—"

"—*Whatever* happened to him was a terrible, tragic accident, one that John had absolutely nothing to do with!"

"Then why aren't you at the fundraiser? Why are you

here, sitting alone in the dark, playing the record your dead brother gave you?"

She rushed past them and down the stairs, shouting, "I see what this is! I see now! I know what you're *really* after. It's the money you want! Your bonuses! It's always been about that. You want it? Fine! You'll take it and forget all about this pathetic melodrama you've concocted—these lies—you'll take it and leave my family alone!"

Sumio, following, "We don't care about the money—"

"—Of course you do!" she spat, bent over the dining room table, back to them and scribbling frantically, "You think you can fool me like that? I know you're type all too well; the pieties you use to disguise the greedy, venal, little men you are!" She whipped 'round, slashing at the distance between her and Sumio with a fresh-cut check, "*Here*! Take it. Take it and shut up. Take it. *Take it*. Take it and get the fuck out of my house!"

Sumio sighed.

Sagged a little.

Stepped off.

Turned.

"You should get out of town, *Mrs. Whitmore*," he said, "They're coming for John. And if you're around when they do..." Another sigh, short and sharp, and the door sealed tight behind him.

"What did he mean by that?" Doreen asked, staring after him, "What did he mean *they're coming for John*?"

Buck shrugged, coming down the last few steps, "He means they're going to kill him."

"Why?"

"Payback."

"Why would they... he... he did what they wanted, didn't he?"

"It's not their payback," Buck said, pulling the picture of Eli from his jacket pocket and tossing it onto the desk, "It's ours."

She didn't look. Didn't blink. Didn't flinch. Didn't move. Didn't breathe. But the denial cracked wide open and, in its place, came something urgent and empty and thick on the skin, "I was wrong about you, wasn't I, Buck?" she said, "I thought it was you that I had to worry about, but it wasn't. I should have seen it earlier—you're a reasonable man. A professional. We can talk, can't we? We can work something out? Help each other? You can talk Mr. Takahashi out of whatever spiteful little scheme he's cooking up—convince him to take the money and forget all this? Of course you can. You're dependable. Discreet, isn't that right? Reasonable. Yes. *Reasonable*," She took up the checkbook, "So tell me, how much?"

"Look, Doreen—"

"—No, Buck. No. No more debate; no more discussion. You tell me what to write and I'll write it."

Outside, Sumio didn't ask about the check and Buck didn't offer. The two of them just piled into the rig and spent the next hour nosing 'round idling flatbeds and troupes of denim-clad work crews; following the closures and detours and a half-dozen dead-end routes until, 'bout a quarter mile out, they ditched the car entirely and walked roughly the way that Malcolm had described the week before that took them through the thick, slough-side shade of the alders, 'cross the rail bridge where Eli'd been taken, and over to what remained of the berm where a loose crowd stood staring blankly at the water. Sumio'd been back most days, apparently, but this was Buck's first time since the flood. He saw the break and how the river'd come through, swallowing Vanport up to the rooflines, breaking it, chewing it, and leaving it stagnant and still and quiet and deep and dead and baking in the sun. A stew of shattered plywood and bent metal; of shorn-roof rafts in purposeless drift alongside the flat-bottomed boats of the rescue crews who, at this point, had little to do other than try and keep their boots dry and tally the dead.

Ida was already there. She and Sumio exchanged a few quiet words before he left them to wander down the berm alone. The lady sighed, fingers threading, shoulders heavy, watching him go. "Good afternoon, Mr. Bordell," she said.

"Ida. How's the count?"

"Better today. Mrs. Gautreaux saw Mrs. Maya this morning, and Malcolm sent word from Sacramento."

"Down there already, huh?"

"He'll be back if we need him. Anyway, that still leaves

Mr. Sawyer and Mr. Vasquez unaccounted for—on our block anyway—but I'm hopeful. I saw a lot of people coming in and out of Peninsula Park today. Somebody will have seen them there, I'm sure of it. How did it go with the newspapers?"

He spat. She nodded.

"Don't suppose you and Sumio've thought any more 'bout legging it?" he asked.

"No, sir."

"And how're you feeling after... you know... Karl?"

"Was that his name?"

"Yep."

"I'm ashamed to say that I've hardly had a moment to think about it. I barely remember it. Or, I suppose, I do remember, it just doesn't feel like it's me that I'm remembering when I do. It's a strange feeling altogether." She glanced over, as tentative as Buck'd ever seen her, "What kind of man was he?"

"Normal kind, I guess," Buck answered, expecting to say more but coming up empty. "Anyway, I don't think you need to worry about any of that. If they ever find Karl's body, I figure they'll let sleeping dogs lie. They already got what they wanted outa him. It's in the cops' interest to look the other way now."

"What about for you and Sumio?"

"Dunno. We didn't make ourselves any new friends outa the deal, that's for sure, but if they come for us it'll be later, after things've cooled off a bit. PPD's got no reason to go through the hassle of shutting us up if nobody's listening anyway. All the same, maybe don't jaywalk for a while."

A new wave of arrivals came over the rail bridge and started mixing with the crowd. One of them called out to Ida. "Well, well," she said, waving back and starting off, "There's Mr. Vasquez now. I have to go, Mr. Bordell, but come by the park, won't you? I'll make you that miso soup you love so much."

But she only got a few steps away before Buck called after, "Hey, Ida. I owe you one."

She turned, smiled, and said, "Don't be ridiculous, Buck—you owe me *two* at least."

After, he went looking for Sumio down the far end of the berm, past the low-voiced snags of people as they picked through whatever wreckage had drifted close enough or whole enough to be dragged up on shore. Air still. Air stale. Shadows flinty on the sun-streaked water. "So, how's the old man holding up?" Buck asked, coming up alongside.

"He keeps telling me how much he likes the Red Cross people."

"The tents don't remind him of Heart Mountain?"

"Everything reminds him of Heart Mountain. But, you know, that helps sometimes. How's the wound?"

"Hurts. Think I tore a stitch back at Pittock. All this rough sleeping hasn't helped either."

"I could ask around if you're looking for a place to stay. We have a couple friends in Albina who might take you for a few days. And I'm sure we could get another cot for the tent if you were interested."

"Thanks."

He nodded. "They did it again, Buck."

"I 'spose so."

"We were too slow."

"Yep."

"I don't give a damn if they bump off Whitmore, but he's not the only one responsible, and if him dying means it's that much easier for them to pin this all on corpse…I don't… it's…"

"What?"

Kid shrugged, dropping to his haunches, priming like a spring, eyes picking through the silence of the wreckage, "It's just not enough, is all." For a while it was quiet. Then, "Nothing to say?"

"Got something in mind?"

"No, I just thought you might say '*fuck 'em*' or something like that."

"Do you want me to?"

"No."

"Didn't think so."

Another still and passing moment. Buck tried squatting down alongside Sumio, but crouching like that made it feel like his guts were gonna pop out, so he sat instead, "Christ that hurts."

"Friend of mine in the army took one in the same spot crossing the Arno. He said for a month after it felt like somebody was waggling a finger around inside of him every time he ate. So, you got that to look forward to."

"Well, don't worry, I'm still plenty ready to roll."

"I know." Sumio said, watching the river like a man meeting a dog in an alley, "You know, I don't care, don't you?"

"'Bout what?"

"The check. The bonus. It's fine that you took it. You are entitled to it. We just shouldn't lie to one another. Not right now."

"I didn't lie."

"But you did take it, right?"

"Sure did, but just 'cause I wanted to see what the name'd look like written out." Buck said, handing over the check Doreen had given him and letting Sumio look it over for a while before nodding out towards what had once been Vanport and continuing, "I can't promise you justice. It's not my bag. Maybe you get there someday, but today, right now, you just gotta burn for a while. We both do. We gotta keep moving, 'cause if we stop, that's when the current'll bite. But if we pick our moment and come at 'em hard, we might just have a shot. Call it spite if you want, or revenge or whatever, but, hell, kid, that river out there isn't ever going to play fair—it's gonna rise and rise—so we gotta act like it means to drag us under, 'cause it does. And so long as we're together in this boat, we might as well make a real go of it and paint our names on the side so the bastards know who's coming."

Sumio took all that in his usual way—without a ripple. Then, reading back the check's subject line, he said, "*Bordell-Takahashi Investigative Services.*"

"Uh-huh. Straight split, right down the middle, whoever and whatever we get."

"It's a generous offer, Buck."

"Yah, well, getting shot really does a number on a guy."

They sat for a while. Water lapping, sky empty.

"What about the check?" Sumio asked.

"What about it?"

"Are you going to cash it?"

"Be stupid not to."

"I know."

"Two-thousand dollars goes a long way towards getting us set-up."

"It would," Sumio said, tearing the check in half and tossing it into the water, "But fuck 'em."

Buck stood, "That's the spirit. Now come on, we got some rowing to do."

ACKNOWLEDGEMENTS

I owe a debt of profoundest gratitude to all the friends and loved ones who lent their time, wisdom, and encouragement towards the completion of this book.

To my wife, Mariska, for all of it, always and forever.

To David Whitney, Johanna Krogh, and Joseph Tiegs for their loving interest in my first serious short stories—both the good *and* the bad.

To Seth Dawson for their enthusiasm and feedback which served as a delivering wind through each new stretch of the writerly doldrums.

To Catherine May for her funny, thoughtful, and wonderfully thorough feedback that helped iron out some particularly persistent wrinkles.

To Stephan Schultz for his unfailing brotherhood and support.

To Nicholas Mirra for sharing the view from the trenches.

And to Jessica Vu, Geoffrey Gund, Brian Schiller, and Sarah Schurr for being early, willing readers.